The
Ballad of
St. Katherine

a novella and stories ———————

The Ballad of St. Katherine

a novella and stories

Norman Simon

iUniverse®

THE BALLAD OF ST. KATHERINE
A NOVELLA AND STORIES

iUniverse books may be ordered through booksellers or by contacting:

iUniverse
1663 Liberty Drive
Bloomington, IN 47403
www.iuniverse.com
1-800-Authors (1-800-288-4677)

ISBN: 978-1-4917-4958-6 (sc)
ISBN: 978-1-4917-4957-9 (e)

Library of Congress Control Number: 2014920379

Printed in the United States of America.

iUniverse rev. date: 12/12/2014

Acknowledgments   A number of these stories have appeared previously in literary magazines, as follows: ESPN in *The Literary Review*; Terry and Egypt in *new south*; The Bargain in *Hawai'i Pacific Review;* You Are She? in slightly different form in *Center*; The Headache in *Fiction International*.

To The Dutchie

The Monastery

Men were Earthbound in the year 1200 and could not fly. But perhaps, as many believed, there were witches who had mastered this art. Such a creature, half human, half demon, would be fearful of holiness, but still might be drawn through the air, out of curiosity or perversity or merely unpredictable winds, to the environs of a holy place. No man of flesh and blood could ever have seen Thoronet from the air, but such a witch or demon might have.

This had also been Robert Hudson's first view of the monastery, from the air. He had been flying his Cessna in Provence, in the region of the Var, and had spotted Thoronet in a sea of trees. There was a steeple, with a church below it; a cloisters; and, among these, quite a number of out-buildings, whose function he couldn't discern. The arrangement was seemingly random. Although the monastery was completely hemmed in by trees, it was open to the air. Was this to let God look in?

As it turned out, Thoronet's layout was not haphazard at all. Only the out-buildings were scattered; the main complex was a rectangle, oriented according to the compass, the church stretching east-west forming one of the short sides, with the green cloisters perpendicular. This was common. If the monastery was a curiosity at all, it was due only to its out-of-the-way location. When he got back to the aerodrome at Frejus, Hudson asked about it while the plane was being serviced. It had been built by the Cistercian Order. Beyond that, nobody seemed to know much.

The next time he was in Provence, he and Hélène drove over on the N7 to take a look. From the air, the reddish roof tiles had stood out, the walls looking gray in contrast. But now, close up, it was clear that the stone slabs were also suffused with a pinkish glow. They entered the church through its west end, Hélène holding his arm. She wore dark glasses and a kerchief covering her hair—she had no need to be recognized. But once inside she had to take the glasses off. Pale light flowed down behind them, entering through an oculus and two small windows. To the front, light shone through a trio of arched windows in the apse, hitting the floor in splotches. There was total silence.

Hélène knew that Hudson disliked churches. He had seen all of the great Gothic cathedrals of Europe—cold, dank places, outsized, full of distance and extravagance. Perhaps they were designed to emphasize how small and cold man was compared with God and therefore how much Jesus was needed to bridge the distance. But Hudson had no business to do with such a God. There were Romanesque churches, of course; they were warmer and more yielding, but, for him, they still lacked an essential element, still left him cynical and bored.

Thoronet, however, was different—it was opposite. The lines were spare and beautiful, without decoration; the vaulted ceiling had a plain, manageable majesty. The two of them walked slowly though the play of light and shadow toward the altar. They stepped up into the apse, looking down at the low, round Romanesque altar, light streaming at their feet. "This is more like it," he said.

Hudson had his enthusiasms. There were certain women, most with short half-lives; Hélène was the one who had lasted. There were a number of companies that Hudson had been fired up about. He bought controlling interests, or bought them outright if they were small enough. But after a time, he lost interest. He gave them over—selling some, keeping others, taking a profit or a loss. There was FORTRAN, the first human language that allowed communication with electronic computers. This was the most durable of his enthusiasms. He had been a member of the team that had created FORTRAN, and the reverence in which he held it had never lapsed.

After a few minutes, Hélène began to hear his labored breathing. Apparently, his nasal passages were abnormally narrow, and he had allergies that flared up unpredictably to block them. Sometimes, at night, his snores drove her from the bed, while other times he breathed quietly, like a sleeping angel. There was something angelic about Robert, his soft, handsome, boyish face, pale eyes, his light hair with its barely perceptible tinge of red, his mild, slightly high, reasonable voice. But he could also be stubborn and arrogant, accustomed to issuing quiet commands and having them followed without question, accustomed to being right.

"Let's go on," she told him.

She led him to their left, a direction that looked interesting, seeing it as the camera might, rolling slowly forward. She had a natural talent for everything visual, for the framing of faces, for camera angles and composition. Descending a few steps, they entered a short arcade. Again, there was light; it streamed in through semicircular arches lining the exterior wall, each arch bisected by a large, squat column. Beyond this wall was the central courtyard of the cloisters, the green rectangle that Hudson had spotted from the air. The courtyard was part in shadow, part in light. When they crossed the terminator, Hélène put on her dark glasses again. Hudson never wore sunglasses and never a hat, despite his light skin and sensitive-looking eyes. His white suit was perhaps too summery for the season, even in Provence, but he was comfortable that way, tieless, his collar open. His hair looked a bit more reddish in the sunlight.

At the sunny end of the courtyard was a small hexagonal structure, whose roof was also segmented into six parts. There were several doors, again in the form of semicircular arches, which let in light. Inside was a round fountain with a central post surrounded by a circular band from which water fell out of protruding fingers, like the udders of a cow.

"It looks like the communal sink in a lavatory," Hélène said.

"The monks must have washed here," Hudson told her, as if he were sure of it.

Hélène had a small house up in the Haut Var. She was more French than American, though the American part tended to show through in times of difficulty. The house had an old-fashioned kitchen, with a midget refrigerator and iron stove. From the compact salon, French doors led into a small garden. The best room was the bedroom, sunny and high-ceilinged with a little terrace that looked out toward a large, rocky formation.

The people in the village knew who Hélène was—her films could be seen in Draguignan or St.-Raphaël. However, they allowed her her privacy. It was Hudson they had stared at, at least at first. He was a handsome presence, and the two of them made a strange contrast—he with his open, boyish face, his light hair, his white suits; she, darker, her hair, when you could see it, dirty blonde and curly, her face hidden with dark glasses, head covered with a kerchief or a hat.

Hudson had been attracted to her before she was to him. She moved in a world of handsome men; for her, his looks had been nothing special. But Robert had pursued her. She'd heard stories about him—he liked actresses and there had been quite a few of them before her, film and theater actresses, from Hollywood and New York, France, Italy, even the Soviet Union. Khrushchev had invited him, the sort of thing that Khrushchev would do; the Bolshevik and the multimillionaire—they got along. The final time, Hélène had come with him. She hadn't met Khrushchev—he'd been called away—but she had talked in French with Robert's Russian actress, a woman who competed with Hélène in beauty. It was not clear whether the woman realized that Hélène knew of her prior relationship with Robert—for this reason they had not spoken honestly. But Hélène had detected a restless energy in her, a dissatisfaction that all three of them seemed to harbor. They had done everything, they had succeeded, they had many years left—what would be next?

"Have you ever considered suicide?" Robert had once asked her.

It was after they had made love. Le petit mort—it had shocked her. His semen was inside her, by that time leaking down her thighs. She had been content. "No," she answered.

"Why not? You've played the roles."

Both had been in French—Ophelia on the stage, and on film a woman who had doomed her younger sister by refusing to collaborate during the war. "Yes, I thought about it, but not in a concrete way, not for myself."

"Unless you believe in God, why wouldn't you? Does it really matter if it's now or later?"

Though it was a number of years ago, she remembered this conversation clearly. Hadn't it taken place in this house, on this very bed? She was almost sure it had. This week, she was not sleeping well, thinking of this or that. Robert was snoring beside her now. It must have been here. Where else—one of his hotel rooms? Hudson had built a house in Florida, but seldom stayed there. He preferred hotels, renting suites for months at a time. He preferred a hotel in Paris to Hélène's apartment there, but he liked to come to the Haut Var—it was an exception.

She had another bad night, tossing and turning. Robert was up early, before it was really light. He tiptoed around, but not quietly enough to keep from waking her. She heard him pulling his boots on, then the click of the door, then his footfalls on the stairs. He would go into the garden to stare at the stars before they faded; that, or set up his chessboard to duplicate a famous endgame. She wanted desperately to sleep more, but found she couldn't. She began thinking of Robert's departure, set for the beginning of the following week. She found herself looking forward to it. She would sleep, then. Their rhythms were so different—they couldn't stay together long.

She threw herself onto her side, lay that way for a few minutes, then turned abruptly and shifted to her other side. It did no good. Sitting up, she forced herself out of bed, into her flats, her robe. Out in the garden, Robert stood with his hands in his pockets, looking up at the sky, though the clouds dominated. An eerie light forecast the dawn. She moved up beside him and hooked her arm in his.

Later, she went back to bed and managed to sleep. This time she woke suddenly, bewildered. The sun must have come out, the room was light. She washed quickly, dressed, and walked out to the Café des Roches, a few streets away. Despite the cool weather, Robert was sitting at a table outdoors with a man she had noticed in the village but never met.

"Hélène, this is Steven. He's an American."

He stood to take her hand. He was broad-shouldered, his hair gray, prematurely to judge from the rest of him, slightly unkempt but not dirty; his face looked wind-seared.

"He stopped here one day to buy a straw hat for the sun," Robert explained, "and he stayed."

Steven looked at her with watery eyes. It reminded her of the sort of expression a dog might put on for its master, a mixture of devotion and disappointment. Surely this gaze couldn't be meant for her. She reached for her sunglasses, was dismayed to find she'd forgotten them.

"I'm working here at the café," he said, as if he owed her an explanation. "I clean up, do some work in the garden. In return they've given me a room."

She wondered what Robert found interesting about him. There had to be something; if not, he wouldn't have bothered.

"Have you been long in the village?" she asked him.

He was wearing a thin, black coat; he pulled up the collar. "About five months. I like it very much."

Robert had a little smile on his face—he was going to say something. "Steven worked on the Defense Calculator in the early days. Afterward, we were together for a while on the FORTRAN team."

So that was it. The Defense Calculator had been the prototype for IBM's number-crunching computers. Hudson had not been there for its development, but had worked on a related problem—the FORTRAN software needed to run it.

Steven, though he was clean, needed a shave. To Hélène, he seemed a lost soul, not a man she'd want to get to know. But some had been attracted. Robert was, and there must have been others in the village. Later, she found out that he had shown up one morning with little money and without resources. Except for a few words he could not speak French. Somehow, the conservative, even xenophobic, villagers had taken to him. Hired for odd jobs, he had proven a good worker. He, also, had a boyish look about him—not scrubbed and handsome like Hudson, but rather an overgrown puppy, loyal and lovable.

They were drinking café au lait; Robert called the waiter and ordered one for Hélène. He asked Steven: "Do you remember Poppa?" They both grinned.

Robert explained to her: "Poppa was IBM's Super Calculator. It came before the Defense Calculator. I saw it in '50 or '51. IBM had it in the window at 57th and Madison. It was a work of art—people stopped to stare at it."

"It was beautiful," Steven said in his soft voice.

"Beautiful—how?"

"It had colored lights, hundreds or thousands of them that blinked on and off. It made a clacking noise and you could see punched cards and paper tapes running through it." He smiled at Hélène. "I had just gotten my degree in electrical engineering and mathematics, knew nothing about electronic calculation. But once I saw Poppa, I was hooked."

He had big eyes, with pupils like runny yolks. The sun seemed not to bother him. Cold light was reflecting off the paving stones and white houses. Hélène's eyes were a hard blue, almost sapphire, but sensitive. She reached for her sunglasses again, forgetting she had left them at home. "What brought you to France?" she asked him.

He stared at her, as if the answer were that *she* had brought him to France. Robert was filling her cup—half milk, half coffee. He was intent at the job, as he was with everything he did. He took no notice of the way Steven was looking at her.

Finally, Steven said: "Nothing. I always wanted to come here. Nothing special."

Robert combed his hair with his fingers. "I never heard what happened to Poppa. Do you know?"

Steven's eyes left her. "They had it in a warehouse, I think, up at Yorktown Heights. There was some talk about it going to the Smithsonian, but that never happened. Look," he said, "I have to go. They're waiting for me inside. The stove needs cleaning. Thank you for the coffee, and for letting me meet your beautiful wife. You don't mind my saying that—that she's beautiful?"

"I'm not his wife," Hélène announced. "I'm his mistress."

Steven stood. He blushed.

"We'll have to talk again," Robert said. Once Steven was gone, he took her hand, which went limp in his. "Are you in a bad mood?"

"When are you leaving?" she asked.

"In a few days. I think I'll drive to Paris. Do you want to come?"

"You have another woman in Paris. Have you forgotten?"

His face was smooth, smiling, unperturbed. "What's wrong with you?"

She looked past him at the cold, bright sky. "It's winter," she told him. "I don't like winter."

Once he was gone, she felt better. She got a good night's sleep, hugging the pillow. Her period came. It had been weeks late. There was no fear about being pregnant—Robert had had himself sterilized. But she had thought—the thought had crept in—that it might be the start of her menopause. A terribly early start, but her mother had also begun early. Hélène had never wanted children, so she wasn't bothered by the possible arrival of that finality. This is what it was: that a new chapter in her life would have to start, one she wasn't ready for; she had no idea—even thinking about it produced a background anxiety. Now that she was menstruating there was no need to think of it.

A package arrived from Paris, a new script they wanted her to read. If she accepted it, there was a good chance that Gérard Philipe would be her co-star. She brought it to the café. The day was blustery and unpleasant—she took a seat inside, sat with a glass of wine. The building was very old. It had originally been a farmhouse, with an attached annex where a few animals had been kept. This annex, now a storage area, had been fitted out with a bed and dresser—it was where Steven slept. She had seen him a few times since Hudson's departure; he always passed with eyes averted and they never spoke.

The script was for an adventure film that would be set in Mexico and also shot there, or perhaps in Spain. One of the important characters was written as an American, who would speak often in English. The actress playing the lead role had thus to be bilingual, an important advantage for Hélène, a native speaker in both languages. Her American father had died; her French mother lived in Nice. She preferred France, but had spent a lot of time in the United States—as a child, then during the making of two Hollywood movies and, of course, with Robert.

The more she read of the script, the more she liked it. She had been exhausted by her last film, quite content to do nothing productive in the ensuing months—visiting her mother, vacationing in Africa, spending some time with Hudson. They contacted each other when they felt like it, Robert more regularly than she, often telephoning in what was for him the middle of the night. Sometimes, she felt she could sense the presence of another of his women, perhaps sleeping in the next room, the bedroom of the hotel suite—in New York or San Francisco or Denver or Chicago—while he phoned from the sitting room. Hélène, of course, could also call him. She would always be put through, but then encounter long silences and monosyllabic replies, until he managed to clear his head of what had been there and focus on her. Slowly, slowly, the spotlight inched her way, until, finally, it arrived. "Let's get together," he might say, then. "I'll come to you."

Steven was working on the lighting in the café. He had to come past her, and he tried to hustle by, his body rigid. "Steven?"

He turned. His face was weathered. He had dark eyes. He was at least her age, perhaps older. "Steven," she said. "Could you greet me when we meet? I would like that."

"All right," he managed.

"*Regarde*," she told him. "I was out of sorts that morning. I was very impolite to you—I'm sorry."

He was wearing an old woolen sweater, which had frayed on bottom. "I thought I had done something to upset you."

"Nothing. Not at all."

She gestured toward the chair beside her. "Won't you sit for a minute?"

"The lights …"

She smiled. "Monsieur will give you a minute."

He seemed to recover his composure, smiling shyly back at her. He sat. "Tell me about the Defense Calculator," she asked him.

He shrugged.

"Tell me about FORTRAN, then."

He thought for a moment—a bit like Robert, running through the things in his head. "Imagine entering a country where the inhabitants speak no language. Each time you want something you must lay out stones in a large and intricate pattern. This, viewed from a hilltop, makes sense to them and they will bring you what you need. Each message, produced and deciphered this way, takes as long as weeks. Then, one day, you construct a language they are capable of understanding. You ask for a tool or a drink of water and someone brings it immediately."

"What was his role in this, Robert's role?"

Steven wiped his mouth with his fingers. "I don't know," he told her. "I was in the group early, he late. We only met twice."

"You left the FORTRAN group before he arrived?"

"It was a long time ago."

"Won't you tell me?"

He blushed. "When the project began, most experts thought it would be impossible to build what later became the FORTRAN compiler. The government ignored us. When they finally realized how important it might be, they intervened. I was called a security risk and was removed." He rubbed his hands together, as if to wash them. "Do you have a cigarette?"

He stared at her as avidly as if he had asked her for a kiss. She looked away, down to her handbag. She found a half-crushed pack of Gauloise, removed two cigarettes and gave him one. Steven produced a lighter from his pocket, lit her cigarette and then his own, his hand shaking slightly.

She inhaled deeply and held the smoke before expelling it. She hadn't had a cigarette for two weeks—Hudson disliked it. "What had you done?"

"Nothing," he said, vehemently. "I went to a few meetings after the war. It couldn't be that. It was mistaken identity, same last name. There was a Steven G.; I knew him in graduate school. I'm Steven J.—it's stupid, isn't it?"

"He was communist?"

"Yes, he must have been. There was no appeal. I would never even have known why IBM dismissed me, if a friend hadn't told me."

Another blush. Hélène took it to mean that this friend had been female. "What did you do?"

"I compiled a dossier of my case and tried to show it to someone in authority. No one would look. Then …"

Over her shoulder she saw the proprietor. He was behind the bar, watching them, while he polished a glass. "I think Monsieur might want you now."

Steven started, jumped up, rubbed out his cigarette in the ashtray. "Perhaps you can tell me the rest later," she said, as he backed away.

With Robert gone, Steven *was* the most interesting man in the village. She invited him for tea. He came, clean-shaven, wearing a jacket and tie, his hair slicked down. It was late afternoon, the light getting ready to fade. She sat him in the salon, brought the tea on a tray. She was wearing her dark glasses but would take them off soon.

She sat with him on the divan at a comfortable distance. They both smoked. She had started again, but limited herself to seven cigarettes a day. Steven watched her eyes, as if he were trying to penetrate the sunglasses. He held the saucer and teacup, his hand steady. "When is Robert coming back?" he asked her.

An unexpected question. She considered, pursing her lips. "I don't know. Perhaps not until next summer. I'll be leaving, myself, in a few weeks."

A small tremor began to develop in his hand. The cup clicked against the saucer. He put them down. "Where will you go?"

"To Paris, and then to Mexico. I'm taking on a new film." She took in some smoke, washing it down with tea. "You were telling me about your unjust dismissal from IBM."

"It was unjust."

"What happened afterward?"

He averted his eyes. "I humiliated myself. I traveled, carrying my dossier. Europe, Africa, South America. I tried to make my case. Of course, I was part of a pattern of abuse by the U.S. Government. Many groups were interested. I would give a little speech, then ask my audience to write letters to the State Department, the United Nations and IBM on my behalf. Usually, there was a little stipend for me, enough to keep going."

"But eventually you stopped."

"Yes." He looked around for a moment, nervously, as if Monsieur were still watching him, growing impatient. "I couldn't bear it anymore to be new in every place, alone in every place. The only thing I had was my dossier." He took the cup, a bit calmer now, drank a few sips of tea. "I'll tell you something, Madame ..."

"Please, call me Hélène if you like."

"Yes, I will. I wanted to tell you. The thing that made me hate them most was not the loss of my salary or my prestige, such as it was, or even the injustice of their accusations. No, the loss I felt most acutely was my estrangement from the FORTRAN group. Can you understand that...?" It seemed he would say her name, then, but something stopped him, almost as if he were afraid. "We were all of us so close," he continued. "Perhaps it's the same when you make a film. We could speak about the project for hours, any one of us to any other. Sometimes, we would complete each other's sentences. We were creating a new kind of language that had never before been possible to construct or even to conceive—a language between humans and machines. The connection among us was almost mystical, as if we were monks serving the same God."

"Monks?"

He looked away from her. "Do you think I am being too extreme? Am I humiliating myself?"

"No." She took her dark glasses off, folded them, put the case on the table. She touched his hand to make him look up. Her face changed dramatically, she knew, when she removed the glasses, exposing her eyes. Robert had told her this, also others. One of her directors had taken advantage of this effect in both the films he had made with her—having her wear her dark glasses, then remove them, the camera watching her eyes. "Have you heard of Thoronet?" she asked him. "It is quite near here."

They went on a Monday, when Monsieur kept the café closed until the evening. Steven wore the same costume he had put on to have tea with her. She chose a dark dress, then saw in the mirror that the neckline was perhaps just too low. She covered it with a short jacket and pinned her hair up.

She asked Steven: "Do you drive?"

"I haven't in perhaps ten years."

She smiled at him. "Would you like to?"

He accepted the keys from her. She planned to take them back after a few kilometers if he drove dangerously, but she need not have worried. He was in full control from the start. Monsieur had told her that Steven was also dexterous and sure at the café, and had been trusted with repairs that were not trivial. It was only in his interpersonal relations that he seemed fragile enough to blow away in any wind.

They stood in the nave of the church and looked toward the glowing light of the apse. Steven was a rapt as Hudson had been. She noticed his physical presence. He was an inch or two shorter than Robert, but large across the chest; and he moved heavily, a weight on the paving stones. If she had been alone, Hélène thought, this place would not have affected her so much; but in Steven's presence (as it had been in Robert's), the emotion he felt was somehow transferred to her. After a few moments, Steven seemed to become weak in his knees, hardly able to stand. The nave was lined on both sides with simple wooden benches, and she urged him toward one of them and sat beside him.

"Are you all right?"

"My God," he said.

His face looked gray in the chapel's strange light. She took his arm and he slumped against her. Then, suddenly, they weren't alone. The nave had begun to fill with children, young girls in school uniforms. Their teacher, a small woman with pinned-up, graying hair acknowledged Steven and Hélène as she passed. "*Monsieur'dam.*"

The girls gathered in the middle of the nave and began to sing under the teacher's direction. Their high, pure voices echoed back from every direction in a hundred rivulets of sound, as if the walls themselves were whispering. Hélène found herself breathing deeply, while, beside her, Steven straightened. A smile appeared on his face. Light flowed in from the oculus and found the group of singers, lighting some but leaving others in shadow. Suddenly, the teacher swung her arm downward. The singing stopped abruptly and the whispers died, but the silence that ensued seemed to contain the sounds as a potentiality that might emerge spontaneously at any time.

"Beautiful," Hélène said.

Steven looked at her without shyness. "More than that," he told her.

They waited to see if the girls would sing again. They didn't. Instead they began talking among themselves, little schoolgirls' talk that the walls turned into a thousand eerie whispers, like the voices of all the dead— not a cacophony but a sort of frail music that might have emerged from the vacuum itself.

The girls left through the chapel entrance on the west, while Steven and Hélène strolled into what had been the monks' quarters. She went first, he behind her; she could feel his heaviness. They followed a stream of light, down a few steps into a smaller space, where they were met by a luminous counter-flow entering through a quartet of arched windows. This was the chapter-house, where the monks had met each morning to read from a religious work, often the Benedictine Rule. The room was supported by two massive columns from which ribs rose like giant stalks, curling upward to support the vaulted ceiling.

Encircling the room were three tiers of stone benches. They sat in the third row and Steven kissed her and stuck his hand under her jacket to feel her breast. His lips were hard and chapped, his tongue delicate, tentative. She pushed him away, forcefully at first, then more softly as his body yielded. "Don't do that."

His face paled. "I'm sorry," he told her. "I was overwhelmed ... I didn't think ... I didn't mean ..." He stopped and stared at her. "I'm sorry," he repeated.

"Never again," she warned him, "if we are to see one another."

"The emotion," he said, "it was overwhelming. This place—and you. I won't ..." he stammered, "I understand ... pardon me."

There was a pool of light at her feet, surrounded by shadows. Steven's explanation, though he hadn't said it outright, was this: The sacred and the profane lie close together, separated by the thinnest membrane, almost nothing. She accepted this. She wondered if the monks had known it as well, living their celibate, cloistered lives? She suspected that they had.

ESPN

In the stars live beings of fire. Their greatest pleasure is to merge—body on body, flame into flame. Maggie is fire. She became that in the crematorium on Long Island, while I was left behind. But I dream that I am fire, too. Soon, I'll join her.

"Mr. Perelman, where are you? It's lunchtime."

"I'm here."

"You think you could sit up for me?"

She helps me. Over on my hip, then push with my legs, like doing the sidestroke. Swimming across Lake Peekskill, my father trailing me in the rowboat, just in case. Strong, I felt strong.

"Come on, Mr. Perelman. Don't quit on me now."

I push, she pulls. She props the pillow behind me, tray on my lap. I can smell mashed potatoes, I can see red jello.

"You want to feed yourself today?"

I look. Who is it? Yelena? No, not her; she's got a Russian accent like my grandmother. Maybe it's Gypsy? No—Gypsy had fat black arms. Used to put me on the toilet. *Do your business, little man.* My Aunt Millie? Sounds like her. But how could it be? She's out on Long Island, too.

"Don't feel up to it this afternoon? You should be ashamed of yourself, Mr. Perelman. Making me feed you like a baby."

Jello red, potato smell. Who gives a shit?

"If you don't start eating better, we'll have to hook you up to the tube again. You want that?"

Beings of fire, blazing up in the stars. Maggie loved the beach, the sun. No wonder she chose fire. We talked about it before she went. Her hair was gone. Red wig. She laughed. It was easier for her. She was going, I was staying.

"Hey, Mr. Perelman. Somebody here for you."

This one *is* black. Not like Gypsy, though. Where's mama, Gypsy? *She gone. Poor little boy—she gone.*

"Sit up, Mr. Perelman."

"That's okay," someone says.

Maybe it's the television. "Turn that set down, Gypsy."

"Some days he's better than this."

"That's okay. I'll just sit with him."

One time we went to Fire Island. Maggie and me. Took the train to Bayshore, ferry out to Kismet. It was early in the season, a weekday, hardly anyone there. We spread our blanket under the dunes, out of the wind. Too cold to swim. I rubbed her with Coppertone. She always had to watch out for her skin. Redhead, lots of freckles and spots. Lying on her stomach, while I rubbed it in her back and legs. "I told my mother," she said. "I told her your name."

Whoever it was must be gone, or maybe it was just ESPN. Yelena turns it on for me. It's nice of her, but what do I need ESPN for? I used to go to Yankee Stadium with my father, down the stairs at 86th Street, the express coming; I got close to the edge, he let me but holding my hand, the train shaking, the darkness rushing by, 125th, 149th, my hand in his, then the train coming out of the tunnel and we saw the Stadium, and the hotel, the Concourse Plaza.

I don't sleep too well at night. I dream of fire, inside me and outside. It hurts at night, even though Millie gives me something. No, it couldn't be Millie. She's out in the cemetery on Long Island.

"How are you doing, Mr. Perelman?"

It's ESPN again. I know the voice. I've never been very good with faces, but voices are another thing.

"You feeling all right? Is there anything you need?"

I can turn myself when I want to. Right hip over to left hip, right cheek of my ass to left one, right elbow to left elbow. ESPN has a jaw like Nixon's, but a big guy, big chest, black hair.

"Richard Boyle."

Another Dick.

"They told me your name is Jerry." He holds his hand out. It's cold. Not like Gypsy's hand.

"I'll be coming around to keep you company—a few times a week, or more if you like."

Jerry's dick.

"Maybe we can talk sometimes."

"Almost nobody calls me Jerry. They call me Salt."

"Were you in the Navy? Merchant Marine?"

I was in nothing. Not even the Boy Scouts. I never liked joining things. Milk and cookies is what I liked. Aunt Millie, one more? *I'm your mother now. Call me Millie, darling, or call me mama.*

"I was in the Navy," ESPN says.

I'm getting tired of talking to him. I wish Yelena would come. Wash me, give me my shot. She had a hard life. No toilet paper in Russia. No eggs. She put newspaper in her boots. Cold winter, long winter, not like here. Shortages. I was called "Salt" because I'd empty the shaker out. Even on French fries, even on eggs and bacon, even in beer. Nobody made me stop until Maggie. Nobody loved me enough before that.

I think that ESPN is gone. He must have walked out when I turned my back for a minute. There was a guy in the bed next door. I had to share Millie with him. She pulled the curtains around him and took a lot of time. They don't come to you here if you make a fuss. You have to smile and be charming. Or, if you can't do that, being shy is next best. I'm pretty good at that. I don't want everyone knowing my secrets.

The guy next door is fire now. Fire or dirt. Gypsy found him, and fifteen minutes later they had him out, stripped the bed and had it ready for the next customer. No one was there when he died.

No one visited. It doesn't matter. He's fire now. Or maybe dirt. If Maggie had wanted that, I would have followed her, but it wasn't my first choice. My father is dirt, and Millie, and my mother, in Los Angeles or wherever she went. Why would I want to be underground with them?

"Yelena, can I have my shot now?"

"No shot. I explain to you. Doctor say pill. Put in mouth. Drink water."

It hurts, Millie. *Don't be a baby. A spanking, it's nothing.* Then, afterward, pressing me against her. Bad cop, good cop. I swallow the pill. "You want TV on?" I can't understand the television. I used to be able. Now it goes too fast. The people jerk around like a cartoon. Only if it's baseball, I can watch sometimes. Joe DiMaggio and Johnny Lindell and Charlie Keller. My father took me.

"Is there baseball?"

"I don't know baseball."

Maybe I should talk Russian to her. I used to know some words. My grandmother spoke the language. Old lady in a *babushka.* That's one word! *Papirosa. Morozhenoe.* "Don't understand," Yelena says. "English bad." She puts on some channel with the people jerking around. She straightens the covers. Pats my cheek, shaking her head.

Maybe it isn't even baseball season, maybe it's winter.

I open my eyes and ESPN is sitting there. Reading the New York Times. I may not be able to understand television anymore, but I can still tell the New York Times from the Daily News. ESPN has got the paper folded like he's reading it on the subway. "Hey, ESPN—where'd you come from?"

"You're awake, Mr. Perelman. I came from home."

"You live up in the Bronx?"

"No, in Manhattan. Actually, I'm close enough to walk over."

I don't know where I live. Does this place have a name? Ask ESPN—I'll bet he knows. "What's this place called?"

"Beth Jeshurun Center."

I'm in a Jewish place. I don't know why. I'm as Jewish as the next guy, but Maggie wasn't. Her mother wasn't very happy about the whole thing when Maggie let her know. We kept waiting for her to die—not a nice thing to say, but it was true—but she wouldn't. Finally, Maggie had to tell her.

"By the way, Salt, I brought you something. Let me open it up for you."

Cookies. They look like Mallomars, but bigger. "They go good with milk."

"I'll try to get you some," he says.

He comes back with a little half pint. Pours it in a glass, holds it up to my lips. "I can do that." It's a big glass. I have to hold it with two hands at first, but then I can do it with my right hand only, cookie in my left hand. "You want one?"

"I brought them for you."

"Go ahead and have some."

He takes out three of them, hand goes toward his mouth. "Hey!"

He puts two of them back, laughs. This ESPN is a joker. When we're done with our cookies, he says: "Well, Salt, what should we talk about today?"

Talk? I think I forgot how since Maggie's gone.

"Salt, where are you?"

I don't want to talk. Why did he come around anyway, Jerry's dick? A big guy, almost a fat guy, hardly fits on the little chair. He's wearing a suit today, blue suit and red tie, like he's a lawyer or a ward heeler. I used to make deliveries to guys like him. Big shot lawyers with their offices in Manhattan and their boats out on Long Island. Have Salt bring over the compass—it's in the catalog, page twenty-four; have Salt bring over the Power Squadron uniform, the Captain's hat.

When I arrived, the secretaries would buzz back on the intercom: Commodore Nauticals is here. The big shots liked to come out front and give me the glad hand, just like I was one of them. Hey Salt, how have you been keeping yourself, how're they hanging?

"Maybe next time," ESPN Jerry's dick is saying. "I'll come around in a few days. We can just sit around and eat cookies or watch television. We don't have to talk."

The doctor came in and told me I couldn't have shots again, but I could have an I-V drip with pain medicine in it. There would be a little button or something I could use to control it. This is because Yelena told him I was moaning and crying during the night. "I think he painful." The doctor always looks bored. I can see he's thinking why can't he be doing real medical stuff, instead of giving pills to old guys and listening to nurses' aides talking Russian in a nursing home? I think he likes being God around here, though. He says pills, you get pills; he says drip, that's what happens. For myself I like the shots best—Yelena or Gypsy or Millie shooting me up, and the good feeling when all of a sudden the medicine starts working.

The beings of fire come and signal to me. I always know which one is Maggie and which are her friends in the star world. Those few are always in front, but there are lines and lines of them, stretching far away, sometimes being taken back into the fire and then coming out again. Even Maggie gets taken back and I can't see her anymore, only the burning star. But her voice is there: Come on, Jerry. When are you coming? You know how impatient I am, how I don't like to wait.

Gypsy used to come around to clean the apartment and watch me while my mother was out. I can hear her voice in my head. *Woman sure loves that Russian Tea Room and them matinees.* Those two didn't like each other. But, without someone to babysit me, the Russian Tea Room and the matinees would be out. My father wouldn't replace Gypsy just because my mother complained. Their fights shook the apartment, rattled the windows. I went to my room, got out my erector set.

ESPN is back again, this time with a couple of donuts full of cream. He brings a glass of milk for mine, coffee for his. I haven't finished the Mallomars yet; there's still one left, which I'll eat later.

"You have a job?" I ask him. "You show up here all the time—doesn't your boss get mad?" Though I could do the same thing when I worked for Commodore, make a delivery then disappear for a while. I liked to go to Chock Full O' Nuts, get a donut and coffee and read the Daily News a little bit.

"I'm retired," he says.

"You sixty-five? You don't look it." His hair is black, but it's true that he's lost plenty up the middle.

"I'm fifty-nine."

"What did you used to do?"

"I was an attorney."

I knew it! "I only used a lawyer once. I was making deliveries on a bike, and some guy opened the back door of a cab and knocked me over."

"What happened?"

"By the time I paid the lawyer off and took care of the doctors, nothing was left. I got a bad knee out of it. It didn't really work right after that. When I met Maggie, I had a little limp. She thought I might have got it in the war."

"Maggie—was she your wife?"

I shouldn't have said her name. Dumb shit! I don't want to talk to ESPN about Maggie.

"Salt, it's okay. I don't want to pry into your life. Let's just drop it."

He puts his hand on my shoulder. Big paw—he could have been a pitcher with that paw. It looks like Allie Reynolds' big paw, when I got his autograph. Outside Yankee Stadium—my father was standing with me. I can't remember if we still had money then, or if my mother was still with us, or if Aunt Millie had already moved in.

"She was like my wife, but we never got married."

He looks like he wants to find out more about it, but he doesn't ask, just says: "I never got married, either."

Millie comes in. She wants to sponge me down, give me a little bath. I like it better when Gypsy does it. When Millie moved in,

Gypsy left. We didn't need to have her anymore and, besides, we couldn't afford to hire anyone once my father lost his job. ESPN says he'll wait outside, but I don't want him around at all when Millie's sponging me. I know if I don't keep talking, he'll go away.

"Does it feel good?"

She hasn't even pulled the curtain. Even if there's no one in the bed next door, I like to have it pulled. The door is open and anyone can walk in. "Close the goddamn curtain. How many times do I have to tell you?"

"Be nice, Mr. Perelman."

"Where is Gypsy—I prefer her."

."Could you turn over for me, Mr. Perelman? I don't know who you mean."

"Gypsy—the black one."

"Letoya, you mean? She'll be here tomorrow."

Millie stayed home to take care of me. When my mother used to be around, she hardly touched me at all, but Millie never took her hands off me. I liked it better when she hit me than when she cleaned my ears, or looked in the toilet to see what I did or scrubbed me in the bath. "Leave him alone," my father would sometimes say; but not very often because it always started a fight, and he couldn't afford to lose her—she was all he had left.

"Come on, Mr. Perelman. You have to admit it feels good."

I'm waiting to become fire. It's more than time already. Maggie made me promise that I wouldn't help the process along. You risk being cast into hell, she told me. I don't believe in God, but if she did maybe there's something to it. Maybe you see God when you dream. He's the fire.

Night comes and there's pain. I use the I-V as much as it lets me. It works, but I can't sleep. Only a little. I can't find the fire. Maggie—where are you? Yelena comes in to check me, takes my wrist. She stares into space, her lips moving while she counts my heartbeats. I feel like my heart is going fast, but Yelena doesn't notice. "Okay," she says. I don't think she knows how to count very well. She takes a thermometer out and sticks it in my ear. Millie used to shove the thermometer up my ass. She liked to do it. She held my hand while we waited four minutes for the fever to register. I pretended she was my mother.

"Perelman alone," Yelena says. "Not worry. Tomorrow. Friend come."

Does she mean ESPN? How would she know if he's coming or not?

He doesn't come. ESPN comes and goes as he pleases. Why should he give a shit for me? Only Maggie cared for me. They put somebody in the other bed. A bad one—he talks out loud. Like there's someone he knows in the room. Sometimes he gets mad and sometimes he starts whining. I'd rather have what I have than what he has. Gypsy's here. She straightens up my bed. "Listen, Gypsy. That guy is driving me crazy."

"I'll put on the TV for you, Mr. Perelman."

There's nothing on television. It's a vast wasteland. She flips through the channels. A ballgame comes up—this must be a Saturday. The players hop around like frogs. I can't keep track of them. I used to be able to keep score. I took Maggie to a game. She watched me fill out my scorecard. "Jerry," she said. "You amaze me."

The guy in the next bed starts talking again. He thinks he's having a conversation with someone named Wilma. I can't stand it. "Shut up," I yell at him, but it doesn't do any good.

Gypsy comes back in. "Be cool, Mr. Perelman." She gives the guy a pill and me a pill. He starts snoring. I can't keep my eyes open, either.

Where's the guy? He's gone. They must have taken him out, maybe roomed him with another nut case. I hear ESPN's voice out in the hall. Before he comes in, I move over to the far side of the bed, pull the covers over my head.

"Come on, Salt. I know you're in there."

"Where were you, yesterday?"

"I'm sorry, Salt. There was something I had to do."

"What?"

"I had a board meeting that lasted all day. I'm on a lay board for the Catholic Church."

"You a Catholic?"

"Yes, I am."

Maggie was a Catholic, too. She thought about being a nun. But it was before she met me. She told me, that after we got together, she never thought of it again.

"I brought you something," ESPN says.

It's cheesecake. I think I already had breakfast, but it doesn't matter. There's always a place in my stomach where I can put cheesecake.

ESPN is wearing a suit again. I ask him if he puts it on to see me, and he laughs and says no he just came from the morning mass. "Maggie used to go in the morning. She never missed one."

"You had a good marriage together, a Jew and a Catholic."

"Who said I was Jewish?"

He smiles. "Perelman?"

He's no dope, this ESPN. I knew some lawyers that were pretty dim. The lawyer for Commodore Nauticals was one. His sister was the owner's wife. Some guy in the Power Squadron slipped on the deck of his boat and sued Commodore because he was wearing our boat shoes. The lawyer made a big mess of it and it cost Commodore a bundle. The owner canned the guy, but then his wife walked out on him. "Hey Dick, are you married? Did I ask you that before?"

"I'm not sure. Anyway, I'm a bachelor. I always played the field and then, I guess, it was just too late."

"I met Maggie when I was fifty-two and she was forty-five. She said I was her last chance, sort of joking, but I told her lots of guys must've wanted to marry her, the kind of girl she was."

"You got a picture of her, Salt? Let's see what she looks like."

The picture is in the drawer of the table, right next to me. I check every day to make sure it's still there. I'm sure that Millie wants to take it, but so far she hasn't found out where it is. To ESPN, I say: "I don't like showing it around."

"I'm sure it would be all right."

It's still there. Maggie and me—her arm around my back and mine around hers. She's taller than me, I only come up to her eyebrows. This is at Coney Island—you can see the Parachute Jump behind us, a little blurry. Maggie's wearing shorts. She's a big girl. She's broad where a broad should be broad, I always told her.

"Terrific legs," ESPN says. "You don't mind my telling you that?"

"She was a chorus girl. She was in Damn Yankees, Bye Bye Birdie, It's a Bird, It's a Plane, It's Superman ... I forget what else."

"That's all right, Salt. I saw all those shows. I must have watched her perform."

I never saw her. I never went to shows until she took me. "After she couldn't dance anymore, she was a secretary at the radio and TV union, I forget what it's called, and I came to work in the mailroom, and we met." I don't feel like crying in front of ESPN. "We had twenty-two years together. After she was gone, I didn't know what to do with myself. I talked to her at night. Like the roommate I had, talking to Wilma. Only I didn't bother anyone, because no one else was there. Maggie is fire now—she asked to be burned. When I get out of here, I want the same thing."

"You want to be cremated?"

"Are you hard of hearing, Dick?"

He laughs at that. "I am, a little. But I heard that. Who else have you told?"

"I told Gypsy, and the doctor, maybe."

"Would you like me to check on it for you?"

"How much is it gonna cost me?"

"There's no charge."

"I heard that before."

"Really," ESPN says. "I'm a volunteer. I don't charge for anything I do here."

"Okay, then,"

He gets up. "I'll tell you what. Before I leave, how about if I hang up Maggie's picture for you?"

"Somebody's gonna grab it. It's my only one. I had more pictures of her, but I don't know what happened to them."

"Don't worry, Salt," he says, "I won't let anyone take it."

He has a cardboard frame that he puts the photo into. It fits exactly right. This ESPN is really something, a mind reader.

"How about over here?" He hangs it on the wall next to my bed. If I look through the middle of my trifocals, I can see Maggie's face. "Tomorrow is Monday, Salt. I'll come in the afternoon."

I'm waiting to see if anyone else notices the picture. I hope that it's Gypsy who comes in. It's taking a long time. I like having Maggie on the wall. I'll bet that ESPN told all of them he'd sue the shit out of anyone who touches the picture. None of them will dare.

"Hey Mr. Perelman—is that you?"

Maybe I slept a little. It *is* Gypsy who came in. I think I'm getting to be a mind reader, too, from hanging around with ESPN all the time.

"Who is that with you?"

"Maggie—my wife."

"Nice looking woman. You were kind of a handsome dude yourself, Mr. Perelman."

"You think you could keep an eye on Millie for me, make sure she leaves the picture alone?"

"Sure I can. Now I'm going to fix your I-V. Have you been using your pain medication?"

I don't know. I can't remember using it. If it means I'm getting better, I don't want to. Maggie has been waiting for me a long time. I shouldn't be late.

Time goes slow in this place, then sometimes it zigzags around, like a bug on the ceiling. I can't see Maggie in the dark, but I know she's there. "You can kiss me, Jerry. If you feel like it."

"Do you mean it?"

"Try me out."

I think I'll sleep a little now. I can't stay up as late as I used to.

They got another guy in the bed next door. They must have snuck him in during the night. This one's no talker—he hasn't said a word. Millie's in there working on him, behind the curtain. Who knows what she's doing? It can be anything she wants, if the guy can't talk. She likes being behind the curtain with people who can't fight back. She better not try it with me, though. Especially now that I've got ESPN on my side.

He comes with a paper for me. "You think you can sign this, Salt?"

"What is it?"

"It directs the funeral home to cremate your remains."

"Did they do Maggie?"

"Yes they did."

Okay, I'll sign. ESPN says both funerals were paid in advance, Maggie's and mine. When my turn comes, he says he'll make sure they burn me like I want. "I've brought you something, Salt." Actually, he brought two things—donuts and a CD player with Damn Yankees, original cast. We listen. "That must be Maggie singing now," he says. "Can you pick out her voice from the others?"

I think I can.

"Hey, what show is that?"

The guy in the next bed—he can talk after all. "It's Damn Yankees. My wife, Maggie, was in the chorus."

"Yeah?"

When I look again, the guy has rolled over onto his back, staring at the ceiling. It doesn't look like he's gonna say anything more. I know what that feels like, the way I was before ESPN showed up. Who sent this ESPN to me anyway? Maybe it was God. Maybe he's an angel.

"Hey, how come you're a volunteer for me and not for this other guy?"

"I picked you, Salt."

"Wha'd'ya mean?"

"There's an organization that matches volunteers with patients. Beth Jeshurun felt you were a good candidate for the program. I looked over the files of a few candidates and, when I chose you, the people here approved it."

The people here? I'd like to know who. Maybe it's Millie. I can see her writing things in my file. *I'm your mother now, Jerry. I want to take care of you.*

"Don't turn away from me, Salt. What's wrong?"

"I don't like people reading all about me."

He puts his big hand on my arm. Allie Reynolds hand. I let him. "I've learned a lot more about you from our visits than I did from the file."

"What kind of program is it, anyway? You trying to convert me into a Catholic?"

"No way, Salt."

"Then what?"

"Well ..."

"Well?"

"It's for people who are dying."

"Dick—you're dying?"

No, he's not. I get it now. It's me. Gwen Verdon is singing: Whatever Lola wants, Lola gets. And, little man, little Lola wants you. Maggie used to play this record all the time. Sit me in a chair and dance around me. Doing Gwen Verdon's part.

"Maggie's calling me. She wants me to be fire."

"I know."

"Why are you doing this? What's the matter with you, Dick? You got nothing better to do?"

"I don't know," ESPN says. He's frowning. "We all think about dying."

"You got no one waiting for you."

"No."

"You're a Catholic, though. You're in good with God. He'll take care of you."

"You believe in God, Salt?"

"Nah. Not much. But I know that Maggie is fire. She talks to me. At night."

"Bullshit."

The guy in the next bed. He says one word every fifteen minutes. Maybe I should time him and have ESPN put a pillow over his head the next time he's due to talk. Not that I care what he says. The poor shmuck. I haven't seen anyone visit him—not so far.

ESPN sits down next to me, doesn't say anything more, just rubs my shoulder, like a massage. His hand feels warm. We listen to the music: Who's got the pain when they do the mambo? Who's got the pain when they go: uh. Who needs a pill when they do the mambo? I don't know who—do you?

I guess I have the pain.

"Hand me that, will you?" ESPN passes me the control for the I-V, and I push on it, a few good squirts. It'll take a while to work, but by time the record is over maybe I can sleep.

ESPN has started coming every day, now. They all know him— Gypsy, Millie, even Yelena. Millie has started being nicer to me. She always pulls the curtain when she cleans me up, and she doesn't boss me around so much. She even straightened out Maggie's picture once when it was hanging on the diagonal. I know why she changed her behavior. It wouldn't be any fun to get the shit sued out of you by ESPN. The pain medicine has been working real good. I get a lot of sleep and I see Maggie most times. We'll be together soon, she says to me.

My mouth is dry. I don't have to ring for Gypsy, because ESPN is here. There's a glass straw I sip with, while he holds the water for me. He's wearing his blue suit. "Is it Sunday today?"

"No, Salt, it's Wednesday."

"How come you have the suit?"

"I came straight from my AA meeting," he says. "I like to wear my suit to remind me it's serious."

"I never knew you were a boozer."

"I should have told you. It never came up."

"Is it real bad? You can't leave off?"

"Five years I have. Almost six."

"If you ever think you're gonna go back on, you can call me. I mean it."

"I will, Salt."

"Maggie had a friend went to AA. She used to call us up sometimes."

"What did Maggie tell her?"

"'Life is golden.'"

ESPN looks at me. He's a little fidgety today. He keeps rolling his shoulders, like he's trying to get his jacket to sit right. "Do you believe that, Salt?"

I have to think about that one. There's pain, and there's pain medicine. Maybe the whole thing is not really golden—only silver. But once you get made into fire, then it's all different. Nothing hurts, and you don't have to think anymore. There's no other people, not really, only flames. Sometimes Maggie is one part of the fire and sometimes she's a different part. I don't know if ESPN can understand all that.

"When I'm fire—what'll you do with yourself?"

He laughs, shakes his head.

"Maybe you can volunteer for another guy."

"I don't know."

"You can ask Yelena. She's the one who comes in the middle of the night, when it really hurts. She'll know which guy needs a dick. You have to talk Russian to her. I can teach you a little. I want you to take the picture, Dick. Me and Maggie, put it on your wall. Don't let Millie get it. Hey, you got something sweet? I feel like it now."

"I'll see if they have something downstairs."

They already sent me a Rabbi. Orthodox, I think, with a skullcap. He looked about twenty, best they could do. I understand you're a Jew, he said. Sure, as much as the next guy. Would you like me to read to you—a Psalm, or something from the Talmud? He's wearing blue jeans and a t-shirt. He's got muscles all over like Arnold Schwarzenegger. They must have a gym in the shul. Or, I can just sit with you, he says. Did Millie send you? He's shaking his head, but I wasn't born yesterday. Rabbi, I don't need you. If I want someone to read to me, ESPN can do it.

"I found a Mounds Bar, Salt. Will that do?"

I can taste it. So sweet. Half for me and half for Maggie. "Hey, Salt, are you okay, wake up." *You're close now, Jerry.* I didn't do anything myself, Maggie, I waited. *I'm proud of you, Jerry.* "Salt? God dammit, Letoya, get the doctor up here!"

That's ESPN, Maggie.

What's he yelling about?

I don't know.

Terry and Egypt

Terry had a strong spiritual side—it was one of the things Egypt had loved in him from the beginning. They met in the desert at a rock concert. She had driven down from UC San Bernardino with her girlfriend, Melissa. Terry had been staying alone in a small, cheap tent that could hardly sleep two. He had blue eyes that sucked you in, like tunnels to another world. After one night, Melissa was sleeping by herself.

Terry knew the Bible; that was nothing special—plenty of people did. But who also quoted the Upanishads and the Tao Te Ching, and knew the Heart Sutra by heart? Who else looked out across the sand, eerily pale in the red sunrise, and chanted in Sanskrit? To continue on with him was an easy choice: it was mid-semester—she had two A's and two C's; she was a junior. She wrote her parents a note, to be delivered by Melissa, who was also a witness. "I'm going of my own free will. I need to do this. In a few years I'll probably have it out of my system, and I'll settle down the way you two did."

Terry had a steely gray SUV that looked from the front like a crouching animal ready to spring. After they had thrown the tent in the back along with Egypt's small suitcase, he asked her: "Where to?"

"I've always wanted to see Texas."

"Texas isn't much."

"Oh," she said.

Terry had long arms. He threw one around her, squeezed her against him. They kissed. "Okay," he told her. "Let's try it."

She was a thin girl, narrow in the shoulders, heavier in the chest; small hips, round behind. She had reddish hair that hugged her head in a tight halo, brown-framed glasses that she wore for show more than sight. When she drove, it was fast, two hands on the wheel, the seat dialed up high then shoved forward so she could bang the pedals. Terry had a laconic driving style, totally opposite; she covered the distance he had left undone. They were a good team.

They took a roundabout route, spent two nights in the tent, the third in a motel in Raton, New Mexico. They got to know each other. Egypt was vegetarian, but willing to compromise. She was afraid of spiders; she wasn't meticulously clean. She had a small scar on her right leg from a childhood fall, but nothing like Terry's knee, which was a mass of scars from two surgeries. In the end, the doctors had messed him up worse than he was before.

Egypt admired his philosophical attitude. He had been on the baseball team at Cal State Fullerton, a first-baseman. He expected to be a high draft choice, but after his one false step on the base path it was all over. He got a degree, a teaching certificate, coached high school ball—there the story stopped. "Enough for one night," Terry said. She knew there was a lot more to come. She estimated that he was younger than her father, who was forty-five, but older than her 34-year-old geology professor. She would have asked him, but she was afraid of breaking the spell.

Terry prayed twice a day at dawn and sunset. He liked to scramble up to a high place (favoring his bad knee, but only a little), where he had a view of the rising (or setting) sun, staring at it while he chanted. At the motel, their vantage point was the tiny terrace which looked east over the desert. The red sun seemed to rise slowly, as if to the rhythm of Terry's prayers.

On their way down the Interstate, he asked if she had any money. She didn't—only a Visa Card that her father had probably stopped by now; but even if the card was still good she didn't want to use it and take the chance he could trace her location. Terry said he was also nearly broke, but that they could rob a bank.

"What?"

He rubbed her thigh with his large hand. "Don't worry," he told her. "I've done it before."

It turned out that her card still worked. In Albuquerque, they bought disguises—ski masks, cheap wigs, stocking caps—and loaded up on duct tape; Egypt wandered into a hippie-store and found long, black, hooded robes like monks might wear. They drove six hundred miles to a gun show. She waited in the car until Terry came back with a couple of semiautomatic handguns. He handed her one of them. When she told him she hated guns, he grinned, looking boyish. "Don't worry—yours won't be loaded."

They drove all day; she did most of it, nearly eight hundred miles. The SUV was dusty and grimy. "They all look alike, especially dirty," Terry said. The first bank was in a suburb outside of Tulsa. They went in at eight a.m., with the first employees. Egypt mummified two of them with the duct tape, while Terry took the third behind the counter and into the vault. The whole thing took twenty minutes—they got just over sixteen thousand.

They drove three hundred miles and camped that night. The air was getting chilly. Terry got his big sleeping bag out of the SUV and Egypt crawled into it with him. She nuzzled her face for a minute in his hairy chest, then shimmied into position along his body. When Terry fucked, it was slowly, silently, reverently—as if he were praying. Egypt loved it.

After breakfast, they found a library in town and read the Tulsa paper on the web. The story described a man of medium build and a smaller accomplice, perhaps a woman, perhaps a boy. They had both been masked and robed, hands covered with latex gloves. Egypt had not spoken during the robbery. So far, so good. But Terry said they'd had beginner's luck and needed to prepare better. The next bank, in Manhattan, Kansas, they cased for three mornings before doing it. Terry disguised himself in a theatrical moustache and eyebrows, sunglasses, torn jeans, baseball cap pulled low on his forehead. He bought a two-thousand dollar car from a lot named "Strange Sam's."

It was beat up on the outside, but ran fine. They left the SUV on a back street six blocks away and did the bank with the old wreck. It was all smooth—this time almost twelve thousand.

They decided to try one at six p.m., grabbing the last employees as they left and forcing them back inside. One of them struggled for a moment, but Terry knocked him down with a swipe of his forearm, like the guy was a bowling pin. He was *strong*. That night, they missed the setting sun, but drove out into the prairie and chanted in the direction where it had gone down.

Egypt noticed that her feces were getting darker and sturdier. She'd once read in a book on Chinese philosophy, or maybe Indian, that the color and consistency of your feces could be an indication of how your life was going. For the last few years, her shit had been coming out in puny little marbles, but now, watching it daily, she saw improvement. When she finally told Terry, he grabbed her, laughing, squeezed her, kissed her ear, whispering: "Baby, I love you."

They did nine jobs in all, netting over a hundred fifty thousand, before Terry called a halt. He put some of the money *back* in banks, all under false names, some his, some hers, using phony driver's licenses; it wasn't hard to get them, or even very expensive, he told her. Another portion of their funds went into a few stocks he thought might be hot. Terry had such a strong intellect, which Egypt loved.

They applied for passports, renting a furnished apartment in the Chicago suburbs while they waited. Terry bought her clothing and jewels, and she marveled at herself in the mirror—could this be me? She called her parents—her mother was tearful on the phone, her father cold. When Terry found out about the call, he was angry. They couldn't rule out that the police knew their identities, he told her; she had thoughtlessly jeopardized their freedom. But Egypt needed validation. She wrote Melissa, enclosing a photo of herself in a short dress that showed her legs off, a tiara at her neck. The letter came back; evidently, Melissa had moved on.

Terry chanted every day—from the lakeshore, the roof of the Prudential Tower, from small parks or cul-de-sacs. He was content to spend his time reading and playing the market, but Egypt quickly got bored. Her feces turned into pellets again. She wanted to get back on the road, do another bank. Terry said no. He took her sailing on Lake Michigan, got her to start writing a journal. It helped some.

When the passports arrived, they drove down to Mexico for some beach time, leaving their stuff stored in Colorado on the way. The ocean tranquilized Egypt, its beat in her ears day and night. She lay in bed and the waves seemed to roll over her. She sat on Terry's chest and felt his stiff, wiry hair tickling up through her crotch and between her buttocks. She made him come slowly, exquisitely—each time slower than the last. Evenings, they prayed into the ocean; mornings, with the waves at their back.

Terry took her to the local casino and taught her to play craps. She had a run of forty minutes, throwing sevens and making her points. The table drew a crowd, all eyes on her. She was wearing a thin beach dress, red sandals, her exposed shoulders bronzed, hair the color of brick. She took her glasses off and handed them to Terry. She smiled, rolled another seven; the crowd applauded. Someone brought her a drink—she didn't need it.

By the time that run was over, she had won almost ten thousand. But in the weeks that followed, she began to lose. It was almost as exciting as winning, and in the end it didn't really matter—they were going to run out of money sometime. As far as Egypt was concerned, she could hardly wait. She was more than ready for the road.

It was winter in Colorado by the time they got back. They stopped for two days in Durango, long enough to organize their stuff and for Terry to study his maps. The snow glinted on the mountains, the sky full of small, fast-running clouds. Egypt felt a fantastic energy. They left at night, driving fast so that they could hit a bank in central Kansas first thing in the morning. They were both a little nervous, out of practice, losing track of a woman, who went for the alarm, practically under Egypt's nose. If her weapon had been loaded, the foolish bitch would have been dead; instead, Egypt clocked her good above her ear, opening a gash that spewed blood. They duct-taped her along with the rest and got a few thousand from the cash drawers. On the highway outside of town, Terry had to calm Egypt down—she was doing ninety.

The next four weeks, they did six banks, moving fast. The last was in eastern Ohio near the West Virginia border. Neither rhyme nor reason, Terry told her; roundabout routes, sometimes the Interstate, sometimes secondary roads—they'll be scratching their heads at the FBI. After the Ohio bank, they made the TV networks—the new Bonnie and Clyde. According to Peter Jennings, the authorities were still not sure about "Bonnie"; it was not ruled out that it could be a boy—a teenager, say—although the consensus was growing that "she" was indeed a woman. Terry looked carefully at a grainy tape from a bank in Iowa. He had worn an old parka that time, jeans and boots, a ski mask completely covering his head. Egypt had her robe, a blonde wig, greasepaint on her face; she could have been male or female, or something in between.

Backtracking through Michigan, they crossed the Canadian border separately—he in the car, she on a Greyhound. Egypt spent the night in a cheap hotel near the bus station in a grimy Ontario mining town. She fed *loonies* to the TV to keep it going. There was nothing about Bonnie and Clyde on any channel. She thought maybe they should do a few jobs in Canada—it would be easy. At midnight, she bundled up with a scarf and stocking cap to go for a walk. The snow was packed down on the sidewalks, the air smoky, no soul on the streets but her. The streetlights flickered in the grainy air, looking remote as the moon.

Terry was carrying most of the money. He had gone to Toronto to buy new IDs for them, and they were scheduled to meet in four days at a Best Western in Winnipeg. The thought briefly crossed her mind that he might not show up, but it lasted only a second. She knew Terry.

Sure enough, he arrived just an hour after she did, driving a new car, a Subaru wagon with Manitoba plates. Up in their room, he plugged in his computer and brought up the FBI website. Their pictures were on the screen. Egypt blushed and fanned her hand over her face. "It's my fault," she said. But Terry made love to her anyway. He had missed her badly—he needed her with him every day.

They tried out a town called Bradley, in northern Alberta. It was a minor resort town, sitting on a large lake two hours from the foothills of the Rockies and close enough to Edmonton for a weekend drive. In summer, the shore sprouted thickly with bushes and tough little trees. Boats sailed quietly out from the two launching docks, fishing into the sunset. On sticky afternoons, giant thunderclouds boiled out of the lake, turning the sky the color of slate and spawning a wall of wind that moved through the town pushing the rain ahead of it.

By September, the nights were already cold. Most of the tourists had gone home, though a few returned for weekends of gambling in the nearby Native casino. The town's focus moved inland from the shore to a large recreation complex, with its gym and hockey rink, its swimming pool, game room, bowling alley and performance stage.

They called themselves Jim Wright and Clay Gleason.

Egypt got a waitress job in a restaurant whose picture windows looked out on the lake. The summer business had consisted of tourists in shorts and local fishermen who barely cleaned themselves up for dinner. But in the winter, there were conventions in town, and there were also customers before the hockey games, and, afterward, the players and boisterous fans who came to drink beer. Egypt had let her hair grow long, tending toward red. Her compact little tubular body radiated energy as she moved among the tables, talking to customers in her slowish, breathy voice. Men liked her, and they tipped accordingly.

Terry spent his mornings looking after investments, and the rest of the days hanging around at the recreation complex. He lifted weights, swam, played squash, and even put on a knee brace once and worked out with the over-thirty-five hockey club. He told people he was Canadian, but had gone to school in the U. S., explaining his south-of-the-border accent. He talked stocks with the small brokerage firm in town; he was believable as a man who made his living as a trader—he knew a lot.

They lived in a house six miles out of town, along a gravel road that bordered the lake. They never socialized as a couple and seldom appeared together in public, except at the Indian casino, which was staffed mainly by Natives and not much frequented by the local population. Even after many months, there were a lot of people in town who didn't know whether or not they lived together; or whether they had arrived in town together, or met after having come separately; or even whether or not they were a couple at all.

There was no craps in the casino, only slots and a few blackjack tables, but Egypt got used to them—they were exciting enough. On weekends, when buses came up from Edmonton, the tables were crowded. Egypt examined her cards with a quick, cagey look. She rubbed her little nose with a finger—hit or stay? Her other hand was at her side—Terry squeezed it. Hit or stay? She almost always stayed. She wanted to be around for the thrilling moment when the dealer's cards came down and the suspense suddenly ended.

The week of Egypt's birthday she took some days off and they drove toward the mountains. Terry had bought another silver SUV, resembling the one he'd had when the two of them met. The two-lane road ran past pine forests and oil wells, occasionally a cleared field under cultivation. Egypt drove with her usual heavy foot, passing the rumbling, chattering logging-trucks, slowing reluctantly to move through scattered towns with their lonely, pathetic, wind-blown streets and makeshift buildings. It was 1995. She was twenty-four.

The valleys were still cold; there was snow on the ground in places, though the days were pleasant. At night, they curled together in Terry's sleeping bag. He slept calmly, with no sound, but she could feel his ribs move as he breathed. There were no sounds around them, either—no wind, no cars, no voices. She felt as if death might come for her one of these nights, as if she might be whirled up among the stars, to descend later in a new guise, perhaps a man, perhaps an animal. They were camped in a stony meadow where a river flowed through in five fingers. In the afternoon they had seen two grizzlies, mother and cub; they were recently out of hibernation, the mother foraging for food. Terry had asked Egypt if she wanted to move to another place, but she had said no. It was beautiful here, spiritual; she wasn't afraid.

The bear came back that evening, before dark. Terry fired over its head, but it kept advancing. When it got too close and he had no choice, he put four quick shots into its body and it crumpled.

"Oh shit," Egypt said. She remembered back to one of the robberies: Terry had the handgun to a woman's head, while Egypt got ready to go with another woman to get into the vault. "Your colleague is the angel of God," Terry had said to the woman he was holding. "If God wants you to die, she will make one tiny mistake back there and you'll get a bullet in the brain. Your life is in her hands." The woman had turned white. At the time, Egypt felt sure that he wouldn't have shot her. Not like that.

"I should go after the cub," he said.

"No."

"He'll starve, or something else will kill him."

"No, Terry. Please."

He shrugged, relenting, but then told her in a cranky voice: "My name is 'Jim,' remember? If you slip up in private, you'll do it again in public. How many times do I have to remind you?"

As it turned out, she never slipped up that way; instead, it was Terry who had left a trail, probably with one of his financial transactions. By pure luck, he found out about it during a squash game, his partner an unsuspecting police sergeant. After the game, he went home, burned papers in the fireplace, trashed the hard drive of his desktop with an axe, then picked Egypt up at the restaurant. They drove west to Vancouver, took a cab into town and hopped different buses, she to Seattle, he to Portland. Terry had two U.S. driver's licenses squirreled away for the occasion: Jim and Andrea Wightman, husband and wife.

They ran—Houston, Charleston, Ft. Lauderdale. Egypt was Andrea Gleason, Cloris Wright, Clay Wightman. She waited tables and hostessed in restaurants, one time in a "Gentleman's Club." She gained some weight in her thighs and her behind. Terry said he liked it. He had also gotten some fat on him. She loved him to lie on her with his full weight, pressing her into the mattress or the rug. They fucked a lot. After her period went off one time and there was a big scare, Terry got a vasectomy. It was no sacrifice for him. He had her; he had his computer, his day trading, his sports clubs, his chanting.

But Egypt still felt moments of nostalgia for the robberies. She was twenty-six, her youth getting away. "Maybe sometime," Terry would say vaguely, when she asked. They didn't need money right now: he was good at stocks, more than holding his own. Terry was good at a lot of things. He could have been a professional ballplayer. He could have earned a Ph.D., but his interests were too eclectic— religion, philosophy, psychology; at Stanford, where he'd gone to try graduate school, they hadn't known what to do with him.

Sometimes, Egypt wondered why he loved her.

They caught a plane from Miami to Paris. Terry said it would be easy to lose themselves in the E.U. "The borders are porous and in a pinch we're one hop from Africa." They wandered a few weeks, then settled in Villefranche-de-la-Mer, in the western Mediterranean near the frontier with Spain. It was early June. Terry's French was passable; Egypt had taken it in college, but couldn't say much. They rented a little box of a house with a tiny garden in back, whose fence gave onto an alley. It was three blocks from the wide, sandy beach.

Egypt got a job as a hostess at Texas Country, a French version of a country-western bar. Her poor, English-accented French was no detriment; nor was her lack of papers—they paid her under the table. She already knew how to line dance. She took customers out on the floor and danced with them, showed them how, tolerating the occasional straying of their hands from her waist or back. It was something to do. Meanwhile, Terry settled in as usual: the computer, the health club, a book on Thai Buddhism, written in French; chanting, meditation.

Egypt was twenty-seven. She tried to list the places she had lived. There were fifteen or twenty, depending on how you counted. After Villefranche-de-la-Mer, they would go somewhere else in the E.U. And after *that*? Africa? Asia? She looked up at the pattern of sky and leaves above her, the single tree in their garden, seeing neither sky nor leaves, only the mosaic. She was drinking a beer, the neck of the bottle cold against her lips. Their stays were getting shorter. Terry had developed a feel for when things were going wrong, a kind of sixth sense. His nerves tingled with the alarm; he'd let it ride a day, two days, maybe a week—then, they'd be gone. They were still on the FBI website, their pictures staring out at her whenever she looked. She was looking more and more.

She had a fantasy about surrendering. They would return the money that remained—it was still a lot. The judge would take into account that they'd never really hurt anyone, that they'd given themselves up. There would be no jail, only probation and maybe some community service. They'd get married, invite her family (even though they were probably still assholes), her friends from college. Melissa—where was she? She smiled, shook her head. Terry would never surrender. He'd rather die.

They took day trips—down the coast, or inland into the Pyrenees. Terry heard about a monastery, hanging off the mountainside. They drove, in rain, to the base village, then had to walk an hour along a paved switchback that zigzagged up the mountain. The sun came out, and the low, red- and blue-roofed buildings appeared out of the trees like enchanted cottages in a fairy tale. There were few tourists—the climb dissuaded most of them. A monk, Brother Yves, gave a tour to Terry, Egypt and three others. They stared into the small chapel, which looked to Egypt like a tableau in a wax museum. Three figures knelt in the pews facing an alabaster Virgin. Two of them wore white hooded robes, a man and a woman; the third was a woman in street clothes. They were so still that she thought they must be wax sculptures or perhaps street performers who imitated statues. But eventually Egypt realized they were real people praying.

Brother Yves took them out on a large terrace, paved with smooth stones, hanging at the edge of the mountain. The supplicants kneeled for many hours, he told them, moving as little as possible, learning the discipline of prayer. The monastery was unique in that it was shared by the celibate and non-celibate. Brother Yves lived on the mountain in simple quarters with his wife and child. Others resided in the monastery for shorter or longer periods, while their families waited below in the village. Still others slept in the village, but made the climb daily in order to pray. A celibate priest was the highest authority on the mountain, but the monastery was actually run by a governing board that included both clergy and laity.

"What does Rome say to all this?" Terry asked.

Brother Yves frowned. "They tolerate us," he said.

The weather turned windy in Villefranche-de-la-Mer. Egypt sat under her tree and watched flickering leaves shift the sunlight. In the alley outside the fence, two women were arguing about parking. The streets were becoming more and more crowded as summer residents returned. Egypt sighed, sucked at her bottle of beer. She could feel the passage of the liquid inside her. She pulled down the waistband of her shorts and looked at herself. Her belly was soft, amorphous, disgusting. Her shit, she'd noticed, had also begun to look that way.

The wind stopped for a few moments, making the air suddenly hot. When it blew again, the Herald-Tribune she had weighted down in the grass snapped like a stand of flags. This morning, wakening with a premonition, she had looked through the pages carefully. Expecting to read … what? That the FBI had removed Terry and herself from the Ten-Most-Wanted list? The President issued a pardon? The police no longer looking? "Bonnie And Clyde Off The Hook!" Of course, there had been nothing. She was pathetic.

Norman Simon

They made a second visit to the monastery. Viewed from just
below, its walls had the imposing rise of a fortress. Once they were
inside, Terry found Brother Yves and asked if he might be allowed
to pray in the chapel. Brother Yves had deep-set eyes, perpetually
pursed lips, not quite a frown. "Both of you?" he asked. The two
men looked at Egypt. She shook her head.

He had stayed on his bad knees almost four hours, imitating the
other statues. The time for tourists passed; the others had to leave,
but Brother Yves allowed Egypt to wait on the terrace. When Terry
finally came out, he looked like an old man, shuffling as he walked,
his back stiff from kneeling. He stared as if he had never seen her
before, then took her in his arms. "It was fantastic," he told her.

The third time he went alone, this time to spend a week in the
base village "to see how it would be." She had declined to come
along, telling him, peevishly, she had better things to do. But what
did she have to do? Line-dancing with phony cowboys at Texas
Country? Sunbathing? Drinking beer and evaluating her shit? She
was feeling a little sorry for herself, she knew; maybe the wind was
starting to get to her. She needed to shower, fix her hair, put on her
smutty dress. It would make her feel better

The morning after Terry returned, they took their bikes and rode
out far along the beach road, until the terrain became rough and
the narrowed beach empty. They found a wedge of sand among the
rocks and spread their blanket. Terry stretched out, hands behind his
head, looking at the sky. Egypt put her palm flat against his chest,
feeling his kinky hair and the contraction of his muscles against her
touch. The tide was low, the ocean calm and blue.

"I want to try it for six months," he said.

"Why?"

He sat up and looked at her, trying to pull her into his blue eyes.
"It's the closest to God I've ever come. I talked to Brother Yves. You
can stay with me in the village. You don't need to do anything, but
if the spirit moves you one day, you can pray with me. Imagine how
fantastic it would be to do it together."

Egypt put her hand in his swim trunks and rubbed gently. "Close your eyes," she said. She took her shorts and halter off, exposing her folded belly, her thighs and flabby breasts. Terry entered her slowly, but came in a second, his body collapsing above her. "Monk's ejaculation." He grinned sheepishly.

After a few minutes, Egypt kissed him. "Let's do some banks in France," she said.

He shook his head. "We'd get caught. I need more spiritual power. Brother Yves told me that some of the monks can pray on their knees for twelve hours, hardly moving. If I could do that, I could do anything. I could fly." He ran his big hands along her ribs. "Come with me?"

She didn't, but on the day he went, she drove him to the base village. He promised to write to her, a letter every day, so that they would feel close. After two months she would visit and they could reevaluate. He kissed her, then stepped back. He had shaved his head, and his neck, emerging from his black t-shirt, suddenly looked massive, in a way she had never noticed before. She thought he looked like Mr. Clean.

The letters came, long letters, handwritten with a thick pen. They were about Zoroastrian light and darkness, Christian symbolism, the cares of the Buddha, the play of light in the chapel, the sea of trees below the terrace, the melting of the world to become God. After a time, she put them in a box without reading them.

Meanwhile, the high-summer crowds flowed down on schedule from the north. The beach began to smell of suntan lotion, and the authoritative voices of the French women reprimanding their children drowned out the slurp of the waves. It seemed that all the women were nude, but Egypt left her clothes on. Down at the edge of the sea, a couple of nuns in white hassocks were supervising a group of five or six older-looking children. At a distance there seemed something strange about these children, and when Egypt got down to the water she saw that their faces had the flat conformations and fixed stares of the severely retarded. The nuns also appeared expressionless, going about their business.

At Texas Country, she recognized two of the women she'd seen earlier at the beach. They were in the line, dancing together rather clumsily, laughing when they lost the steps. Without their children, they looked flimsy and unremarkable, light as air. If the wind rose, blowing them away, their places in the line would be filled in a minute by others equally light. Egypt was dancing with a man in a black vest, his chest bare otherwise. He smelled of beer, pulling her to his hip. Directly above her, a ceiling fan spun slowly, like time passing.

Early in the morning, when the bar closed, she stopped at a beach café for a small coffee. Five or six of the tables were occupied, the rest already done up for closing. The waiter mopped his brow and stood for a moment staring out at the dark, invisible ocean. A man came along, moving silently, almost gliding; the waiter nodded as he passed. He stopped at Egypt's table to offer her a flower, a pathetic rose wrapped in plastic. She took out a few euros and gave them to him. She had seen him around many times, given him money before. He was dark, North African no doubt, probably an illegal like herself. He looked tired. She held out a hand, indicating the chair beside her, and he sat down. They spoke in rudimentary French. He told her that he lived in a small room with four other men; they were all trying to get to England, where things were supposed to be better. There was no bed; they all slept on the floor. He seemed to Egypt like a stray animal, and she brought him home. Why shouldn't she?

In the afternoon, when he wouldn't leave, she took a carving knife from the kitchen and held it ready above her shoulder. He looked at her for a long time. Finally, he took a creased photo from his pocket and held it out to her: a veiled woman with a baby in her arms; two more children standing by; an old man with a cane, face wizened, his stare as fixed as those of the retarded children she'd seen on the beach. The pathetic unfortunates and losers of the world! She gave him a handful of bills and he walked out the door.

A few minutes later, Egypt also left. It was high afternoon, the back streets quiet. It was strange what her eyes stopped on: an old woman in a hat and dress being helped, slowly, into the back seat of a car; a wall of bougainvillea, bleached colorless by the light; a one-armed girl on a bicycle, her intact hand on the handlebar, leaning slightly toward her bad side to keep her balance. Egypt walked around until it got dark. She didn't go to Texas Country, but instead walked inland a few blocks to the Gendarmerie, where she told them who she was. They let her go home to wait. Two days later an FBI agent came down from Paris to interview her. When he got around to asking where Terry was, she told him.

Barges

The apartment I inherited had been in our family for many years. It was in a building with fifteen flats, three to a floor, and a tiny, slow-moving elevator that seemed barely able to climb. The flat had three rooms. The bedroom was narrow and dark, the kitchen just large enough to include a little, square table and three chairs. But the front room looked out on the water.

I sat in the window well, watching the barges go by. Though they were under power, they moved up or down the river, through the coal smog, as if floating under sail. Their progress was regular, seemingly timed. There was a barge every ten minutes, or perhaps fifteen, moving left to right or right to left. This train of barges continued at night, lights floating on the water.

My binoculars were beside me. They had been brought by my brother, Kes, on one of his trips home from the war. Cheaply manufactured, their lenses were not powerful enough for long distances, but sufficed for looking out at the river. From my high perch, I watched the decks and wheelhouses. The barge crews often consisted of families—a couple and their children or, not infrequently, only the mother, the man having been swallowed up in the fighting. In these cases the elder children, boys or girls, would spell the woman in the wheelhouse or take command while she slept. Even when the crew members were not all related, they were still referred to as "barge families" in the common parlance of the city.

My bed had been in the front room on the sofa. It was long enough for me, but I woke every morning with a backache from the lumpy cushions. I had long since grown used to this, but once Kes and his wife, Annika, were gone I slept in their room, when I went to sleep at all. More often, I simply sat in the window watching the boats and, occasionally, dozing off.

The barges sailed up and down. There were fortified cities, smaller versions of ourselves, in each direction along the river. Beyond these, the territories were held by various warlords—English in the north, Franglais in the south. They fought among themselves and launched sporadic attacks on the cities and along the river. U.N. patrols went regularly out from the cities, and, occasionally, a larger expeditionary force would be sent, backed by the U. N.'s two aircraft. Villages would be destroyed, only to be rebuilt shortly afterward, from earth, from stone, from stray materials, tin and wood, whatever was available.

I seldom went out, except for food and beer. Before Kes and Annika died, I attended the *Lycée*. Though it was Franglais, it was considered to be somewhat better than its English counterpart. Shortly before my graduation, I sat the exams for the two universities, in Paris and London. Success in either examination might provide a ticket out of the city, depending upon whether a place could be secured in one of the convoys. At any rate, this was one of the few possibilities for getting away, apart from military service. It was during the short period after Kes' death and before Annika's that I received the results from my exams: unfortunately, I had not succeeded.

Our building was largely Franglais. There had been three English apartments, eleven people in all; now this count was down to nine. I had lived in the building since my parents' death, moving in with Kes and Annika. Even then, the little elevator had been aged and decrepit; it amazed me that it still ran. Inspections were a thing of the past, and there was a long wait to get machinery repaired once it failed, assuming it could be fixed at all. Some of the residents never used the elevator, preferring the relative surety of the stairs. The car was so small that three adults would fill it. You could stuff four in, but not without their bodies touching. When I encountered other tenants in the elevator, particularly the Franglais speakers, we would largely maintain silence. This was partly out of natural reserve, partly as a matter of security. No one knew what would happen if the U. N. left. One possibility was a bloodbath, fueled by differences in language and religion.

I met Eloise and Maribelle for the first time in the elevator, late one night when the little girl should have been in bed. They were the newest residents in the building—Annika had told me they bought the flat of M. and Mme. La Bas, an ancient couple who dated back to the time of my grandfather. Eloise was tall and thin, her skin pale. Her dark hair was clipped severely across her forehead and fell straight down over her ears; the effect was of a three-sided frame setting off her rather delicate face. There was no shortage of hair-dressers in the city; they worked cheaply and were visited often by the city's women.

The elevator descended. Maribelle stood sideways from her mother, her back against the fading faux-wood of the car. She had Eloise's wiry build, but her hair was lighter and complexion darker; her eyes looked hazel in the dim light, wider and softer than her mother's dark eyes. The father had been in the building at least once—Annika had seen him, though I never had.

In between Maribelle and Eloise, there were three small valises piled on the floor, one on top of the other. They stared down at them, or at the door, saying nothing. We would not have talked to each other at all, except that the car jerked suddenly and stopped moving. The weak light went out at the same time, leaving us in total darkness. It was clear we were in between floors; between two and three, I estimated. The city had an old hydroelectric power plant, which still functioned and was well-guarded by the U. N. troops;

but sometimes there were local outages at night when minor repairs were made on the system. These were generally unannounced.

I had a small flashlight in the inner pocket of my jacket, but I didn't want to use it unless I had to. There was a severe shortage of batteries in the city, and I was down to my last two. Kes would have brought more had he returned—I was reminded of his death once again. We waited. Eloise inhaled heavily, letting out the air in a coarse burst. Finally, after a minute or two, she said: "Will it be long?" She asked this first in Franglais, but repeated it in English when I was slow to answer. I wondered why she was asking me. She was older.

"Probably not too long," I finally told her.

We stood in the close darkness, in the limbo of our arrested motion, with Eloise's breathing the only sound. Around us, the building was also silent. The time went by. Though my watch had a luminous dial, I didn't look at it. What was the sense of counting the minutes?

"What is your name?" Eloise said.

"Paul."

She introduced herself and Maribelle, then reached out with her hand, searching until it found mine in the darkness. "We must go," she said. "We are already late."

Late for what? I extended my foot and touched the little tower of valises. During that epoch, there were many things that might be carried inside a suitcase late at night: black market items such as eggs or pork; illegal arms; jewels; drugs; euros. Ostensibly, there was a curfew, but it was lightly enforced. It's presence on the books allowed the corrupt city police to stop anyone who looked promising for a shakedown. Eloise and her daughter might or might not be stopped. There were always people on the streets carrying their meager belongings, especially women and children, searching for a better place to stay. Curfew hours were good for this—any place found empty was likely to remain so at least for the rest of the night, perhaps longer.

Eloise's disembodied voice floated out of the darkness. "Can't we get out?"

I tried to think what Annika would say. "It depends how close we are to the floor above. I think we are better off waiting for the power to come back."

Eloise ignored this. "We will try." She slid the valises a few inches, until they were positioned approximately at the center of the car, below the escape on the ceiling.

"Wait," I said.

I pointed my small light upward, finding the escape panel and sweeping the beam around its perimeter. "*Voilà*," said Eloise.

"We will need something to work open the outer door once we reach it."

"Don't worry yourself." She tapped me on the arm, and I swung the light in her direction. It lit up a retractable knife; the long, heavy blade slid out as I watched. This was an item of contraband in the city, though many people had them. Being caught with it could conceivably get you into the large, very unpleasant jail built on one of the hills that overlooked the river. Or, even worse, if you ran afoul of the U. N. rather than the police, the penalty could be summary ejection into the dangerous countryside. There was no appeal.

I wondered again what was in the valises.

"Help me."

Eloise had climbed up onto the stack. She removed the panel, which clattered to the floor, exposing the dark rectangle above. With a boost from me she was able to hook her elbows on the roof of the car and climb out. The reaction force caused the suitcases to tumble. From the sound they made hitting the floor, it seemed they were empty.

Maribelle went next and then myself. The landing was only a meter above the roof of the car. Eloise held the light for me. It took just two or three minutes of work with the knife before I was able to slide the door open enough for us to get out. We were on three—the hall was dark. We made our way down the stairs, Maribelle jumping the last three steps at each landing. I gave her a compliment in Franglais. "Speak to her in English," Eloise said. "She must practice." I reissued the compliment. Maribelle smiled.

When we reached the small lobby, Eloise asked me to put the light on her. She was wearing the ubiquitous costume of the city— fatigues and a t-shirt. The fatigues were cheap and easy to come by; there were warehouses full of them—clothing for an army, pre-U.N., that had never shown up. Her shirt was yellow, the logo worn into illegibility. She took a mirror from her bag, and I lit her face while she checked it. The cosmetics available in the city were cheaply prepared and smeared easily. Annika had complained about this.

Eloise finished fixing her makeup. She looked at me. "Do you want to sell the light? I'll give you five euros."

Euros were dear. The city ran on U. N. scrip, but euros were always accepted, and if you wanted to buy anything out of the ordinary, only euros would be good. It was legal to possess the currency in small amounts, and people tried to accumulate it. I still had something left in Kes' and Annika's bank account, but it was in scrip. I was out of euros.

"All right."

Eloise counted out the three coins and I gave her the flashlight. Immediately, Maribelle took it and began to shine the beam around the lobby. Her mother slapped her, rebuking her in Franglais. Maribelle shrugged.

Retrieving the light, Eloise illuminated the door. She pointed with her hand, palm up. "After you." She wanted me to go first, perhaps fearing I would follow them. The suitcases were soon to be filled, and I was not meant to know where or by whom.

Once outside, I turned left, following the river toward the center of town. Though the surrounding streets were without lights, it was clear that the blackout was local. The glow in the sky from downriver provided more than enough light to navigate the sidewalk. I had no destination but was merely out to take the air; perhaps some instinct for mental preservation had ejected me into the streets.

The atmosphere was dense with coal dust, moist from the river. Though the water was not visible from the sidewalk, I could hear the loud, coal-fired engines of the barges as they passed. The boats were already slowing down for the stop at the *Douane*, where their cargos would be tallied for import duties and searched for contraband. The inspectors looked first and foremost for weapons, including material that might be used to fashion bombs. The greatest fear was that a small force might infiltrate the city and attack from within, while a warlord army simultaneously besieged the walls. After weapons, the gravity of contraband declined through currency to coca and hashish and then down to products whose smuggling was a matter of tax avoidance rather than security. Of these, the prime item was cigarettes.

While Kes was alive, Annika had not allowed me to smoke. When I did it at the *Lycée*, I had to cover my breath with mints to avoid her annoyance. But after he was killed on the Russian front, Annika herself began smoking, and I was also free to do so. Cigarettes were very dear—because the wars had destroyed tobacco farms worldwide and because of the taxes. The legal product could be bought with scrip; contraband cigarettes were cheaper, but you had to pay euros. I felt in my crumpled pack—there were three left.

Abruptly, my steps carried me into the light. I turned and looked behind me toward the streets I had left—a dark canyon, the roofline barely discernable, the gunmetal-gray sky streaked with black. I was conscious of Eloise's euros in my pocket. A couple passed me, walking arm in arm, kissing. Perhaps they were going to a place by the river, where they could make love; or perhaps they had just come from there. There was little privacy in the city—people did what they could.

Suddenly, I had a destination—a restaurant, ironically called "Paul's." I went left, away from the river, in the direction of the hills. The street began to climb slowly. Already I could see the lights of the wall fortifications high above me. This barrier, surrounding the city on its landward sides, had been constructed about a kilometer out from the old medieval wall that had once defined the city's boundary. The new wall excluded centuries of growth—both the expansion of the city proper and the extensive suburbs which had spread out around it. All of this was beyond the hills and had thus been considered indefensible.

Paul's was a night-restaurant, open from ten in the evening to ten in the morning. It was a plain-looking place, located a few streets from the *Lycée*. I had passed it many times, but never been inside. A bell tinkled as I entered and a white aproned *serveuse* rushed over to cut me off.

"*Monsieur. Vous désireriez?*" She looked me up and down.

When I answered in my slightly accented Franglais that I wished something to eat, she switched to English. "We are euros-only."

"I know."

She nodded, indicating the counter, still looking skeptical.

I scanned the price list, ordering up to the extent of three of my five euros: roast pork and rice, a glass of wine, a North-American candy-bar, real coffee. The *serveuse* showed me to a booth of plain wood, dark with age. She brought the wine and I sipped it sparingly while waiting for my food. It was not that I preferred wine so much to the ubiquitous, affordable beer. No, the truth was that I had surrendered my euros in exchange for nostalgia, those warm memories of the time when my parents and brother were still alive, when the war had not yet reached us and wine was a stable element of my mother's table.

The pork and rice also represented a voyage into the past. The centerpiece of the city's diet was now potatoes; these were grown in large quantities in the agricultural fields outside the wall and stored for the winter. Meanwhile, our animal protein came from the sturdy but stringy chickens that the city raised. There were also pigs, but not many. This made pork a euro commodity, as was rice, which came in on the overland convoys or aboard the barges.

I ate as slowly as I could, looking around between bites. The restaurant seemed to me crowded for this hour well past midnight, but the people looked subdued and sad, unlike in the "potato cafes," where the beer flowed freely. There were couples at most of the tables; they talked quietly and stroked each other. The women were lucky to be paired. Because of the draft, there was a shortage of men, despite the army stationed inside and outside the walls. The war, to greater or lesser extent, was everywhere, and the draftees were sent where they were needed—Kes, for example, had been killed on the Russian front, thousands of kilometers away.

The *serveuse* brought a plate with my candy-bar, still in its wrapper, bearing the city's decal to certify it had entered legally. There were also smuggled candy-bars on the streets, where they could be bought for scrip. All of the candy-bars came from North America, where the war was more confined and large territories more or less pacified. Kes told me that certain items such as cigarettes and chocolate were overproduced, the excess going into the black market and winding up in fortified cities all over the map.

When the *serveuse* came with my coffee, she covered my palm with hers for a moment; after she left, I looked and there was a bonbon. Earlier, I had seen a box of ten of them at Paul's counter—the cost of these was a full euro. I followed the girl with my eyes. She was younger than Annika, older than me. When I was twelve years old, in the seventh form, a girl had put a note into my hand: "*Jardin des Astrologues*. 16:30 *heure*." She was a year older than myself, one class ahead. I had been watching her at the recess, perhaps staring. Though I wanted to meet her, I was afraid. I could have asked Kes what to do, but I felt embarrassed. After I had let a week or so pass, I knew my chance was over.

I finished my coffee with the bonbon and took out a cigarette. The *serveuse* came over and lit it. "What time do you finish?" I asked her.

"At four."

"I'll meet you outside."

"No," she said. "At the corner." She pointed in the direction she meant.

"Okay," I told her. "*À bientôt.*"

But after I left the restaurant I started feeling sad, and it kept getting worse. After a while, I decided I wouldn't meet her and went home instead to sleep.

The barges moved back and forth under my window. The smaller boats had their own coal-fired engines; the larger were pulled by tugs also burning coal. The decks were like stages, where vignettes of life were acted out before my eyes: a child hanging wet clothing on a line, carefully placing each piece with great concentration; a woman in a shower stall, exposed from the shoulders up, water cascading on her from a pipe; a family picnic; pets—a dog curled up near the wheelhouse, a bird flying around the deck; a little boy getting into a pile of coal, emerging with a dirty face, his mother slapping his bottom.

Coal was the major cargo—modest piles on the smaller boats; large sooty pens stacked full on the long decks of the tug-powered barges. It was coal that made everything go. There was almost no gasoline to be had. The U. N. troops managed to fuel a complement of armored cars, and the police drove patrol cars; the two U. N. fighter planes were gassed up and ready. But it was coal that provided heat and a portion of the electricity, coal that powered the city's modest factories, coal running the clumsy tractors in the agricultural lands that furnished most of our food.

The coal came down from our fortified sister city to the north, where the one remaining regional rail line intersected the river. The trains were armored and carried a detachment of soldiers in addition to those who ceaselessly patrolled the tracks, watching for sabotage. Sometimes the trains had to fight their way to the river, but once the coal was loaded on the barges, it was more or less safe. The warlord armies seldom fired on the boats. By unwritten agreement, the barges had been accorded a special status. The river was navigable into unpacified territories both north and south of the fortified cities, and the boats penetrated there, carrying on an illegal, and even illogical, trade, tolerated because it was making money both for the warlords and for entrepreneurs in the city. Although people kept expecting this charmed existence of the barges to end at any time, so far it hadn't.

One afternoon, while I was sitting in the window well watching the boats, the door buzzer rang. I had not heard this sound for so long that it startled me. The thought came to me that perhaps Kes was not really dead; that it was a case of mistaken identity and now he had come back. I ran to the door. But when I opened it, Eloise was there, with Maribelle just behind her. For a moment I stood watching dumbly, as if one of them might magically turn into my lost brother. Finally, Eloise held out her hand. "*Bon-après.*"

I moved aside to let them in. Eloise was dressed in a feminine way—skirt and soft sweater, shoes with heels. Her hair was waved and she had made up her face. "*Écoute,*" she said. "I need a favor."

The favor was to watch Maribelle, while she was away for a time. "A few hours," she promised. "No longer."

"All right," I said. I had nothing to do, anyway.

"Thank you." Eloise pulled Maribelle out from behind her. "*Soit sage,*" she told her. And then, as if the little girl would not be able to understand Franglais in my presence, she translated. "Be good."

When her mother was gone, Maribelle went straight for the window. She picked up the binoculars, but couldn't focus them. "How does it work?"

"We can speak Franglais," I told her.

"My mother says I must speak English."

"All right." I fixed the glasses for her.

We sat watching the barges, sharing the binoculars. After a while, it began to rain. The wind blew in off the river, pelting the window with drops, which formed into long streaks. Maribelle slid from the window seat and started toward the rear of the flat, while

I followed. We entered the narrow, dark bedroom, where, on the same mattress and wooden bed frame, first my grandparents and, later, Annika and Kes had slept. The slats had been replaced many times, and a sheet of plywood inserted, but the old mattress still sloped downward on both sides, depositing the sleepers together in the middle.

The bed was nearly as wide as the room, leaving an alley of only forty or fifty centimeters between it and the wall. At its foot, there was space only for a chair—Annika and Kes had piled their clothing there before going to sleep. Behind the headboard, a dingy window looked into a small courtyard. Maribelle pulled aside the curtains to take a peek out; there was nothing interesting to see.

We sat side by side on the bed, dangling our feet. Maribelle was a girl who knew how to be silent. She kicked her heels back against the footboard, drumming quietly, without rhythm. No one had been with me in the apartment since the day Annika died in a mortar attack on the agricultural fields. They had buried her nearby in the large cemetery, just outside the wall.

Maribelle moved closer to me. I put my arm around her, and the drumming slowed. "How old are you?" she asked.

"Eighteen. How old are you?"

"Eight." She thought for a moment. "How did you get the glasses?"

"My brother brought them."

"Might he bring some for me?"

"He was killed," I told her.

"Oh," she said. Then: "Have you any games to play?"

"What do you do with your mother?"

She hunched her narrow shoulders. "We play at cards."

I looked in the bottom drawer of the *garderobe* out in the foyer. There was a deck of cards in a withered box, not ordinary poker cards but Mille Bornes. The instructions were long since gone, but I remembered some of the rules. Kes and I had played the game with our grandparents years before.

We went back to the window well. It was still raining. I explained the game to Maribelle. The idea is to complete a thousand mile road trip by putting down cards from your hand; some cards say "Two Hundred Miles," some "One Hundred Miles," or "Seventy-five Miles," and so on. The other players try to hinder you, by slapping on a Speed Limit, for example, or a Tire Puncture, or Empty Gas Tank. But there are also cards to take these hindrances away—for the puncture, a Spare Tire; to fill the empty tank, Gasoline.

Maribelle and I started to play. The game came back to me. When I made my thousand miles, Maribelle grimaced, nodding her head—she had no miles. The next time, I did the thousand again, but now she made six-hundred and twenty-five. She began to put her cards down gleefully. I slapped her with an Accident—she threw down a Repair, and on her next turn stopped me with a Puncture. Finally, on the fifth deal, Maribelle got to one thousand while I had only three hundred. She shot me a look of triumph.

Eloise returned. Her lipstick had been freshly applied, and it glowed wetly. The little girl ran to her, jumped into her arms. "She was good?" Eloise asked.

"Very good."

I expected her to give me a euro, maybe even two, but instead she took two packs of cigarettes from her bag. "Thank you, Paul." She clicked the bag shut.

Maribelle had to be prompted to deliver her thanks, but, as she did, she gave me a long look, her eyes opened wide. Behind her, I could see in the hall two of the valises, along with an umbrella, sopping wet. Eloise had put on a camouflage cap, which was also dotted with rain. Beneath it, her hair had lost its body and hung down limply. "We must go now," she said.

I told her goodbye, and again to Maribelle. As soon as they were gone, I lit a cigarette. To conserve my scrip, I had been limiting myself to two a day; now, I was in the mood to smoke as many as I pleased. I decided to go out for beer. I put on the raincoat that Kes had given me when he went into the military. Though it was a little large across my shoulders, it shed the water fairly well. There was a Printemps two blocks away, inland from the river. They sold beer and legal cigarettes, local foodstuffs, ersatz coffee and tea, simple pharmaceuticals. These stores existed in all the fortified cities, under a contract with the U. N. Here, there were ten of them.

In addition to the local beers, the Printemps sometimes carried one of the technically-contraband beers that were brewed up- or downriver in the unpacified territories. These were generally bitterer, stronger and more expensive, though you could buy them with scrip. There was a crowd in the store and I had to wait my turn. The woman at the cash register had worked there for years. But though we had seen each other many times, we might as well have been strangers. Her only acknowledgement of me was a nod. I nodded back.

That night I smoked and drank in the window well. I imagined that Annika was still there—touching my shoulder, calling me to dinner, admonishing me to study. The fantasy gave me a strange sort of comfort, mixed with bitterness. As I watched out the window, the sky slowly darkened and lights came on across the river, wavering in the rain. My grandparents had sat in this same window seat, holding hands. I could easily picture them. Their marriage had produced two sons. My father had also produced two boys in his turn, while his brother had been childless. We were a small family, divided into even smaller parts by the wars. I had four cousins on my mother's side, whom I had not seen since my parents' death. Two had gotten to North America, while the others disappeared into the chaotic geography of the battlefields.

My uncle, however, my father's brother, was near at hand—across the river in the English enclave of Newbridge. I had not visited him in many months. He had always made me feel welcome—the difficulty was on my side.

There was no way of knowing if he would be at home. I went on a Saturday morning. A stiff easterly wind had blown away the coal dust and the sun had come out. I crossed the high steel bridge, standing for a time in the wind, watching the barges pass under me. Many of the smaller boats looked alike; they had the same design— engine in back, with its smokestack spewing black smoke; long flat expanse; crew quarters and squat wheelhouse on the foredeck. Often, the boats distinguished themselves by small features. One moved by as I looked. On the roof of the crew quarters, a pale green disk seemed to float in a white sea, an effect created by painting the disk with an indeterminate circular boundary. The paint looked fresh; it would have to be, since the dirty trip downriver would quickly negate the artist's work.

My Uncle Hal lived in a building not unlike my own, but located many streets back from the water. The elevator had long ago ceased to operate, but the stairs were swept regularly and kept clean in a cooperative effort by the residents. No word of Franglais was ever uttered on the premises.

Before my father's death he and Hal had had a correct relationship for a number of years, neither wanting to break it off. Hal had been equally cool toward Kes, but his attitude toward me was always warmer. He felt that I was not hardened in my wrong beliefs, and might come around at any time. I believe he thought of me, in a certain way, as his son.

Hal's common-law wife, Alice, met me at the door, kissing me once on the cheek, in the English way. "Paul—how nice."

My uncle was in the living room, working at his desk. He wrote tracts complaining about the arbitrary power of the U. N. regime. This was legal, so long as the grievances were general, with no mention of an English community, and, most infuriating to Hal, so long as a translation in Franglais was included. The same restrictions, of course, applied reciprocally to the other side. Violation of these rules could put you in prison. My uncle tried to say as much as he could without crossing the line, but it was difficult. Most people in the city were grateful for the U. N. They believed that, despite the restrictions, life in the fortified cities was preferable to that in the countryside, where ethnic cleansing was practiced and civilians frequently targeted. The hope was that, eventually, large regions surrounding the cities could be pacified and the walls come down. If it had happened, at least somewhat, in North America—why not here?

We sat in the living room, around the low coffee table, Alice and I on the couch, Hal in a wing chair he had pulled up. Alice brought ersatz coffee and crescents. I offered them cigarettes from the last of the packs Eloise had given me. Both accepted.

"Are you working now?" my uncle asked.

"I'm watching a child." Of course, I had done it only once.

"English?"

I shrugged.

Hal shook his head. "Paul … Paul," he said, my name an admonishment. He wiped crumbs from his lips. "Is the conscription harassing you?"

"No, I still have some months."

But my uncle continued as if I had answered affirmatively. "Vultures!" he said. He sipped from his cup. "You think those U. N. bastards are drinking this shit? They have African coffee convoyed in from Paris. And wine. And chocolate. And frocks for their women. Look at what Alice is wearing."

She was wearing camouflage. She gave me a weak smile. Alice and Hal had been together for seven years. She was a hair dresser by trade, but wasn't doing much of it now. When the U. N. took over, it had become illegal to restrict a business to English, or Franglais, only. Finally, the inspectors had come around and closed her. The U. N. was lax in many areas, but kept a tight watch on anything ethnic. Hal had lost his job at one of the munitions factories for talking out of turn, and now they both worked outside the wall in the agricultural lands. It was dangerous, but it brought in scrip.

Alice asked me: "Are you going to sit the examinations again?"

"You should try for London this time," Hal added.

"I'm not sure." My thought was to let the conscription take its course, but I didn't say so.

After a few minutes, Uncle Hal brought out the chessboard and two beers, and we began to play. Alice announced that she would walk in the sunshine. "Won't you two come along?"

Hal shook his head. "I've already gotten enough of the outdoors to last forever," he told her.

We played for an hour in the tight, little flat, tight as mine but without the river. I made reflex moves, defending myself but not bothering to attack. Hal was intent. He was intent most of the time, I realized—he didn't dawdle or dream. Finally, my defenses broke down and he checkmated me.

"Another game?"

"No thanks," I said, though I had no place to go. I just wanted to get out of that flat.

Eloise asked me to watch the little girl again. She brought Maribelle around in the afternoon, but the job was going to be at night. Maribelle ran for the binoculars, while Eloise and I sat at the kitchen table and talked, over a beer. She was back in camouflage again and without makeup; her face looked tired.

"Perhaps I return late," she said.

"It's all right."

"No, I mean very late—not until morning, even."

"Maribelle can have my bed," I told her. "I often sleep on the sofa, anyway."

"Are you sure?"

I said yes, I was sure. I wanted to ask her where she would go. Was it a man, the smuggling, perhaps both? But I was silent—it was too soon for that sort of question.

She delivered Maribelle in the late evening, just after it had gotten dark. Quiet had settled onto the river. By a strange quirk of sound, the deep croak of barge horns was audible from far along the water. Eloise handed me a cloth bag with the little girl's pajamas, towel and toothbrush; also, a small, beat-up panda that Maribelle slept with. "Put her to bed when you want. She likes a light, a small one. She will talk and play in her bed until she has sleepiness."

"All right."

"Perhaps I will return early, perhaps not."

"Don't worry."

She nodded. Kissing Maribelle, she left quickly, the door clicking shut behind. She was not carrying the valises—whatever she would be doing tonight apparently would not require them.

"Can we play Mille Bornes?" Maribelle asked.

The best cards in the Mille Bornes deck are the Safety Cards—Gas Truck, Driving Ace, Puncture Proof, and Priority—which protect irrevocably against hazards an opponent can place on you. Of these, the most powerful is Priority, which allows you to roll on through many hindrances. That night, Maribelle seemed to have Priority in all her hands. Each time, she would wait for the right moment to play it into the game, laughing as she did, announcing her move with a flourish. She rolled up the miles, while I struggled against her, slowing her momentarily with hazards, which she was able to quickly brush away, driving on to victory.

"I've won!"

She sat in the window well, glowing and smiling, while I felt a childish resentment that I could not overcome.

"Let's play again," she said.

"No, you need to go to sleep now."

She argued a little; then, perhaps to forestall the inevitable, she asked: "Did you have a car, Paul?"

"Me?"

"My mother drove to Paris once," she told me.

"Yes, when I was your age, we took car trips."

"Outside the wall?"

"There was no wall, then."

She nodded at this, slowly, as if confirming a great truth.

"Can we watch out the window?" she asked. "Just a small time."

She brushed her teeth and pulled on a nightgown. Then, I put her to sleep on fresh sheets in Kes and Annika's bed—a little girl in a strange place, with only the cloth panda to sleep beside her and the small night-light I had plugged in to mitigate the darkness.

"Good night, Paul," she said to me, formally.

"Good night, Maribelle."

I returned to the front room. The flat seemed different now—not as it had been in the near past when my brother and his wife were still alive, but more as it was years before, when I would visit my grandparents and, sometimes, if it got late, be put to sleep in that same bed, until my mother and father would come to pick me up.

I sat in the window watching the slow parade of lights, but quickly grew restless. There was beer in the refrigerator. I opened a bottle, finished it, then opened another. After a while, I got a blanket from the closet and lay on the sofa to rest. I imagined that Annika was still alive. She put her arms around me, held me. I felt her lay down beside me, squeezing me against the sofa's back. "Just for a minute," she whispered …

I woke to a hand on my shoulder, shaking me gently. "Annika?" I thought she was waking me for school.

"You left the door unlatched."

Eloise. Her face was pale in the room's dim light. "What time is it?" I asked.

"I don't know. Perhaps four."

I smelled her breath. It was overpoweringly sweet, as if she had rinsed it many times with a sweet mouthwash. Her arm brushed against mine, and I could feel the coarse cloth of her fatigues.

"Where is Maribelle?"

I swung my feet to the floor, covering a yawn. "In the bedroom. She's asleep. You can leave her, if you like."

"I had better take her," she said. "Thank you."

She went back toward the bedroom and came out with the sleepy girl, who carried her panda, her eyes closing as she tried to walk. I felt sleepy myself, clumsy in my disheveled clothing.

"Thank you," Eloise repeated.

I stood aside to let them pass me. The door clicked behind them, and they were gone. I stood for a few minutes before I could find the energy to move. In the bedroom, I saw that Eloise had pulled the sheet up and straightened the blanket. You could hardly tell that Maribelle had slept there.

But underneath the blanket the bed was still warm. I lay on my back in Maribelle's warmth and looked at the ceiling. There was a bad spot that Kes had plastered a number of times. Now it had come loose again, and a large flake of plaster hung off vertically, ready to fall. Shortly before she died, Annika had asked me to fix it, but I had never gotten around to the job. Once I had resolved to do it the next day, I was able to fall asleep.

In the morning, I found two euros that Eloise had left on the night table. Adding the euros that still remained from my sale of the flashlight, I now had four. I decided to go to Paul's again that night. In the meantime, I attended to the ceiling and went out to buy some groceries. Before putting the food away, I cleaned the refrigerator and the kitchen cupboards.

Later, sitting in the window well, I looked at Kes' bankbook. If I were careful there would be enough scrip left to keep me for a month. After that I would have to find a way to earn more. There was *chômage*, of course, available from the city, but in return for the small stipends you had to work twenty hours a week in the agricultural lands. I had no desire to do this.

I had brought home both the English and Franglais newspapers and now opened them to the job ads. There was work in the lands and in the munitions factories, which made shells and small arms. The skilled trades seemed in high demand—ancient buildings and aging infrastructure were in constant need of repair. But for a young man with a fresh *diplôme* from the *Lycée*? I knew there were teaching positions, but these required special training beyond *Lycée* and were never advertised in the newspapers.

What more? One could serve a long apprenticeship in a legal firm, eventually learning the law and becoming licensed oneself. The U. N. and the city administration hired a certain number of bureaucrat trainees, but these positions could not be obtained without a certain amount of influence, familial or financial. To top all this off, any of the better jobs required that military service be completed. If worse came to worst, I could always advance my position in the draft, following my brother to the Russian front, perhaps to share his fate. If Annika had lived, she would never have allowed this. But there was no one left to weep for me now. I could do as I wanted.

That night, I took a nap from eleven to two-thirty; then, I washed, dressed, and went out to Paul's. I wore a suit that had been Kes', along with my best shirt, open at the collar. The *serveuse* looked at me as I entered, then quickly looked away. I went directly to her at the counter.

"*Monsieur.*" She greeted me formally, as if I were a new customer, not speaking English to me, denying that we had ever spoken before.

"I'm sorry," I said. "I had just lost my brother at the Russian front. I was too sad to be with you."

Her expression softened. She had big eyes, a prominent chin, hair a shade darker than Annika's. Her black and white uniform fitted her loosely.

"What can I give you?"

I asked for coffee and a North-American candy bar, a different one than I had ordered the previous time. When she brought it, she said: "Monsieur has a sweet tooth." She didn't smile.

"Do you have the same hours?" It was forty-five minutes until four.

She brushed a hair from her forehead. "Why?"

"I'm all right now," I said. "I'll come this time. Same corner?"

We walked toward the river, exchanging names. After a few minutes of silence, she put her arm in mine. She was wearing her uniform, with a camouflage jacket over it against the night chill.

Reaching the embankment, we descended the steep stairs. Karine slipped slightly and hooked my arm to steady herself. At the bottom of the stairs the quay swept off in both directions as far as one could see, lit by ornamental lamps, relics of a long-gone time.

There were benches along the river, placed about five meters apart. When I started to sit, Karine blocked me with her arm. "Your suit," she said. She took a large handkerchief from her bag and wiped the bench seat and back.

We sat and looked out at the dark river. I put my arm around her. At the next bench a couple was kissing heavily. When I tried to kiss Karine, she said: "Let's talk a bit."

She turned toward me. "I never saw you at Paul's, except these two occasions."

"I was a student at the *Lycée*. I used to pass the restaurant every day."

"Ah, you have a *diplôme?*"

"Yes."

She took my chin in her hand and turned my head gently, examining me with her large eyes. Finishing this, she lowered her hand to smooth the lapels of my jacket. "I have admired your *costume*," she said.

I began to tell her that the suit had been my brother's, but I stopped myself. Instead, I said: "I put it on because I hoped I would meet you."

"Thank you." She smiled at me. She had large, strong teeth. "I suppose that you wear it for your work."

If I did, it would mean I was a budding lawyer or bureaucrat, someone with prospects. I began to understand that she was administering a test I must pass in order to get closer to her. "I don't work now," I told her. "I'm studying for the university examination."

"Which one?"

"London is in January, Paris in March."

"Both, then?"

"Yes."

"You must be very clever."

"No ..." I hesitated. Why was I lying to her? The answer came clearly: Because I wanted to kiss her, hold her against me, to see her naked breasts, to be with her, body to body, breath to breath.

"If you succeeded in both," she asked, "which would you choose?"

"My father and mother lived in London once—before I was born."

"How wonderful," she said.

She settled back against me and we sat comfortably, watching the river. A barge came by, floating with dreamlike slowness, its dark spume of coal smoke visible against the faint lights from the opposite shore. On the long, flat deck a man stood, seemingly staring in our direction as we watched him. More likely, he was looking at the bench next door, where the couple had now begun to abandon themselves to each other, as if they were in a private place.

"Do you think about the boats?" Karine asked me.

"In what way?"

"Sometimes I imagine myself aboard, leaving by way of the river."

"But they go nowhere," I said. "Only out into the unpacified lands, and then back again."

"How do you know?"

"I see them passing my window; sometimes the same barge, moving one way and, later, the other."

"You have a window on the river? How I envy you! Perhaps sometime you will show me."

We leaned toward each other and kissed. For a moment I felt badly about lying to her, when she hadn't really taken precautions to conceal from me what she wanted. But then the kiss took over, and all I could think about was how her body would feel naked against mine, and how long it might take before it happened.

I watched Maribelle again on a wet afternoon. We took a walk in the rain, shielded by a large red umbrella that my grandmother had used. Maribelle was a good walker. We reached the large square in the middle of the city, which had once been Liberation Square, for the Anglophones, but *Place de la Espérance* for the Franglais. When the U. N. took over it was renamed Place of Hope.

A procession was passing. There had been a skirmish outside the wall, where a group of English irregulars had tried to set up a mortar position to shell the city. A U. N. patrol intercepted them, and, in the ensuring firefight, two of the defenders had been killed. Maribelle stood at attention as the coffins went by pulled by a small electric trolley. Above us, the live wires sparked in the rain. Maribelle was a straight little soldier, hand over her heart. It looked as if this were not the first time she had watched a funeral procession.

We stopped at a café to interrupt the walk back, sitting outdoors under a large awning. The wind had let up and the rain slowed to a drizzle. The city looked sad. I ordered a faux coffee and Maribelle a chocolate, hers constituted from a thin powder that hardly looked brown. She took a sip and frowned.

"Is it bad?" I asked her. "You can order something else."

"My real father died in the war."

I nodded. "My brother, too."

She took another drink, holding the cup with both hands. "I know—you told me."

"Do you have another father now?"

"Étienne," she said.

"He lives with you?"

"Sometimes." She took a handkerchief from her little purse and wiped some chocolate from her mouth. "Can we play Mille Bornes when we get home?"

We sat in the window well, I on the left, she on the right, as always. Everything went right for me. I rolled up the miles, while Maribelle was stalled. She studied her cards, holding them in close as a canny player would, her face stoical. Just as I was about to complete another trip, her mother walked in.

"We didn't expect you so early," I said. If she had stayed out the night, I could have anticipated as much as a few euros. This way, a pack of cigarettes might be all I would get. I needed the money to take Karine on a barge ride up- or downriver. It was the most expensive thing you could do in our surroundings—six hours by boat to one of our sister cities, a night on the barge, then six hours back. It was what I wanted.

"Do you have a beer?" Eloise asked. She had pushed her cart into the foyer; all three suitcases were on it and they seemed to be full. She didn't bother to hide them from me anymore, although I had never seen their contents.

"Mama, will you play?"

"You know I am not useful at cards."

"Please! Paul will teach you."

"I will," I said. "There is plenty of beer."

We began a three-way game. My magic quickly vanished, and Maribelles's face became triumphant. Eloise had been right—she couldn't play cards. She mistook accidents for flat tires and discarded mileage when she could have played it to the table. She sat with a vague smile on her face as Maribelle corrected her. Before this, I had never had the chance to watch the two of them together for more than a few minutes at a time. They conversed in a mixture of English and Franglais. The daughter was methodical, while the mother moved and twitched with nervous energy. I wondered about Maribelle's father, dead in the endless war. The little girl was perhaps all that remained of him. Even so, Eloise had more than I did. Kes and Annika had left nothing.

"Look, Mama!" A barge was passing. The rain had given way to a gray sky, bruised with gunmetal patches. On the boat's deck, a man and two young boys were kicking a soccer ball, directing it carefully within the narrow confines. Maribelle picked up the binoculars to watch. The boys took positions in a makeshift goal, a partnership of keepers trying to stop the soft shots that the man kicked at them.

"Let me see," Eloise said. She took the glasses from Maribelle, adjusted them, then swept slowly back and forth over the deck. The boys blocked the soft balls, so the man began to kick harder, more often with his right foot but sometimes with his left. A woman came out on deck and called to the others. Though I couldn't really tell, it seemed to me she was smiling. The man put the ball down for her and she kicked it at the boys, who returned it with too much exuberance. "Uh-oh," Maribelle said. The ball headed for the edge of the deck, with one of the boys after it and the man after him. Catching him before the edge, he shook his finger at him. When the boy began to cry, the man hugged him.

Eloise followed the boat until it floated out of view. We resumed the game, but now without enthusiasm. After a few minutes, Maribelle finished her thousand miles and that ended it. Eloise stood. "Time to go," she said. I expected her to give me a pack of cigarettes, but she didn't. Instead, after Maribelle had run ahead into the kitchen, she said: "Will you come upstairs later tonight after she is asleep. I want to talk to you. You know where it is?"

I knew. Eloise had the middle of the three apartments on the floor above mine. It was small and dark. The door opened into a narrow kitchen. Passing through, you entered the living room, whose window looked out on the courtyard. There were few furnishings—a worn sofa, padded rocker, a desk, a small, square dining table with two chairs. For light, there was the weak, overhead bulb and a single floor lamp.

Eloise sat me on the sofa and opened two beers. She wore a camouflage outfit, the jacket open, the long pants rolled up at her ankles. The clothes were too big for her—they might have been meant for a man. The jacket fit fairly well on her broad shoulders, but swam on her where she narrowed through the chest and torso. Her height was made mostly of leg. When she removed the jacket, her high waist stood out; the pants bunched there, tied tight with a cord that threaded the waistband, her short, plain white blouse barely tucked in. She had a complicated body; by contrast, Annika's had been even and compact.

She sat down on the rocker. "*Bon*," she said.

"What did you want to talk to me about?"

"Maribelle likes you," she told me.

"We get along well."

She pulled her chair closer. "I must leave for a time."

"You want me to watch her?"

"Yes."

"For how long?"

She pulled her chair closer. "I need a person I can trust."

"For the suitcases? What is in them?"

She sucked at the beer bottle, wiping her lips with her tongue. "Things."

"Cigarettes?"

"Yes."

"And more?"

She acknowledged this with a nod.

"My brother said to stay away from smugglers. It's dangerous."

Another nod. Then: "I knew your brother."

"What?"

"A long time ago. We were together in school."

"Which school?"

She named it. Kes had attended for a year or two, when he was eleven or twelve. I wished he were here now to advise me. I felt a pang of loneliness, the worst sort. Eloise got up and put a hand on my shoulder. "I'm sorry you lost him," she told me.

I shrunk away from her. "What is in the suitcases?"

"Currency," she said.

"Euros?"

"Yes." Smuggling euros was more dangerous than smuggling opium. Euros could be used to buy weapons and influence, to bribe officials, even to put together a private army if enough money were brought to you.

"Did you know Annika, also?"

"I heard about her," she told me.

"How?"

She had the habit of rubbing her eyes, the way children do when they are tired. Maribelle did the same thing. "Paul," she said. "The city is not so large." She pulled the rocker even closer. "I am afraid I have been recognized."

"By whom?"

"Who can tell—the police, a competitor, thieves. They watch me. I give a certain consideration each month to the authorities, but sometimes one is not protected enough by this. *Écoute* ...""

"How well did you know Kes?"

She cupped her face in her hands. "We were only children."

"Even so."

"We never really spoke. I knew who he was." She smiled. "He stared at me sometimes. I was tallest in the class, more than the boys. I had a pretty face. But I attended only for half a year. If I had remained we would have spoken."

I told her: "You still have a pretty face."

"No," she said. "That time is passed."

Eloise proposed that I take Maribelle for a few weeks, perhaps as long as a month. Her plan was to disappear for this time, finding a temporary place in our fortified sister-city downriver, waiting there until the eyes that had been watching her began to look elsewhere. Following this hiatus, she would decide whether to return to the city or to summon Maribelle to a new home downriver. "Perhaps," she had said to me, "you might choose to move as well, commence a new life."

The summer was nearly over, school would soon begin. Eloise planned to leave then. In the meantime, there were some things she thought she must do in order to assure her safety and that of

Maribelle. When I asked for some money in advance of the time I would take the little girl, she gave me ten euros!

I asked Karine to come with me on a trip, choosing the city downriver, perhaps because Eloise had chosen it before me. Karine smiled at me but held back. It wasn't that she didn't want to sleep with me—she offered to come to my apartment. Her objection, finally voiced, was to the money that would be spent, seven euros or even eight. This currency—she didn't ask where I had gotten it—would be much better used to assure the future. While she did not spell out *whose* future, it was obvious she meant hers and mine.

Still, when I insisted, she gave in. We left on a dark morning, the thin wind bringing a northern chill but also the possibility it would blow the dust away as the day progressed. We sat on the narrow bed in our cabin, holding hands, watching out the immovable glass of a crude window. Karine was subdued and silent. At the city's border, soldiers came aboard; unsmiling, they ushered us out onto the deck while they searched inside. A sad beginning—but once we were out into open country things changed.

"Put your arm around me."

We stood at the rail, watching the shore go by. Crumbling walls overgrown with summer vegetation; a gnarled, decaying tree and, then, a small copse of healthy trees; rough, makeshift docks, extending a few feet into the water, some with small boats tied up. And people!—an old man with a white beard, standing near a tree; a woman in a thin dress; a pair of children waving.

Karine leaned against me. She was wearing her best outfit—a patterned cotton dress, slightly too large for her, and real leather shoes. Over the dress, she had buttoned up a fatigue jacket, also too large, the sleeves rolled up to her elbows. Her hair was brown and thick, a mass of heavy curls. At the crown she wore the present I had given her before we left, a silken cap, made in China, with a dragon embossed on the front. Kes had brought it home from the Russian wars. She asked me: "Where have you been?"

"What do you mean?"

"Traveling. Before the wars."

I had been to Maastricht, now a pile of ruins; to Köln and Thionville; to Ostende. Karine told me that her parents had taken her once to Paris, but she was a small girl and remembered very little. "Are they alive?" I asked.

She shook her head, then gave me a small, rueful smile. "No one is left," she told me.

We came into each other's arms and I kissed her. Her face was cold from the wind, her breath sweet. I felt tears coming into my eyes and I pressed her against me so she would not see. But the moment passed. Karine shrugged and laughed. She put her arm around my waist and we turned again to the shoreline moving by.

The wind worked on the coal dust, allowing the sun to appear as if in silhouette. At noon, the barge commander found us to ask if we would take coffee and sandwiches. She wore bluejeans (a contraband item in the city, almost impossible to obtain), an old, old blazer, which might once have been lilac, with threadbare collar and sleeves, and a campaign cap in green and gray camouflage. A young boy, perhaps twelve or thirteen, brought the food to our cabin, where the bed folded into a table and benches. There was also a girl aboard, somewhat older. Karine had tried to start a conversation with the woman and girl, but without success. It was clear they wanted to keep to themselves.

After lunch, we went outside again to watch the shore. The air had cleared further, exposing a milky blue sky. Karine took her jacket off and hung it over the rail. We were far from the city. Here, the shoreline was rougher, rising in hilly formations strewn with rocks. We saw three men cooking over an open fire. Though their weapons lay near them, they made no move to threaten us or even to acknowledge our existence.

"If this was mine," Karine told me, "I would sail it as far as the rivers went—to Paris, if I could."

"You can't get anywhere near Paris—not a great deal farther than the U.N. fortifications, everyone says."

She leaned her head on my shoulder. "They don't know! I would sail as far as I could go and then leave it, Paris or not."

"You would be at the mercy of some warlord, without the immunity that the barge gives. The barge families have the best lives, the most freedom. Everyone envies them."

Karine smiled. "Your plan is better—I agree." She rubbed my back with her hand, massaging gently. "Once you get to London or Paris, you will be free."

We walked through the sad city, arm in arm. It was coarser and more raw in every way than the city we had come from. The site originally encompassed fortifications constructed in the nineteenth century. Rendered an anachronism by the technology of airplanes and missiles, it had become useful again in the post-technology era. The population of a few thousand consisted almost entirely of U.N. soldiers, a few family members, and support personnel, including shopkeepers, bartenders and prostitutes—exactly what you might expect in a military frontier town. The soldiers' duties consisted of defending the fortifications, launching patrols into the countryside and tending the agricultural fields, which were, in this case, enclosed within the walls.

There was one euro café in town, certainly not the equal of Paul's. Karine and I dined there. The pork was gray and dry, the coffee just a cut above ersatz. Afterward, we went to a nearby shop; among the groceries and beer were two small shelves of souvenirs. Passing up the pennants and cheap scale models of the fortifications, Karine found a single metallic sculpture of the Tour Eiffel, about thirty centimeters high and rendered with seeming precision. I spent a full euro on it and she rewarded me with a kiss.

Back at the barge, a bottle of sparkling wine awaited us. Karine had put on a wispy blue nightgown that once belonged to her mother. Underneath, the contours of her body showed themselves as mounds and shadows. We kissed—softly, then harder, then harder still. I shifted down to bury my head in her breasts with their silky blue cover. Karine dropped the straps of the gown and it fell around her. I tasted her skin, smelled the aroma that arose from her breasts, her belly, from the entrance to her.

And then, the moment came that I had imagined a thousand times. Inside her I stopped, suspending myself, while we continued kissing—once, twice, then again, until my thoughts became a series of brilliant flashes and I lost my mind. "Paul," Karine said, her voice breathless. "Paul, oh Paul."

We sat naked together on the bed, drinking wine. Karine took my hand and put it between her breasts. I could feel her heart beating. After some minutes, I was ready again. This time, without meaning to, I thought of Annika.

The little cabin became stuffy. The window could not be opened—there was only the bed, a small table and the two of us. Bundling up, we climbed out onto the deck. A steady breeze was blowing from the east, clearing the air and parting the clouds to show a few stars. Karine began to talk about the time to come. Even if I succeeded in the examinations, it would be necessary to pay a large bribe to get into one of the convoys. She told me she had nearly forty euros saved and in the coming months could perhaps put away four or five more. Adding to that what I had, there might be enough to buy passage for two on a convoy to Paris. From there, one could cross the Channel. London, she agreed, was the best choice—only the examinations stood in our way.

The boat rocked lightly in the mild flutter of the river. All around us the stolid fortifications rose toward the dark sky. Paris and London seemed bright and distant as the stars. At that moment I wanted nothing more than to return to bed, to Karine's body and sweet breath. A warm passivity ran through me, heavy as syrup. Soon I would have to confess the truth to her, that the examinations had been too much for me, that I would never get to university, that my future held no promise. Soon I would have to tell her—but not tonight.

#

The barges cross in front of me. It is dusk now, the day slowly fading. In the quiet streets across the river, lights begin coming on. The quay is empty except for a boy and girl, who sit sharing a cigarette. They are wrapped up in each other, ignoring the coal dust and the thin wind that is blowing in along the water. The sight of the smokers ignites my own appetite. There is a pack of American cigarettes in my pocket and ten more in the closet. I can barely remember how it felt to ration my cigarettes for fear of running out. Those days have been left far behind.

The barges have numbers now, large white numerals painted on both their sides. When it pleases me, I chart their comings and goings. I have written short descriptions of each boat in my journal, noting their physical attributes and, particularly, their crews. As changes occur, I enter them. Following our defeat on the Russian front, men have trickled back. More and more of them have been appearing on the river.

The boats move slowly, bubbling coal smoke, their running-lights winking in the dusty air. I watch them to the farthest edge of vision, then imagine their passage beyond. Sometimes, I picture Eloise standing on a dock far downriver, searching the decks for Maribelle and myself as the barges pass. She removes her cap and waves, dark bangs flowing on her forehead in the river breeze.

These days Maribelle seldom sits with me in the window well. She has school assignments to occupy her, friends at the *Lycée*. She has grown tall and thin, her mother's daughter. I have found her to be mature beyond her years, and, mostly, I allow her to do as she likes, despite cautions from Gwen, who tells me that girls need rules. Maribelle sleeps here in the outer room, as I once did, while the narrow bedroom belongs to Gwen and myself, as it did to my grandparents long ago.

In retrospect, it is obvious that Eloise meant to disappear; we have heard nothing from her over all the long years. But I know that Karine is in Paris. She managed to get there with one of my schoolmates, a boy two years behind me, who succeeded in the examinations when his turn came. Although there are stories of food shortages and riots in the Paris streets, I have a deep feeling that Karine is all right.

Here, the life we live is not so bad. The small fortune that Eloise left for Maribelle enabled me to buy my way out of military service and leverage a position in the city's bureaucracy. Since then, I have risen a bit through the ranks and earn a decent wage. Enough has accumulated for Gwen and me to begin to discuss marriage. Perhaps we will even have a child.

The daylight is all but gone now. Gwen and Maribelle have been away for many hours, but should return soon. I expect Gwen first, Maribelle later, reversing the order in which they entered my life. I seldom ask myself if I might have done differently, but when I do, as in this long afternoon, a steel net of inevitability seems to imprison my actions and I can hardly imagine that anything might have been changed. Below me, the sidewalk is empty; but beyond on the river the barges are still passing, their forms ghostly now in the accumulating darkness. Back and forth they move, a ceaseless procession that ever leads outward—comforting, mesmerizing, proclaiming, over and over, the illusion of freedom.

The Bargain

The lake is below her. How old? she wonders. Ten thousand years? Ten million? On nights when there is mist, the surrounding trees slowly vanish, seemingly melting back into the old water-world from which they came. The wind drops, and the moon, more ancient than them all, struggles through clouds. Frogs call, their voices far off. And Deidre wonders.

Her son arrives, making his way onto the deck. Allowing for everything, he is an hour late, though his plane was on time. But Deidre expects this. Merrill is a true antiquarian, comfortable in the freeze-frames of the past. The present's quick time eludes him. He has a shop of antiquities in Ann Arbor, out west. Some years it makes money, some not. It was the accident that provided this shop, and it is the accident that now buffers its losses.

Merrill kisses her. "Hi, Mom. You're out here."

Without getting up, she pulls out a chair for him. "Where else would I be?"

"It's lonely," he says.

"Yes." She turns her own chair to face his. "How is the baby?"

Her son grins. "Good. Did you get the pictures?"

"Recent ones? I guess I haven't read my e-mail. And Carlota— how is she?"

"Also fine. You should look at your mail."

She knows Merrill so well. He must have arrived with a mission in mind. It is not easy to get here. You have to fly to Albany, then rent a car for a two-hour drive. Deidre had always dreamed of living in a place like this; it was Merrill's father who kept them in the city.

He starts: "You know, Mom …"

But she won't let him. Not yet. "Have you eaten?"

"A few slices of pizza, when I changed planes."

"That must have been hours ago," she says.

She warms up some pasta for him, with a glass of wine. For herself: a cigarette and a Drambuie—she brings out the bottle. Slowly, the moonlight begins to disperse the clouds, and the stars appear, still threaded by strands of mist. Too hot to burn, they nonetheless roil with a luminous energy, strong enough to reach out through vast space. None of this is really comprehensible to her. How? she wonders. And why?

Merrill eats slowly, as if considering each mouthful. He is her eldest; thirty-three, but he looks older still, with his head of heavy blond curls, his rimless glasses, his corpulence. His life, she thinks, has been a function of the accident. Not just the shop—but Carlotta, whom he never would have met otherwise; and, then, by extension, the little girl, Deidre's new granddaughter. This progression, this *generation*, she understands even less than she does the light of the stars.

"It's good, Mom," Merrill says.

Pasta, with sausage and green peas—her son eats with appreciation. This has been a constant, persisting while other things changed. Merrill, who has always loved to eat, and his sister, who could not care less. She asks: "Have you heard from Brette?"

Merrill puts his knife and fork down. Talking and eating do not coexist for him. "Not since March," he says.

Brette lives in a desert town in New Mexico. She seems to get by, though neither Merrill nor Deidre knows how. Before that, she had gotten herself into real trouble with credit-card debt and a forged check. Deidre bought her out of it—another thing made possible by Herb's death. He had washed his hands of Brette, decided he'd had enough of her recklessness and selfishness. But after the accident, when the money was there and it was Deidre's decision to make, she found she could not deny her daughter. Now, Brette is doing what she's doing, effectively excluding her mother from her life. And Deidre is not sure if she did right or wrong.

Merrill eats slowly, meticulously. Deidre refills her cordial glass halfway and lifts her face to the now bright moon. The light enters her eyes, but when she closes them, there is no heat on her face, not the slightest sensation, nothing. The moon's light is cold.

"Mom?"

Merrill is done, his utensils set neatly on his empty plate. She says: "There's some ice cream, I think. Do you want coffee?"

He declines. He'll get a container on the way. He plans to drive back to Albany tonight to catch a plane to Boston in the morning. "Mom," he says. "We want you to come to Ann Arbor. To live. Carlotta and I."

She looks at him, his red, fleshy face in the moonlight; stares, as if he had spoken in a strange language she must struggle to understand. "Why?" she asks.

Merrill curls his hair with a finger, a gesture he has had since boyhood, so long ago. "You're so alone here—it's not good. And we need you, now that we have Vanessa."

She wonders which it is, her loneliness, or their need, the baby she could help care for? Vanessa—the name had meant nothing for an instant after he had said it. The name of a stranger.

She tells him: "I'm content here." But she adds: "Of course, I will come out. Maybe Thanksgiving, or Christmas."

"Mom, we're asking you. Carlotta and I. You could buy a condominium, or a nice house. We want to have another child. Two grandchildren—you could see them every day."

Merrill has always liked his mother. He has indulged her, and she him. As for Carlotta, his wife, Deidre and she have gotten along, nothing more; cold and neutral as moonlight on skin. "I'll think it over," she says.

"You will really? Promise me."

She promises. Merrill looks at her. "One more thing."

This "one more thing" is a request for money, another indulgence for the shop, twenty-thousand worth of renovations to enlarge and enhance the display space. She wonders if she should give him more than that; a lot, say half a million, and the same for Brette—let them do what they want. If Herb were here, he'd say no. But Herb is gone, and the money has replaced him. She thinks of it that way from time to time, as if it were a trade, a bargain made with the Devil. And, sometimes, she thinks of this Devil coming to ask if she would revoke the arrangement. But though she has invented this question, constructed it out of words, its logic cannot be comprehended. What could it mean to be returned to a world that no longer exists?

She says: "Let me think about it. I'll let you know soon."

Merrill is satisfied. This is the way she always deals with his requests: a delay—short, or a bit longer—followed by a check. He stands and they kiss. "You really should come to Ann Arbor, Mom," he tells her. Deidre thinks: He is sincere. And then: How little he knows me.

When he is gone, she pours herself another drink. She has always had a weakness for alcohol, always consumed a little more than she ought, and now, she is drinking yet a little more than that. But it is a great pleasure for her to sit above the lake with a cigarette and a glass. A spiritual experience—yes, very close to that—the creeping warmth of the alcohol in her chest and the thrill of smoke drawn deep into her lungs, then exhaled slowly though her nostrils and lips.

Yes, a spiritual experience. But some mornings, when she wakes, there is a slight sickness. She is, after all, fifty-eight years old—what can you expect? And, sometimes, she will reach for Herb and feel a greater sickness, an emptiness that lasts—a minute or an hour—until she drinks a cup of coffee, or enters her atelier and picks up a brush, or paints, or mixes paints.

There is no way around the loneliness; it is part of the bargain. This is how she has come to see it—an exchange of one world for another, accomplished in a moment. Less than a moment. She imagines the unimaginable. *In the gym on Third Avenue, Herb kneels to tie his shoe. He is exactly in the wrong place. Or—the right one? A TV falls, one of the thin and heavy LCDs that front the exercise bikes. Herb's neck is broken, and, in an instant, he is gone.*

There was an investigation, of course. It found that one of the mounts, designed to hold the TV against practically anything, had inexplicably failed. The only theory—offered to Deidre not in the official report but, informally, afterward—was this: immediately preceding the accident, two lifters had dropped their weights to the floor at the same moment, setting up the perfect vibration to make the TV fall. Had these incidents occurred in other locations, or with an interval between them, nothing would have happened.

Could this be? How could this be?

Now, she has her loneliness. She has made only one friend in town, a woman, whom she sees weekly, for lunch or dinner. There is also an art gallery, open regular hours in the summer, by appointment otherwise. It has shown Deidre's paintings, intricate pieces, with birds, flowers, geometric shapes, repeating at skew angles, bizarre perspectives. These works seem to her to have made themselves, from colors and white canvas, from time—no, from out-of-time—instants passing beneath notice, becoming hours, until … there is a click, or a change in the light, or the air, and the other part comes back, suddenly, all that she has lost.

Out on the lake, the moon hovers, pancake-sized and bright as a streetlamp. When the frogs rest for a minute she can hear the syncopated rush of water against her wooden embankment. The stars, subdued by moonlight, hide themselves in the remaining crevices of mist, and, out on the road, a car passes, its high-beam sweeping briefly across the deck. Light, she thinks, and a new painting begins to come. Bold streaks of light and darkness—electric blue for light, green for an undersea realm, the thick black of the mineshaft, deep purple of Hades. It is so radically different from the fishes and birds she has been painting, tiny, colorful creatures trapped in geometry, that her first impulse is to reject it. Where could it have come from, this sudden, drastic shift, this new vision? From her brain cells? From God?

She recalls the time she and her town friend took the train into the city. They went first to lunch, then to the Whitney and the Frick. But Deidre found she couldn't be there without Herb. The museums made her cry, and the city made her cry—it had always been Herb's city more than hers anyway. She felt relieved when they returned late in the night—to the dark village and the black sky full of stars. Here, she had thought, she had everything she would have chosen—the lake, the house, the atelier, yes, even loneliness.

It comes to her that human beings are not meant to be happy. Or, perhaps, only in out-of-time moments that can't bear any thought; or, in sensual pleasure. Her shoulders are aching now, and her legs feel nervy. The spiritual feeling has slipped away. Vanished. The Drambuie, the smoke in her lungs, the thrill of nature, or of making love—they're all the same, she thinks, brief streaks of light across a dark, mysterious world. Not happiness, not really.

She wonders if God's gaze is on her. What might it see, that secret Eye peering coldly through the moonlight? Perhaps what Merrill saw—she can still feel her son's earnest, heavy appraisal. She looks down at herself. She is wearing a man's shirt, Herb's, with its sleeves rolled up and tails flying. Her faded jeans ride low on her hips, tighter than they once were. She has no bra on—could Merrill tell? Perhaps the change in her has shocked him; she can understand how he might think she has let herself go. But that is not how it feels to her. It feels as if she is dead, and, at the same time, something has opened up in her. She no longer pauses in front of her closet, previewing what's left of the day, thinking: which top, which shoes? matching this with that. The shirt is there, she puts it on; the jeans go with it. She does the wash before her underwear runs out, hanging the wet clothes on a line at the back of the deck. She cooks in big batches, freezing what she doesn't eat. From time to time, in the middle of the day, she is conscious of her own breathing.

She still worries, of course. For one thing, about winter—she has never lived through the entire long, cold winter here. When the snow falls for months, covering the deck, and the frozen lake fades into an early twilight—how will it be then? She'll paint, she thinks; she'll paint her way to spring.

And she worries about her daughter. She worries that Brette will get back on drugs. Or get pregnant in her little hut in the desert that Deidre has never been invited to see, and there won't be any father around. Or get herself killed one night by some man who follows her home from some bar. The wrong place at the wrong time. If it was a bargain that changed Deidre's life, she wonders if all its terms have been fulfilled. Or is there more?

In her glass, there is a bit more—one more sip. She drinks it, shivering at the cordial's sweetness. She yawns, stretching her arms out in the moonlight. Tomorrow she'll wake early, she thinks, to begin experimenting with the new style. Hard colors in broad swaths, the paint on the canvas thick as house-paint. She doesn't have it yet, but it's coming—she can feel it. And next week, Monday morning, she'll call her lawyer. She'll instruct him to make over large sums to her children, a chunk of the money from the insurance and the settlement, the fruits of the accident. She has decided to stop watching over them, give them their chance. Let it come, she thinks. If there is more to the bargain, let it come.

You Are She?

It dawned on me for the first time that Marianne Knauer was Joyce Carol Oates one afternoon when we sat together out on the deck watching the ocean. Together but separate. The others were elsewhere, engaged in their various pursuits—Ruth and Caroline shopping in West Palm, Allison walking on the beach, Hector down at Gulfstream Park watching the horses run. They would all be back soon. When you are better than seventy, a few hours in the heat, or even in the air, tires you out.

Marianne is the newest of us. She arrived about a month ago—from Pennsylvania, she said. Going by the way she talks, when she talks at all, it could be. Also, it could be New York or New Jersey, or even Maryland. Her voice is thin and breathy, and she speaks in well-made sentences, but there are few of them. Her glasses were the first thing that put me in mind of the author—big, round, owl-eye lenses like you always saw on the jackets of her books. She has not written anything for a while now, nothing that I know about.

Whenever a new person arrives there is a formal gathering in The Parlor. This room has an old-fashioned look, with large potted plants and soft cushions. The chairs are hardly ideal for people our age, but consistent with a house that makes few concessions in that direction. We all have to walk stairs and we share two bathrooms. This is all part of the Agreement. The new arrivals are always escorted in by June Petersen, who has been Foundation Secretary for years. Marianne was wearing a blazer and calf-length skirt, despite the heat. She is tall but rail-thin. You could see plenty of June behind her, sticking out at either side. When the Secretary introduced her, she smiled shyly and seemed to sink into her jacket. "Hello all," she said. "I'm happy to be with you."

She was a widow from Scranton, she told us, conveniently a librarian so she knew a lot about literature. She had applied to the Foundation two years ago, a year after her husband had died. Like most of us, she had been rejected the first time, but tried again. She was shy, she said. Her husband had been the gregarious one; her life in the social world had been due to him. Naturally, she had had great difficulty after he was gone, but hoped that in this environment, this special environment, she would be able to open up, even to bloom. These sentences, strung together, were as many as I have ever heard her produce on any occasion since.

June took her to her room. It is located between mine and Caroline's, about equally far from the two bathrooms which are at either end of the hall. The rooms are small but comfortable—in each a double bed, night table, dresser, large closet, small desk and a terrace overlooking the sea. According to the Agreement, no one can stay who can no longer negotiate the staircase leading to the bedrooms on the second floor. I watched Marianne climb, following squat June. Though her body swayed like a thin tree in the wind, her tread looked strong.

All of us are single—there is little space for two in the bedrooms. This does not mean that you can't bring someone home for a night or two. Nothing in the Agreement forbids it. We are all independent people, free to come and go as we choose, to see whom we want, even to sleep with someone if we fancy it. But the small size of the rooms, the bathroom accommodations and the communal meals preclude any permanent arrangement.

"Marianne, did you ever try to write?"

"What?" The wind carries away her voice. It is blowing in off the ocean, clouds covering and uncovering the sun.

"Fiction, poetry, essays—something."

"Oh," she says, "no. I have no talent for that."

There is a slight blush on her cheeks. Pale cheeks, high forehead, round glasses. Why should she hide her identity from me? Doesn't she realize that I would keep her secret?

So, we exchanged a few words and, shortly afterward, she gathered her things and left the deck. A large cloth bag, white wrap, straw hat—I turned to watch her walk away. Her wooden clogs clunked on the deck, up the flight of eight steps to the back door. Then, one of the shoes shuffled off, bounced and fell between the steps onto the shadowed boards under the staircase. She turned and gave me a weak smile, perhaps only an open-mouthed look of surprise. I scrambled under the stairs and retrieved the clog. "Thank you," she told me. Breathy, blushing.

A short while later, Ruth and Caroline came home from shopping. Ruth is the oldest of us, at least eighty. Her upper lip is severely lined, her skin hangs in wattles from her neck. She has never liked me and has poisoned Caroline's mind against me. I watched them hesitate when they spotted me from the top of the stairs. But then Caroline moved ahead and Ruth followed. Caroline said hello to me, the other one nodded. They sat down by the railing.

"Marianne was just out here."

"Oh yes?"

At that moment I might have confided my suspicions, if only we had gotten along better. Caroline is a big, bosomy woman with a head of thick gray hair. One of her heavy breasts is a prosthesis—she lost the real one years ago. She first confided this to Hector, who later told me. There are no real secrets in this place, except the big one concerning Marianne. June Petersen is always encouraging us to reveal things, to be a "community," as she puts it, "even a family." The Agreement also mentions this, but there is no coercion, of course; everyone is free to do as he chooses.

I have nothing against Caroline, or even against Ruth. It would be comforting, even exhilarating, to be able to reveal my thoughts to them, the way I could to my wife when she was alive. I can talk to Hector, of course—we do talk—but I don't think real intimacy is possible between two men. And Allison—she is so often isolated in her own world, listening to soft music in her room and walking along the beach; resting, then walking further at the edge of the surf, into the surf. One day the ocean will swallow her.

Really, we all ought to get along better. When Rima Richmond created the Foundation and bought the house, her principal desire was to provide a small community for healthy people in their latter years. She hoped that a communal style of life might be possible—a small number of people sharing a house, sharing the chores, small, separate living quarters, always someone to talk to. The first six, hand-picked by Ms. Richmond from hundreds of applications, had remained intact for seven years until the first death. Their photographs are in The Parlor, along with all of our photos.

Yesterday, Marianne's picture was put up. I stopped and stood in front of it on the way to my room. The photographs are made by Joe Barker, who is our gardener and chauffeur. He is a big-muscled man, strong enough to break up trouble, but also with a gruff charm. I could see from Marianne's photo that he had worked his ways on her. Her big eyes were wide behind the glasses and there was a curl of amusement in her mouth. Her hair is jet black, dyed so carefully that no trace of gray shows, not in the photo nor even when you actually see her up close. In the picture, she is the spitting image of the author. Why would she do this, I wondered, if she wishes to hide her identity? Gray hair would have provided a much better disguise. Could it be possible that she *wants* to reveal herself—to the right person, that is, someone who could read all the clues?

We had our weekly meeting in The Parlor and everyone spoke. The Agreement encourages this and June is pretty insistent. Ruth said that one of the planks was loose in the long stairs that lead down to the beach. Though she seldom uses these stairs herself, she said she was afraid that Allison might fall. She is very protective of Allison, even custodial. When she tried this same tactic on Marianne, it didn't work. Marianne recoiled from her.

Hector offered to fix the broken stair. He keeps his toolkit in the utility room just past the kitchen. June thought this was a good idea, but said that Hector should collaborate with our handyman, Manny Fernandez. Manny is another muscle builder. He and Joe lift weights almost every day in our gym. Manny and Joe like to sit in the back at meetings, one on either side of the door. They look like two bookends, or like the fierce Gods you see in front of Buddhist temples. During the meetings they seldom speak, although Joe will once in a while crack a joke.

June asked me for a report on finances. The group elected me treasurer before Marianne arrived; the vote was unanimous, although I saw that Ruth was hesitant in raising her hand. We were over budget on food, but doing well on maintenance and supplies. Our escrow would be sufficient to take care of the real estate taxes, due the following month. According to the Agreement, the Foundation pays all the salaries, including Manny, Joe and Mary Coffee, our nurse. It also provides a yearly amount, quite generous, which we use to run the house. Pocket money, the same for each of us, is furnished as well. This makes for equality, one of Ms. Richmond's main principles. When we were accepted and signed the Agreement, each of us turned all of our assets over to the Foundation, in return for lifelong care, including residence in the house so long as we were able and care in an appropriate facility afterward. None of us has children or other heirs—a condition that the Agreement specifies.

The question came up as to whether we should allot group money to an outing into West Palm to see a play. This was proposed by Caroline, but I could see that Ruth was behind it. She was drinking bottled water as the discussion went on—she is never without it. Hector was in favor of budgeting the outing, Marianne and I against. Marianne spoke up about it, as her contribution to the meeting. "I am content in my room," she said, "and outside, watching the ocean. I don't want to go into the city."

"I am sure that Joe would be willing to take everyone in the van," June said.

Marianne shook her head. She was sitting on the loveseat, sunk into the cushion, but with her back straight and her long legs crossed. Though she was slightly apart from the rest of us, she had turned her body at an angle that opened her to my direction. I didn't miss that.

The vote was three to three, Allison also voting against. Since, according to the Agreement, budgetary matters require a majority, the outing failed.

I never imagined that I would wind up in Florida. In his later years, my father bought a house in Key Biscayne and I hated visiting him there. He was an important man, briefly head of the CIA, though you probably would not recognize his name. He could have retired anywhere, but chose a life of ceaseless golf and inner decay. I tried to talk to him about it, but he was used to giving advice, not taking it. When he died, the house became mine and I sold it to Jodie Foster.

These were my only brushes with celebrity—my father, who hid his true identity, and Jodie Foster, whom I never actually met. My father rose from the streets of South Philly. He was a Golden Gloves boxer, a World War II vet, went to Rutgers on the GI Bill. All of this I found out later; I had to do research. My father would never talk about those early years; and my mother?—whatever she knew, her lips had been sealed.

Caroline sulked a little after the outing was voted down, but Ruth showed nothing. There was only the slight twitching of her thickish lips—probably, I was the only one to notice. Anyway, why should they react? They can and will schedule their own trip to the theater, they don't need us. I think it is symbolic for Ruth, who has a need to control things. Caroline, on the other hand, is disappointed because she knows that Ruth is. She has few opinions of her own.

Sometimes when I look at the members of our group, I seem to see them as they were years ago, long before I knew them. I don't know how I can do this, but somehow I feel with certainty that these transformations are accurate. Of course, over the years, I have been in everyone's room (not Marianne's, not yet) and have seen snapshots from the past. But the figures in these flat and sterile photographs do not seem related to their current selves, those beings who have emerged through the corridor of time. No, it is some inner power of mine that enables me to reformulate their faces and shapes, some power that I don't understand.

Caroline used to be a beauty. In this case no special insight is really needed—it is obvious enough. She was the first one I really *saw* after my arrival at the house. At that time she wasn't yet under Ruth's thumb. One morning, down in the Dispensary, I was behind her in line, waiting to receive my pills. Caroline got hers and turned to leave, and at that moment I saw her as she *had been*. I reached out and brushed her bare arm with my fingers—I couldn't help myself. She stared at me, amazed for a moment, and then she smiled.

It was hard for her to show the disfigured side. We had been together a lot of times before she finally took off one of the heavy bras she always wore. The reconstructed breast was lumpen, discolored, creased in the wrong place. Nonetheless, I stroked it and put my lips to the nipple. Of course, I preferred the other breast, but I was careful after that to give them equal attention.

The Dispensary, along with the gym and the rooms of Joe, Manny and Mary Coffee, is in the "basement." Though we all call it that, this underground word hardly does justice to the lower level. Natural sunlight is filtered ingeniously into the rooms, supplemented by a subtle fluorescent glow. The feeling you get is of light and space. The Dispensary has also been lighted discretely, but its white hospital luster is hard to camouflage. Though there are no beds, the stark, hard massage table, with its heavy straps, also puts you in mind of the hospital setting.

The Agreement requires each of us to get our medications (pills, shots) daily from the nurse. Mary Coffee has had the position for about a year. She is a big, sour-looking woman with a utilitarian haircut and blonde highlights, maybe forty years old. Despite her looks she has a good sense of humor, and I have sometimes seen her and Joe joking with each other. Mary has nicknamed each of the pills she dispenses and refers to them with names like "the little blue guy," "the big mother," "dilly," and "Rosie." She is also the masseuse, and very good at relieving muscle tension. Still, there is something about the hard whiteness of the table and Mary's hearty brusqueness that puts me off. Usually I get out of the Dispensary as soon as I can.

The gym is another thing entirely. The Agreement also mandates daily exercise, and Manny puts us through our individual paces. He is a great believer in weight training. The strongest of us is Hector, followed by Allison, who was an athlete in her younger days. Ruth and Caroline are powder puffs; Manny keeps them busy on the mat and with the lightest weights. They are merely going through the motions, and I can see that they frustrate him.

One morning I happened to be alone in the gym when Marianne walked in. The gym has been difficult for her all along. At first she had nothing to wear. She came in a baggy sweatshirt and a pair of shorts. The sweatshirt hung on her narrow shoulders, giving her a scarecrow's look, while the shorts exposed her stork-thin legs. Manny took her into West Palm and they picked out a warm-up suit similar to Allison's. Marianne wears it zipped to the neck.

"Don't you think the ocean is in a tumult today?"

This is the way she speaks to me, a kind of code. I understand her to be talking about our inner weather. On that morning I also woke in an uneasy state, my heart beating hard, as if something were going to happen. Out on my terrace I could see the waves crashing, and the seagulls screamed like frantic souls locked in the bodies of birds.

"I know," I said.

Manny had given me my program for the day, then left to do an errand. He knows I will be conscientious about my training, no need to keep tabs on me. After we had exchanged a few words, Marianne surprised me. She unzipped her jacket and threw it on a bench. Immediately, I saw her as she once was—thin, too thin, but graceful as a dancer, her larynx rolling as she swallowed, angular breasts thrusting up into her t-shirt.

We worked out side by side, each using a machine, then switching. I felt like an adolescent. To show off, I loaded up more weight than I had handled before. Marianne stopped to watch me, as if she knew. I managed nine repetitions and, when I faltered on the tenth, she stepped in to help me raise the load a final time. I stood up, breathless, staggering a little.

"We should cut down," she said. "There's no need to work out every day."

"If we do, Manny will send us to the Dispensary."

"We don't have to go."

"It's in the Agreement."

We sat together on the bench. I was afraid that Marianne would put her jacket back on, but she didn't. Lips parted, she stared at me with her big eyes.

"We should never have signed," she said. "We are not free."

"We are. Of course, we are. We are lucky to be here. Many others wanted to, but weren't picked." But I argued this way because it was required, not because I was sure. I felt that Marianne was swaying me.

We had moved closer. Our knees touched. I saw the wrinkles in her face, the sagging skin at her throat, a skeleton; but, at the same time, the author, her chest fluttering, a pair of silver earrings in her ears.

But at that moment we were interrupted. Ruth and Caroline. "Well, well," Ruth said, "what is going on here?"

It had been Ruth's doing that my affair with Caroline ended. Caroline is a weak person and needs reassurance. She discussed me with Ruth. I didn't mind this. I had nothing to hide, neither about what I did in bed, nor my life's story. I often noticed Ruth staring at me, as if she were wondering whether the things Caroline told her could be true. I returned her look. Under my gaze her washed out blue eyes cleared, her gray hair turned the color of sand and her craggy face became smooth.

Eventually her propaganda succeeded. Caroline left me. Ruth came to my room. "I hope you don't blame me," she said. I answered that I didn't care. "Can I sit down?" She sat on the bed and I closed the terrace doors to keep out the tumult of the waves. After that, she didn't speak another word. I sat down beside her, and she put her hand inside my shirt. She kissed me, using her tongue. She had been a doctor's wife; she knew how to smile and kiss. Her breasts were intact, not like Caroline's. To make this point she took my hands and ran them down across her nipples and underneath to her ribs. She lay on the bed and I pressed down against her, down and down and harder and harder. The wind blew open the terrace doors and I smelled salt.

In the gym, Marianne shivered. For a moment she looked wildly around the room as if she would run. Ruth smiled at her. "Are you cold?"

Marianne found her jacket; she put it on, zipped it.

"We didn't mean to interrupt," Ruth said.

She smiled. Marianne ran.

After I got out of the army, my father tried to recruit me to the intelligence business. I was physically strong like him, and I had both analytic and literary skills. We had a good relationship, but I wanted to make my own way. I joined the faculty of a high school in far upstate New York, near the Vermont border. I taught English and I became the basketball coach. I won a regional championship, then did it again. In my classes, I assigned the author's books: a short story to the sophomores; to the juniors, the more or less simple short novels; and, to the seniors, the longer, more complex works.

There were complaints. The Principal called me in. He was not very familiar with the books, nor were my colleagues in the English Department. He started out talking nicely, but then threatened me. I held out. I had read almost everything she had written. I wrote her a letter in which I emphasized how important it was for high school students to get a realistic picture of the world, the bad as well as the good. No answer came.

The Principal's office was on the third floor, as high as you could climb. Far away, in the basement, was the realm of Brady, our superintendent-janitor. An intelligent man, he was often reading. He could have been more than he was, but a mental illness had determined his fate. I gave him one of the author's novels. He read it in a few days, then wanted more.

I won a third championship. This helped me to hold out a while longer. My father was appalled by Joyce Carol Oates and considered her deranged. He agreed with the Principal. Still, he said he was proud of me for defending my beliefs. Eventually, I was relieved of my duty, and my wife had to support me.

Once a month we have a party, with special food, dancing and a glass of champagne for whoever wants it. We first voted for this at a Board meeting more than a year ago and it is popular. The entire staff attends and, generally, all of the residents, even though it is not mandated by the Agreement. Since the women outnumber the men, Hector and I and Joe and Manny are kept busy dancing.

I brought Marianne a glass of champagne and we drank it together. She had put on lipstick and makeup and had an intense look, her face flushed. I found her very attractive.

I took her hand and we went out onto the floor. Manny and Joe had rolled up the Turkish rug, exposing the polished slats underneath. The chandelier glowed with a hundred lights. A waltz was playing. Marianne was light as mist, her touch damp. I felt her fingers on my back, soft, wet; then, after a while, sharper, digging in with long nails (had I noticed them before?) down under the skin until my blood flowed. This was a revelation more certain than any she could have made with words. I returned the message by squeezing her hip, pulling her toward me.

The music stopped. From the corner of my eye I watched Ruth make her way out toward us across the floor. She tapped Marianne on the shoulder. "Cutting in."

"What do you think you're doing?" I asked.

"Only men are allowed to cut in? Is that it?"

"It's all right," Marianne said. Soft, breathless, her little girl's voice.

She broke contact with me, and Hector was there to put his arms around her, while I held Ruth. The music played. Ruth danced far from me, barely in reach, but also out of synch, so that she fell against me as if through clumsiness. As if I didn't know she had been married to a doctor and must have had dancing lessons. The dance became slow and heavy. I could feel the arthritis in my hips, the sluggishness induced by the Dispensary's pills, the metallic taste in my mouth.

Ruth came close and whispered in my ear. "Are you enjoying this?"

Over her shoulder I could see Marianne, watching with bulging eyes. She mouthed a word, her lips barely moving, but I was sure of it. "Cunt."

Once Brady had gotten a taste of the author, he couldn't get enough. I brought him her novels and short-story collections and he devoured them, sometimes at the rate of two or three a week, but sometimes at much longer intervals, depending upon how his health was. After he had finished a book, we would discuss it. He was the only person in the high school, or for that matter in the entire town, who could, or would, talk about her. I confided the ideas I had developed over years of reading, and he came up with insights of his own. His sharp thinking amazed me. But during those times when his illness took over, he was all but incoherent and talked nonsense.

As the months went by, I was driven more and more to the basement. I found my way down there after school and during planning periods, even during the half-hour allotted us for lunch. I was running away from my above-ground life, which was becoming more and more intolerable. Even my wife seemed not to be listening when I worried aloud about what was happening to me. Gradually, my colleagues, who had seemed sympathetic at first, began to yield to the constant pressure applied by the Principal. He met with the English Department and, singling me out in public, said: "We'll have no more Joyce Carol Oates here." No one spoke up on my behalf.

I never talked to Marianne about this part of my life. I didn't want her to think I was sucking up to her in any way, trying to impress her with the sacrifices I had made.

Seen from the beach, our house is a brilliant presence in the dun grayness of the dunes. The long flights of stairs leading up to it seem like the stairway to a yellow, phosphorescent heaven. Although the beach is public, it is generally empty. Southward along the ocean from us is a State Park which few people visit, and, beyond that, a country club with private access. Apart from the Park, the nearest public entrance to the beach is well up the coast. For nearly a mile in each direction, our house is the only one visible.

I sat with Marianne on the lowest step. We had begun coming here in the afternoons to avoid people on the deck, particularly Caroline and Ruth. Sometimes we met Allison on the beach; this was inevitable since she spent so much time there. She would come over to talk for a few minutes, all shoulders and long legs. The three of us were comfortable together.

One day Marianne asked me about Ruth. Allison had just left. We could see her dark warm-up jacket receding down the beach in the direction of the country club. Marianne was wearing her similar jacket, though the afternoon was warm.

"Was there something between you two?"

I felt myself blushing. I couldn't control it. Marianne watched me. "I was with her once."

"You fucked her?"

This kind of language is shocking, mesmerizing, when it comes from her lips. The effect is so strong because she never uses it. Almost never.

"Yes," I answered. I told her how Ruth had come to my room, kissed me, how I entered her. Then I also told her about Caroline. Caroline was different; it was easy to talk about her. After a few minutes, Marianne looked bored, as if I had been bragging. She stared silently at the ocean. I felt that Ruth and Caroline had come between us. The sun came out from behind a small cloud and the air got quiet.

"How could you?" Marianne asked. "You with Ruth?"

"I'm a man," I said. "You of all people should understand that."

Abruptly, she stood up and started walking toward the water. At the edge, where the waves strained toward the sand, she stopped, and I caught up.

"I've tried to imagine you with her," she said. "I couldn't. It was like trying to imagine your parents."

A big wave came in, breaking late, washing over our feet.

"I swam in the ocean with my father," I told her. "We had a summer house in New Hampshire My mother never swam."

"Does *she* come down here?" I knew she meant Ruth.

Another wave crashed down toward the beach and rolled in over the sand. I felt the ocean's wildness inside me. It dissolved all my remaining constraints and I finally began to tell her about Brady. As time passed his condition got worse. It was as if our two circumstances were linked—as I became more and more of an outcast in the English Department, he grew sicker and sicker.

"Suppose you asked her? Would she come then?"

Though we seemed to be talking at cross purposes, I suddenly realized that Marianne had heard and considered every word I said.

"The stairs would be hard for her."

Marianne put her hand on my chest. Her ring finger was bare, the wedding ring gone. A wave came in, hard enough to knock us over, hitting all the harder for having been delayed. I held her as we struggled to stay on our feet.

"Do you want to go further?" I asked her.

I listened for her thin, breathless, little-girl's voice. "There'll be another day," she said.

All of the medicines I take are for heart trouble. Though they seem to work—I have good checkups—there are side effects. Sometimes the metallic taste, sometimes the dull, imprisoned feeling of wading through liquid. My father had a heart condition, though I can't remember him ever mentioning side effects.

All of us have complained about our medicines from time to time, except for Hector and Marianne. Hector is absorbed in his handicapping and lives for the thrill of picking perfectas; June Petersen allots him money for modest bets. Side effects never seem to cross his radar. And Marianne—she never complains about anything. Except privately, except to me. "We are not free," she told me again, and again I disputed this. According to the Agreement, we can leave at any time.

But, the age we are, where would any of us go?

I began to talk more with Marianne about Brady. She already knew so much about me that I no longer worried she would misinterpret my telling of the losses I suffered in defense of the author. One day, when I brought Brady a new novel, it seemed to confuse him. I remember his repetitive movements—taking off his gray stocking-cap and putting in on again and taking it off—as we spoke. It was already spring but the basement was cold. I tried to counsel him as best I could. "You won't tell?" he said. He was clever at concealing his mental problems, making sure that he shaved and kept his clothes clean. Even as he was becoming incoherent, he could still do minor repairs and cleaning, slowly but competently. As for the basement, hardly anyone ever came down there. Only the Assistant Principal, who was nominally in charge of him, made periodic visits.

Marianne let me visit her room, but kept the door open. I could hardly blame her, considering what she knew about Caroline and Ruth. We sat together on her bed. Some days her face was leathery, deeply lined, almost wizened. She tried to conceal it from me, speaking from behind a raised hand. But her voice never changed; thin, childlike, breathless, it distinguished her from all other women.

One day, again in her room, when her face had cleared, I told her about how it ended with Brady. There was a mild spring that suddenly turned cold, a chilly May. The furnace had already been shut off. Brady was never supposed to touch the furnace—the room was locked. But somehow he got in. The pilot light had gone off, or maybe it was turned off. When Brady tried to light it, there was an explosion. Marianne said nothing, just stared at me with bulging eyes. I assured her that no one was hurt except Brady himself, and he not badly. But under an old couch in the basement, they found sheets of paper filled with scribbled sentences. There were quotations from the author's books as well as ramblings from Brady himself. "… a titanic conflagration," one said, "… a flame large enough to consume the world's bestiality." Brady was hospitalized and I was fired. At my hearing, they read from Brady's papers as well as passages selected from the works of J.C.O. that I had taught. "Sick, disgusting material," the Principal said, holding one of the books. "It makes you want to wash your hands after you've touched it."

How could I defend myself?

Marianne still said nothing, but she took my hand and placed it on her chest.

I met Hector in the hall. "What's your secret?" he said to me. I asked him what he meant. "The ladies. I never get past second base." I felt myself blushing. How could he know? Maybe about Caroline—we were together a lot. But the others? Could Ruth have talked? Could he have been passing by and seen my hand in Marianne's blouse?

The time for another meeting rolled around, and I gave my treasurer's report. June Petersen asked for comments or questions. Ruth stood up to dispute one of my numbers. It was for a basket of tropical fruit that Allison had bought for the dining room table. Ruth said that it shouldn't be a group expense; some of us didn't like tropical fruit. We all knew what was really on her mind. She was still mad about the theater outing that had been rejected the previous month. It was my job to rebut her. Everyone looked at me. Marianne's eyes, gigantic behind her glasses, beamed her thoughts at me. Ruth was smiling. Her skin was firm, hair dark—had she dyed it? She was wearing a soft sweater; her arms, slightly plump, extended from the short sleeves. She smiled, daring me to speak. After a minute or two, June Petersen said: "Let's get on to the next thing."

In his last years, my father stayed in his house on Key Biscayne, unable to do anything. He had full time help to take care of him—a rollicking Haitian woman, big enough to budge him, and a Jamaican sub who worked weekends. My father had the shakes and sat in a wheelchair, watching golf on television and sleeping. He could still talk and he gave orders to the women. The Haitian said "Yes, yes" to whatever he asked, "all right, loverboy." The Jamaican combed his hair whenever she had the chance. The last time I visited, my father asked me: "Can't you get me out of here?" He dictated a phone number in Langley, Va. and watched while I wrote it down. "Ask for Mr. Harris," he told me. "He'll know what to do."

I learned the lesson of my father's last years. The Agreement is a much better way. There were hundreds of candidates—I was lucky to get it. It didn't matter that I had money. Even before my father got the shakes he was de facto housebound; it wasn't money or mobility he lacked, but companionship. How much better that all of us live together; in the sharing of our lives, our souls are revealed. That was Rima Richmond's philosophy.

The young believe that it's bad to be old, to have everything behind you. But there had been a time, long before my father's disintegration, when I envied the old. They had been relieved of the burden of their responsibilities and were no longer accountable. When my condition was first diagnosed by Dr. Housman, this feeling was particularly strong. His office was on the ground floor of the house where he lived with his wife. No children. He had many old patients who came and went, passing me on the bricked sidewalk. They had made it—to sixty, to seventy, to eighty. I wished I were one of them, that I had made it so far.

Dr. Housman said I still might live a long life—"in reasonable health," he told me. It all depended on not missing my medication. There were side effects, of course, but he said I could manage them. A heart condition—think of it that way, he said. My wife was with me. I remember she pulled her scarf tighter around her neck, as if to get ready for the ordeal.

We had three days of rain—heavy storms with thin, gray showers in between. The weather cooped all of us up. Hector wanted to go to Gulfstream as usual, but Joe was against it. Finally, June had to be called to settle the dispute; she ruled in Joe's favor. After that, Hector stayed in his room.

Marianne and I went outside to the rear of the deck where there was cover. We sat with our backs against the house, looking out at the tumult of the ocean, gray and green. Occasionally, a gust of onshore wind would blow spray in our faces. The rain tasted of salt.

Marianne told me about growing up in Pennsylvania. Many of the details were similar to passages that the author had written in her novels. *She* was well educated, but Marianne claimed that she had only two years of college; after that, she got a job in the public library. Her husband was a professor at the small college she had attended.

"You must be on scholarship here."

I meant nothing pejorative by this, but I saw the muscles in her neck tighten. None of the residents knew who was on scholarship and who had come with money and surrendered it to the Foundation. Ruth, for example, gave herself airs, talked in a clipped accent bordering on British—but I suspected she was a scholarship girl, despite her doctor husband. It didn't matter—all of us were equal now.

"I'm sorry," I said to Marianne. "My money came from my father. I take no credit for it."

I told her how I had sold the Key Biscayne house to Jodie Foster after he died. All those rooms, the palatial staircase, the bathing-house on the beach—what good had they been to my father in his loneliness? Before he got the shakes, he used to wander the house. I'd talk to him on the phone and he'd say, "now I'm in the conservatory ... now I'm in the guest wing ... now stopping in the bronze lavatory to take a leak." Who wants to wind up alone? When I heard about the Foundation, it seemed the natural solution for me. I was elated when I found out I had gotten in.

I must have had the saddest expression on my face, because Marianne looked at me with pure pity, then she leaned over to kiss me. She tasted tart, as if she'd been chewing lemons, and I prolonged the kiss until she broke away.

"I know you," I whispered. "Not only the way you look, but your name. "Marianne" from *We Were The Mulvaneys*, "Knauer" from *Marya: A Life*. To me, it's so apparent—though, don't worry, I don't think the others even suspect. They don't have the sophistication to realize who you are."

Finally ... it was out. The two of us were joined in a secret knowledge that set us apart from all the others. All my life I had dreamed of sharing such a secret. Marianne was silent, but the little, knowing smile she gave me said everything.

"Oh, the breeze feels so fresh."

Ruth and Caroline—it was impossible to avoid them. "May we join you?" Ruth sent Caroline inside for a towel, which she used to wipe off two chairs. She pulled hers up beside me and then Caroline sat next to her. Ruth reminded me of Dr. Housman's wife. She had the same way of talking, as if her words were women walking into a fancy room and sitting daintily on the furniture.

Ruth monopolized me. When I finally turned my head to peak at Marianne, she was staring out at the ocean and wouldn't look at me. The Ruth's of this world, and the Mrs. Housman's, never bother to consider the feelings of the Marianne's. They should be put in the hottest corner of hell.

Yesterday, when I went down to the Dispensary, Mary Coffee said, "We're going to give you two of the little blue guys this morning instead of one—is that all right?" I knew that if I said no, Mary would try to talk me into it; if she couldn't, June would be called to arbitrate, and probably would rule against me. Besides, I felt that my heart was acting up, beating strangely for no reason and hardly calming down.

Marianne always came for her pills late in the morning. She wanted to avoid meeting anyone else. I waited for her, hanging around to get a massage. When I took my shirt off, Mary stared at my chest. I had worked my muscles in the gym over many months, until they looked the way I wanted. My body felt to me in better shape than at any time since I left the military.

"Lie down, big guy," Mary said.

Marianne came in while I was still on the table. I saw her out of the corner of my eye. She was wearing her warm-up jacket, open, with her swimsuit underneath. Her thongs exposed her toes, which were long and shapely, except for a single yellowed nail.

"Be with you in a minute, hon," Mary told her.

Keeping in my sightline, Marianne backed up a few steps to wait. She shoved her hands into the pockets of her jacket. This took away some of her body's awkwardness, made her look lanky and athletic. Watching her, and feeling Mary's strong hands on my back, I began to get hard. Marianne sent me her slight, shy smile, lips barely parted. *She knew.*

We walked down the steps to the beach—Marianne in front, myself close behind. The stairs were steep, like a staircase descending from heaven. Once in a while, there was fog on the beach, so that, looking down from the house, it seemed you were above the clouds. The beach was the profane earth, where the waves crashed. Today, though the sun was powerful, the water was terribly rough.

"Are you coming?"

She grazed my fingertips with hers and took me with her though we barely touched. The waves scared me—even though my father had taught me to swim in the ocean, even though I had had military training. There was a point of no return, a moment when you lost control and the ocean took over. That moment terrified me.

Marianne took off her jacket and let it drop from her arm. It floated out a little, then rose on a massive wave that enveloped us a moment later. I fell, choking and coughing. When the wave passed, I looked out through a film of water. Marianne was still there. "Slide off my straps," she said.

Her exposed breasts were wet and heavy. I touched them. The next wave came, not as high as the last. Some moments of calm followed. We stepped out of our suits and she pressed against me. "Trust me."

I could barely whisper: Yes.

I followed her further into the ocean. The menacing waves came toward us from the horizon, like the slow fulfilling of a prophecy. Standing on tiptoe, I tried to keep contact with the ground. The wave hit and I fell again; rose gasping. For a moment I was turned around, facing the beach.

Marianne raised her arms toward the yellow sky. Her wet hair flattened along her neck. "There is a riptide," she said, "it can take you out."

"I know."

"Are you afraid?"

"No."

It was true. I had gone beyond *the moment*. I was ready.

But the ocean pushed us in instead of out. The sand clung to me. I took long, hoarse breaths. Marianne came out of the water and fell beside me. The salt had withered her—slackened her breasts, wrinkled her face; her Adam's apple swung loosely in the weathered skin of her neck.

High on the dune, the house glowed yellow. Ruth was standing at the lip of the stairs, watching. After a moment she called down to us. "What are you two doing down there?"

"She's flirtatious," Marianne said. "She'll come down to the beach if you ask her."

The time for our weekly meeting came around again. I could see that June Petersen was in a bad mood. She was wearing glasses instead of contacts. There was a pimple on her nose. When Joe did a little joking, she glared at him.

Ruth raised her hand. "I saw the two of them down on the beach. Disgusting!"

June looked in our direction. "What could you have been thinking?"

Marianne shrank back in her chair, as if she wanted to disappear into the cushions.

"So what," I said. "We are free adults. The Agreement says so. We are free to sunbathe on the beach if we want to."

June took a breath. "That doesn't relieve you of the duty to exercise some discretion."

"I agree with them," Allison said. "They can sunbathe if they feel like it."

Ruth's hand went up again. "They were doing more than sunbathing."

I looked over to catch Hector's eye. He winked.

Ruth proposed a motion of censure. She and Caroline voted for it, but Allison, Hector and I were against. Marianne didn't vote. She kept her hands folded across her chest and stared down at her knees.

"The motion fails," June announced. But she swung her gaze from Marianne to me, then back again. "Next time use a little caution. The beach is a public place."

Marianne came to my room. Her knock was timid, but she stood straight and her face was composed. The first thing she said was: "One of the knives in the kitchen—we must have it. It's the one with a brown handle, about nine inches long; it's never used, no one will miss it." The robe she was wearing fell from her shoulders in loose folds, almost regal. I thought of Lady Macbeth. I have always understood Macbeth, how he couldn't resist her.

I asked Ruth if she wanted to go to the beach.
"I don't know." She smiled. "The stairs."
"I think you can handle the stairs better than you let on."
"Could be," she said.
In the afternoon, she came down from her room in a new swimsuit. Her usual suit was black and white, an old fashioned one-piece that fastened at the neck. She must have bought the new one in Ft. Lauderdale or West Palm. The blue bottoms were short-shorts, the white top barely held her in.
She modeled it for me. "What do you think?"
I thought of the body that the suit covered; she had let me see it just once.
I was wearing a white terry beach robe that I rarely used. It had been my father's. Ruth looked at me, flirting. "Why do you have that on?"
"I feel a little chilly."
"I'll bet," she said. "Could it be that you have something big you want to hide?"
The knife was shoved into the elastic of my swimsuit, at the back. Marianne had sheathed it for me in a heavy sock.
Ruth had no trouble with the steps. She took my arm and we descended loosely, easily, not even bothering to hold on. Marianne

was sitting on the sand near the staircase, staring out at the ocean. At the edge of the water, Allison was dipping her toes in. Ruth didn't care that we had an audience. She reached inside my robe and embraced me, her hand too high on my back to feel the knife. I kissed her, then stepped back, dropping my robe to the sand. I drew the knife.

Ruth flinched, but she stood her ground. "I know who you think she is. How gullible can you be?"

Who could have told her? Was it Marianne? I raised the knife.

"You fool—it's a toy. It's harmless."

"No." I stabbed at the bare apron of her chest, just below her suit's white top. I stabbed twice, three times, four times. But each time, the knife retracted into its handle.

Ruth started laughing, and then a chorus of laughter resounded from the beach. Hector and Caroline were on the stairs, laughing; Allison laughing near the water. And Marianne? She had her fingers to her lips and was laughing softly behind them.

They laughed for a long time, and I kept looking at Marianne. Her mouth was laughing, but her eyes stared straight back at me, sending their unmistakable message. I am she. It is just as you thought.

The brutality of the laughter, the reversal, the quirk—doesn't it all reveal *her* trademark?

I was—and *am*—more certain than ever that she and Marianne are one. One of these days she will walk with me into the ocean again, or reveal her true self in another way. *Something violent will happen. Something no one could predict.* Who is better than she at inventing such a scene?

One thing I know for sure: I am not going to end up like my father.

Suicide

He sees Edie at a film. Her looks attract him: narrow eyes spread wide in her face, glinting green; the lashes short, her eyebrows two sandy smudges. Nose long and thin—elegant from straight on, but in profile the irregularities show. Her sand-colored hair is cut severely, exposing delicate ears. She has thin shoulders, bare except for orange spaghetti straps that can't quite hide the elastic of her bra. She stops in the lobby, and he talks to her.

She's on the faculty at the University—Assistant Professor in the Department of Logic, Semantics and Philosophy. Originally from Croatia—her family is still there but she doesn't get along with them. She has been married and divorced. She seems amused that he has begun a conversation with her. "Shall we drink a coffee?" she proposes.

The coffee bar is three doors down from the theater. It has a corrugated tin roof supported by raw wooden poles. They sit across from each other in a narrow booth. The place is crowded, mostly with students, the older, more serious ones. It is not far from the University, where he graduated a number of years ago, a degree in engineering. He has his own business now—not engineering, but carpentry. He turns out cabinets and furniture, elegant banisters, mantelpieces, all beautiful and precise. She is eating a chocolate bar—he can smell it on her breath. He tells her what he is working on—a small deck at the back of a house, just above a lake.

115

There's a dim light on the wall beside them. It makes her eyes look darker. She offers him a piece of her chocolate, hands it over with warm fingers. When the candy is finished, she leans back and hugs herself, crossing her arms over her chest. She has thin lips, which now compress further, a little frown of concentration. "Are you happy, Arthur?" she asks.

This question is so abrupt, direct, surprising, that he forgets to defend himself—or perhaps this is because he wants to answer. He tells her: "Not particularly." But even this shades the truth; it is part evasion. He has never been happy, has suffered all his life, even as a child. He has been through therapy, through anti-depressants. There have been respites but they've never lasted. At times he's thought that the right woman might save him, but, if such a woman exists, he has never found her.

Meanwhile, Edie has said nothing in reply, merely nodding at him, rocking slightly in her seat, her mouth tight.

They make love for the first time. Her sharp little breasts abrade his chest; he disappears inside her, loses himself. They lie together awhile in a soft cocoon, an egg. He doesn't want the shell to break, but eventually it must. Edie dons a purple robe, lights a cigarette. He pulls his jeans back on.

They're at her place; they have known each other just four weeks. "Wait," she says. She finds some chocolate on her dresser. They share it. Arthur has grown to like chocolate since he met her. He buys it himself now, eats it slowly with sensual enjoyment.

He wants to find out everything about her. For example, they have never discussed philosophy, her field. She has deflected this subject whenever it came up. But now, faced with his persistence, she says: "All systems of belief are so much smoke. There is only one question that really counts, the one posed by Camus."

"What is that?"

She looks at him. There's a bit of chocolate on her lip. "Whether or not to kill yourself."

He thinks she is posturing. He has met girls like her before. Hippie chicks in college, who dressed in black; pot smokers; girls in therapy. You would have thought she had outgrown that. How old could she be? She has never told him. Something over thirty, he estimates. She doesn't have the look of those others, though. Sitting in her robe, with her legs crossed, long legs, she looks very much at ease. Sure of herself, nothing to prove.

Now, she laughs, a soft, tinkling laugh. "You are not familiar with Camus? Are you shocked?"

"No," he says. "I don't know Camus, but I have studied philosophy a little."

"Yes? They teach it here to engineers?"

She is sitting on the bed, he on a chair close by, their knees nearly touching. Her robe is parted, exposing her chest. He notices a small blemish between her breasts. "I was a bad fit for engineering," he confides.

He hung out with the unconventional students, he tells her, the pot-smokers, misfits. They were mostly inside their heads, though there were some artists who made things. He was different, because he could do practical jobs with his hands; not only put designs on paper, but execute them; things people would pay for.

"What about you?" he asks. "Did you always like philosophy?"

She shrugs. "I was interested only in politics, until one day I decided it was useless."

"Because of the way Croatia is?"

"Because of the way human beings are."

"How are they?"

"Naïve." Smoke trails from her nose. "Selfish." More smoke. "Misguided. Without purpose."

"And you and I?"

She smiles, her thin lips parting; she has small teeth, slightly irregular. "The same," she says.

He asks to sit in on one of her classes. In return, he'll show her the deck he is building.

The room is on the original campus, dating back almost a century and a half. Despite dozens of renovations the building still creaks with age. He arrives first, takes a seat in the back row. The classroom is small; he counts the chairs—only eighteen. The students glance at him as they enter— he is a stranger.

Edie is the last to come in, just before the bell rings. She is wearing jeans and a dark blazer. She puts her notes on a table in front of the blackboard, then takes her jacket off and lays it down. Underneath is a short-sleeved blouse that accentuates her thinness.

But if there's a hint of frailty in her body, there is none in her manner. The class is an advanced seminar on linguistics and epistemology—Edie's specialty. The students are intellectual— graduate students and advanced undergraduates. Edie stands quietly, framed by the blackboard, leaning slightly back, her palms behind her on the ledge where the chalk and erasers are. Her voice is more penetrating than the voice she uses with him; and she laughs a lot, much more than he is accustomed to.

But when a student challenges her, she is all business. The student is male; tall and long-haired. She answers him briefly; then, when he persists, more at length. Arthur understands hardly anything. A young woman comes to the challenger's defense. Edie listens, nodding. Abruptly, she turns her back and begins writing on the blackboard—short phrases connected by arrows; or by symbols, some of which Arthur has never encountered. Finishing, she steps aside so the class can see. The students are silent. "Well?" she says. She waits but still no one responds. The challenge is over.

They go to lunch, a small place alongside the campus. Spring is beginning; the air is moist, not quite warm. The hostess sits them at the front window, looking out onto the street. "Well?" Edie asks. "What did you think?"

"I'm impressed."

"Yes? That is because you lack the language. It's only a game."

He says: "I don't believe that."

Outside, a wet wind is blowing; students walk lackadaisically, talking into their phones. "There is no content," Edie tells him. "It's all empty."

"Not all of it."

"Yes."

He says: "There is only Camus."

He has made his voice teasing, but underneath the joke his question is serious. Edie is looking out the window—at the atmosphere at once hushed and bright, at the aimless stroll of the students, boys and girls really, just getting started. "Yes," she finally tells him, her voice distant. "You have it right."

He has been feeling well and thinks it must be her doing. He had been relying on Xanax, trying to keep the dosage down to the two a day his physician agreed to prescribe. The doctor was reluctant to maintain him on tranquilizers, but Arthur has been through a slew of anti-depressants, which only made him worse, made him want to climb the wall, or affected his stomach, his skin, withered his penis. But now, in these last weeks, he has taken a total of just three pills. Could he finally be getting better? He doesn't dare to think that.

He is still working on the deck. Rainy weather has delayed him, but now it's almost finished. And Edie has been asking when she can see it. The house is a vacation house; now that spring has come, the owners have been driving out intermittently on weekends. But this weekend, they will be out of town. Edie suggests they bring sleeping bags. If the weather is good, they can sleep out on the completed part of the deck; if not, they can roll out the bags in the living room.

They leave on Saturday morning. The air is unusually warm. The forecast is for more rain, but there's some brightness behind the clouds that perhaps promises better. Arthur is proud of the deck. The main part of it is done; all that's left is a winding staircase leading down to the water. Until then, there is only a slippery path. He goes first, Edie following, taking his hand. At the dock, a rowboat bobs in the little wind-blown swells. "Let's go out," she says.

He takes the oars, propels them into the lake under the gray cover of clouds. Edie sits behind him in the prow; she's humming softly, under her breath, but he can't quite get the tune. It begins to rain, quietly at first, then harder. Arthur doesn't like getting wet. He hates the feel of wet clothes against his skin; even on the beach, in the sun, his wet suit bothers him. But Edie doesn't mind at all. She holds her face up to the rain, even takes off her jacket. A roll of far-off thunder sounds softly over the lake. Large drops fall, splattering in the boat. Arthur pulls with the right oar, trailing the left. They begin to swing around. Edie is hugging him, hanging on his back. It's as if she doesn't want them to return.

In the dull light, the lake is gray. The little swells have become chops, though there is no lightning; not yet. Arthur drops the oars, which hang in their locks. On the boat's floor, at the lowest point, a small puddle has formed. "How long do you think it would take to fill?" Edie says. She stretches forward until her lips are next to his. He twists his head and they kiss.

He answers: "A few hours. At least."

She withdraws, but still holds him around the waist. "Have you ever thought how you would like to die?"

A provocative question—but Arthur has become used to that. He has seen her do it in her classes. And in recent weeks she has initiated wild philosophical conversations between the two of them, often morbid—life and death—but ending in her dismissive laugh, as if she had decided that the subject was trivial after all, not worth speaking about.

"Not by drowning," he tells her, his voice light as he retrieves the oars and begins to row again. But he has considered it seriously, of course. If it came to that he would like to fall asleep and never wake up. Isn't that what anyone would prefer?

When they get to shore, Edie helps him drag the boat out of the water and turn it over. Both of them are soaked. There's a big tub in the master bathroom. Arthur fills it and they lie side by side in the steaming water; a fantastic pleasure, but … something is nagging at him, a tiny worm. He has learned to fear this small disturbance at the back of his mind. It is a warning.

Edie's skin is white, milky, so pale. Her veins show through in blue tangles, which he traces with his finger. The gloom holds off through the evening while they make love. And through the night: They're in their sleeping bags, half in half out, naked because there's no dry clothing; she's holding him from the back, arms around his waist, as she did in the boat. Each time he wakes in the long hours he feels her that way.

But in the morning the black gloom takes over. Though it's a beautiful day, Edie needs to leave early. She has lectures to prepare; and, at the end of the week, there will be a meeting in Chicago; she needs to finish up the presentation she will give. Arthur drives her home—then, suddenly, he's alone. What shall he do? His mind is churning—he can't think.

He takes some Xanax. After an hour, it helps. He decides to go back to the lake, work on the deck. But once he's out there he finds he can't concentrate. It's not that he feels so badly—he's rather calm, in fact. But there's no desire in him. He needs to begin the stairway, but it's just too much. Instead, he launches the boat, using a piece of plastic to cover the still damp seat.

The air is cooler than it was the day before, but there is no wind at all. Today the water is blue and green. Reaching the middle of the lake, he lets the oars go, as he did yesterday when he was with her. A moment of peace comes over him. He feels as if he's on the verge of that final sleep. It's not a hill that you slip down, but more like water, tiny swells that carry you up and back, while time seeps by. When the moment evaporates, he thinks of Edie—how tough she is, despite her thin shoulders and transparent skin. She seems to be made of a crystalline substance, hard as diamonds; a diamond drill cutting through the world, indifferent to fear or even death. If she were to leave him—what would he do?

The next week is terrible for him. He forces himself to get started on the winding staircase. While he's working, the storm in his brain holds off. It's just over the horizon, though—the swirling black gloom clouds, and the panic, like rolls of deep thunder that follow one another, never, never ceasing.

He phones Edie at her hotel in Chicago, the philosophy conference. She's not there, but he leaves a message. It's after midnight when she calls back. He took a Xanax—he's dozing. "I have established myself as a nihilist," she tells him.

"A nihilist," he repeats. He longs to have her beside him.

The panic recedes, but gloom settles in—not black, but cloudy, as if he is enclosed in a plastic shield. This fog is worse than anything. He sleeps late, works in the long afternoons, finishing the deck. When he's with Edie, he feels a little better. They walk arm in arm; hold each other in bed; he enters her creamy body, comes—the clouds part briefly.

They talk, drink coffee. She doesn't like to speak about her past. In a universe of meaningless events, the past is most empty of all. He knows that she is an only child—her doctor father, a vacuum, an absence; perhaps her model for emptiness, he thinks. Her mother blonde, vain, stupid—Edie dismisses her. She would rather talk about the nature of the world, about the books she's reading, the films they occasionally see.

He doesn't want to be in love with Edie. He's afraid. She is not particularly sympathetic to his symptoms, and he suspects that she won't continue to want him. Eventually, he'll be relegated to the empty past—it's only a matter of time.

And then one night, seemingly out of the blue, she says: "I have always known I would kill myself."

This is a typical Edie-ism, but more extreme than he has heard from her before. "Always?" he prompts.

"Since I was a child."

They are in a coffee bar, the same one as the night they met, the same booth. She's sipping her drink, holding the cup with both hands, staring at him over the rim. Is she daring him to pursue this? He asks her: "How?"

She shrugs, the movement abrupt enough that a few drops of coffee spill to the table. "What does it matter? It's merely suicide—not a dance that requires brilliant choreography."

"Yes, but you've never imagined it?"

She puts her cup down. Her fingers spread out on her upper lip, almost into the nostrils. She watches him with her slitted eyes. "There are many possibilities," she says. "The outcome is the same."

That night he dreams of the lake. There is a cliff, its edge sheer, vertical as a building. On top is the house; the staircase he constructed leads downward, but into endless distance, the bottom invisible. He is out on the deck with someone. Is it Edie? Perhaps—or it might be the woman of the house, the one who commissioned the construction. You can jump from the deck into the water, the woman is saying. It's not really so far down. Everyone has done it. Arthur takes her hand and they fall together, slicing through the air. The feeling is incredible.

He awakes thinking of his final sleep. It stays with him through the day. In the evening he calls Edie. She's a little out of sorts—she was in the middle of a difficult paper; he has interrupted her. "What is it?" she says.

The words come out seemingly on their own; he hadn't meant to say them—not yet. "Let's do it together," he proposes.

They plan it for July, two months in the future. Edie has decided to give a paper: The Ontological Puzzle of Suicide—her parting gesture. She has been thinking about this for a long time. She's going to tell them what she is planning—the final irony. Arthur feels again her cutting edge, her crystal purity. No one is like her. As for him—his parents are gone, but he has a brother and two nephews in California. They aren't close, but he'll go there for a few days during the time remaining. He is also in the midst of another job, which he'll be able to finish. With these plans made his depression lifts; he moves with a surer step, through a world that has suddenly become simpler, clearer. Is this what happiness is like?

Edie and he make love. His senses fill with her: her white body on the sheet; her sharp, little breasts with their flows of vein like tiny rivers; her tongue darting at his lips; her breath. He comes with a mad shout of release and she screams too. But when they are lying together, their sweat cooled, she grabs his lower lip and squeezes it between her fingers. "You are not going to chicken out, Arthur."

He laughs, his confidence bubbling up in laughter. "No way in the world," he says.

They talk about how it will be. Going to sleep together—that's what Arthur wants. It's all right with Edie. When he deliberates too much about the details, she brings him up short. It may be that she still doesn't quite trust him, still worries that he might back out. But Arthur is committed. The final sleep is the answer to the riddle of his personality, that excruciatingly tight weave that could not be loosened by drugs or therapy or even love. It is the arc of completion to his life, the end of his torment. For the first time in many years, perhaps since his childhood, he feels safe.

Could he have come to this point without her? No, he thinks—not now, not soon; maybe never.

What would be easiest, most practical? Carbon monoxide—all it takes is exhaust. They decide to do it at the lake. There's a place where a gravelly bank abuts the water. They can drive the car practically up to the edge. The spot is sheltered by bushes, almost invisible from the road. For Arthur, it's the perfect location. As for Edie, she frowns, sweeps her forehead with her palm. "Fine," she tells him. "It's as good as anything."

Edie's presentation is in a small amphitheater in the Humanities Building. The occasion is a regional meeting of the American Philosophical Society. It's a conference that she helped organize, and they have afforded her the honor of an invited talk, thirty-five minutes long. Arthur takes a seat in the third row, near the center. He's wearing a short-sleeved dress shirt, a good pair of slacks. He has paid seventy-five dollars for a guest registration.

The talk starts out with background. There are the Greeks and the Stoics; the condemning Christians; the Enlightenment—Hume and Kant; the existentialists; the contemporary arguments concerning euthanasia. The topic of suicide is not common in this venue, but it's respectable. Edie is a scholar; she knows her stuff. But when her thesis strays to the personal, the audience grows uneasy. There are whispers; glances exchanged. Though Edie is known to be young and brash, provocative, this time she may be going too far. She's wearing her trademark blazer, this one white, with a light blouse and dark skirt. She has come out from behind the dais, microphone in hand. She has no make-up on, except for lipstick, a red slash in the paleness of her face. There's a slight down on her cheeks, impossible to see from where Arthur is sitting. In his mind he recreates the soft feel of it on his fingertips.

Slowly, she begins to reveal the details of what they are planning. Of course, her language is conditional—"should," "could," "what if?" It's really not possible to tell if she is speaking literally or merely personalizing her thesis to heighten the effect. When she finishes, the applause is hesitant. And in the question period afterward, no one dares to ask what many are thinking. Is she serious?

In the evening—a cocktail party. He stands beside her as a little group gathers. She introduces him: "My friend, Arthur." Some people drift off but others remain. And more appear. They are attracted to her. Her cutting edge, her ethereal look—she has removed her blazer in the hot room—the protruding shoulder bones, milky skin, the white down now noticeable if you look closely enough. But from all of them, she has chosen him. And he has chosen her—to sit with him in his car at the lake, to go off together into the final sleep.

Warm, muggy, cloudy—the day arrives. They have breakfast in his house. Arthur has left a short letter on his kitchen table. But Edie, true to form, has sent a brief note to The Bystander, that most iconoclastic of all philosophy journals. She doesn't think they'll publish it, but who knows?

Arthur is ready for the moment. The respite he received weeks ago when the decision was made is now beginning to wear thin. In the last few days, the worm has made its reappearance at the back of his brain. The thought of what is coming no longer seems to magically comfort him, not as it once did. He looks at Edie. She's still in her nightgown, chewing her toast. "Do you think we should be naked?" he asks. "Go out without anything?"

Her eyes look unfocussed, as if her mind is somewhere else. It takes a moment before she replies. "Why not?" she says.

Arthur has bought a length of hose that he attaches to the exhaust pipe. He runs the other end into the driver's-side window, sealing the opening with heavy tape and a cardboard cutout that he made the night before. They are both wearing shorts and t-shirts; nothing underneath—why make extra bother? Removing the clothes, they stuff them into a gym bag, which he weighs down with a tool from the trunk. It sinks slowly, then it's gone.

He gets in the driver's door, Edie on the passenger side. He feels warm in his skin, and her flesh is even warmer to his touch. He asks: "Are you ready?"

"I've told you," she answers quietly. "I have been ready since I was a child."

He turns the key. It's a quiet car; there is almost no sound, only the engine's slight vibration. But, almost immediately, he can smell the exhaust. They sit holding hands, watching each other. Arthur stares at her face. It seems so familiar—and yet ... something is wrong. It's making him uneasy. He stares and stares, but can't understand.

And then, *he notices the pain.* He gapes in surprise, his breath catching in the fouled air. Her whole body suddenly cries out to him with her terrible pain. It's there in her delicate skin stretched to transparency over her thin cheekbones; in her green eyes narrowed against the light; her thin lips pressed tight as if to contain her anguish. He stares at her little breasts, which are pathetic now, weightless and vulnerable, mottled with their pale, blue tangles of veins. Edie is suffering horribly—how could he have missed it all this time?

A sigh rises in his chest, rushes out of him. At last, he understands: Edie is not strong, not pure, not made of impervious crystal. *She is merely a sufferer like himself—a fellow sufferer.* And now, scratching like thorns in his memory, there are others he's known: a smug professor he had at the university; his brother, whom he never loved; the seemingly strong, seemingly assured woman, who ordered the deck. He sees their piteous faces, Edie's first of all.

How could he let her die?

"No!" she moans.

He has dropped her hand, reached across her to open the door. "Arthur—no!"

She scratches him, scoring his chest with her long nails. But he manages to push her from the car, scrambling over the passenger seat to follow her down onto the gravel. He has to wait to catch his breath, but when it comes, he stands and takes her by the ankles. She tries to hold on, but her fingers are weak, rubbery. She comes away face down and he drags her over the pebbles and dirt along the lake's edge away from the car.

The effort leaves him exhausted, and he has to sit down. His eyes close; he could sleep now, but he won't let himself. Lying beside him, Edie has become quiet. He forces himself to his knees and manages to turn her over. She's smeared with dirt from the belly up; the ride through the pebbles has bruised her delicate skin, filled it with scratches. Gravel clings to her chin and mouth. Using a finger, he clears her nostrils, sweeps dirt out from between her lips. He turns her head to the side and sits astride her, pressing her chest down with his palms, push and release, push and release. Pausing, he breathes into her mouth—push, then breathe, over and over.

Finally, Edie groans. She coughs dirt, and, out of her half-open eyes tears suddenly begin to run. Arthur sits over her and stares. He has never seen her cry before.

Reality

I know that Eve is busy in the kitchen. She has a small task tonight, baking bread for tomorrow's breakfast. Though she has never done this before, we have cookbooks that describe it. Eve is very smart and capable. All three of us are, else we wouldn't still be here. Earlier in the evening, I helped her to set up. She asked a few questions; I answered as best I could. Somehow, I don't want her to fail, though such a failure would move me closer to success.

Just to be sure, I check the kitchen. She's there. I watch from the doorway, while she bends to the hot oven, then kneels. Her long, dark ponytail bobs on her back. She pushes a loaf pan into the oven, pausing to stare at the cavity she has just filled. When she stands, the camera above the stove swings up to follow her. She wipes sweat from her forehead. I know that thousands are watching, perhaps millions. Watching her at the stove, me at the door.

She turns her head and sees me. Gerda, you are still awake? Yes, I say, but I'm going now. There's never enough sleep around here, she remarks—is there?

No, but we have grown accustomed to this deprivation by now, after nearly fourteen periods. Tomorrow, as always, before dawn, the producer's assistant will be here to talk to us, individually, and set us our small tasks. At the beginning, when there were sixteen of us, this took hours. But now we are only three.

I stand listening at John's door. He is asleep, snoring lightly. I turn the handle and the door opens without a sound. John is lying on his back, arms outside the sheet. Even at a distance I can see the sharp protrusion of his collarbones. I am not sure what to do. What is the Main Task? Could it be to make a child?

The cameras operate with a slight whir, audible only amidst total silence. The one over the bed has angled down to point at me, its green light winking. Lately, I have been noticing the cameras again, after many periods of having ignored them. The vast audience is watching me—many from their own bedrooms, I imagine. Involuntarily, I brush my hair back off my forehead. It is blonde, and thin. Sometimes, I wonder if Eve and I have been retained because we look so different: Eve, with her muscular legs and heavy, beautiful breasts, her olive skin bronzed from time spent out on the patio; and myself—lithe and pale, tall, small-breasted, my complexion delicate and sun-averse. Or, perhaps, it is not our looks at all, but other qualities that have enabled us to survive. Will we ever know?

I am wearing jeans and a tank-top, my feet bare. I could easily unzip the jeans and step out of them, pull the top over my head. John's bed is narrow, but there is room enough. I worry that he is younger than I, he and Eve both. And she, not I, has the wide hips and sturdy build ideal for carrying a child. But, lately, her menses have dried up. If this is the Main Task, then why did not the producer remove Eve and leave another woman instead? My own menstruation last came two weeks ago, so I think I must be fertile now.

It is only a few steps to the bed. If I go, the second camera, above the doorway, will follow me, watching John and me together. I am long past shame, but … suppose he refuses me? I have been intimate with only one of the other men, the first time following a raucous party with much drinking. The producer's assistant keeps us well-supplied with alcohol and urges us to relax. Matteus took me to his bedroom. We flailed drunkenly at one another, but it was sweet enough. We slept together a number of times and talked many hours, until he was removed.

Sometimes, I envy them, the ones who have been removed. They have returned to the world from which we all came, a universe of endless choices and possibilities. In that world I was the curator of a small museum, planning exhibits and dioramas. One day, the producer's assistant paid us a visit. He stood before a diorama in which a small boy gazed from the foreground at a wonderland of jeweled trees, birds with magnificent feathers. I came out of my office, waiting behind him as he watched through the glass, mesmerized by the same strange and beautiful world that the boy saw. Finally, he sensed me there and turned to face me. The producer has chosen you, he said.

Abruptly, John moves in his sleep, kicking the sheet off. He is nude, and when he turns onto his side, his ribs stick out. His hair is the color of straw, almost white. Would the audience be pleased with us—two pale scarecrows locked in an embrace? Better Eve for him, dark and voluptuous. But John would have to court her. There are flowers in the garden, wine to be poured into her glass. There are silken pillows on the sofas. The tools of seduction abound in this house—nothing is lacking. But John, though he is twenty-seven, has the sharp-tongued insouciance of a teenager; perhaps, also, a slight smugness, born, not of good looks, but of a certain animal energy. He would court Eve quite differently from the way I might imagine.

When John moves again, I back from the doorway and stride down the hall, the camera swiveling to follow me. In the kitchen, I find Eve still engrossed in her baking. She has strong powers of concentration, but can become petulant when she gets very little sleep, as will be the case tonight. I thought you were in bed, she says. No, I answer, I came for some vodka. There is a bottle in the freezer, John's drink of choice. I am bringing him the bottle, I tell Eve. I take two shot glasses from the cupboard, and Eve gives me a wave of her hand, permission of a sort. She can afford to be sanguine. If there are any odds-makers among our audience, surely they must by now have made her the favorite.

Sitting by John on the bed, I touch the icy bottle to his skin. He stirs and his eyes open. He is in a state of taut excitement, perhaps from a dream; after a few moments, he realizes, and draws the sheet up to cover himself. I pull the cork from the vodka, put it to my lips and then to his. The near camera angles down at us. I know what the audience wants. But, the producer—what does *he* want? The vodka burns as I swallow it. John smiles at me, his crooked smile. When I kiss him, he tastes of vodka and sleep. I tilt my face up for a moment, so the camera can see it. Then I look at John. What do you think it is, I whisper, the Main Task? He puts his hands on my breasts, caresses them through the fabric. I don't care, he says.

The producer's suite of offices is on the thirty-second floor, in a building of a thousand windows on the Avenue of the Americas. We, the chosen, were brought there to receive our final instructions and sign our contracts. The producer was also present that day—in his corner room with its view of two rivers—though we never saw him. In fact, we know little or nothing about him, while he knows everything about us. We should have tried to find out, I realize. Before we were sequestered here, and the chance evaporated.

Our story is aired on television once weekly. There are nude glimpses of us in each episode, just enough to titillate. But, online, subscribers can find feeds from all the cameras. There are no private places. The room's light is dim, John and I little more than shadows. There are lights, of course, that we could switch on. Matteus and I did so once, hoping it might increase our longevity in the show. But he was removed two periods later, while I remained. It is the producer alone who decides, and no one understands what he wants.

Later, when John is sleeping again, I make my way back down the hall. Eve is still in the kitchen. She is sitting at the table, waiting for the bread to rise. A cookbook is open in front of her, but she is not reading. Instead, she stares across the room at the refrigerator's white door. Her voice is also toneless and white: You were with John? I sit down beside her on the bench of the breakfast nook, with its comfortable back and soft padding. I have brought back the vodka, and I put it on the table between us. Would you mind if I was? She does not look at me. I uncork the bottle and offer it. Her eyes move. Eve—I say her name. She turns her head, and on the near wall the close-up camera makes a small adjustment.

Now that we are just three, the house has become smaller. Many of the rooms have been locked off, subtracted from the game. I do not mind. My previous apartment was also small—bedroom, living room, small kitchen and tiny bath. But, a few blocks away in an old, barnlike loft, I had a studio. There, I assembled my installations— extensive, room-sized pieces with many parts, and more modest ones that could fit in a space the size of a closet. For years, I installed the work of others, while mine was ignored, even by own museum. The producer knows all this, but I have never told it to any of the other contestants. Until now.

Eve drinks from the bottle, hands it back, and I take my turn. I am somehow sure I have become pregnant, and, tomorrow, I will begin my abstention. But not tonight. Eve has loosed her ponytail; her black hair hangs down her back. She stares at me with her dark eyes. I was in love with him once, she says. John?—but I have never noticed anything between you. From before, she tells me—I knew him before. I listen, I nod, but I cannot imagine why the producer has allowed this. Two contestants with a full-blown relationship that preceded even the first period. And, now, these two are among the three of us who have survived.

Eve tells me that she and John met on the job. They are both engineers and were working on the same project. They began to date. There was a strong attraction, and, after a few months, she moved into his apartment and they started to live as a couple. Then, the producer's assistant contacted Eve. In their interview, he told her that the producer was interested in her because she so strongly breached the stereotype of the female engineer. Beautiful Eve, with her dark hair and voluptuous figure. Perhaps she should have been insulted by this, but instead she fell strongly for the lure of notoriety and stardom. When John objected, the producer offered *him* a place in the house. It was too much to resist.

At first, they imagined they would merely continue as a couple. A week into the first period, she began coming, discretely, to sleep in his bed; during the day, they would touch each other or kiss, when only the camera was watching. But the producer's assistant began to assign them small tasks that made it difficult or impossible for them to meet. John had a weakness for vodka, which was plentiful, while she reacted unstably to the loss of sleep we all had to endure. In their early morning conferences, the producer's assistant hinted to Eve that John had interest in one of the other women. Perhaps this was true, perhaps not; but in Eve's sleep-deprived state it was enough to sour the relationship.

Eve asks: But who will take care of you? I have told her everything—my theory about the Main Task, my absolute conviction that John has made me pregnant. They will be forced to get a doctor, I say. She shakes her head. No, I'm meant to do it. I see that now. But you are an engineer, not a medical practitioner. I know how, she tells me. And she says this with such authority that I cannot doubt her. I offer Eve my lips and she kisses me, as the camera looks on. This is what the audience wants, what will keep them watching, what will elevate Eve and myself to the final two positions. Provided that the producer agrees, provided that we are in tune with *his* desires.

The camera now closes in on us. It has its expectations, but I have learned to tease and confound it. I believe this to be one of the reasons I have survived so long. Eve, her face only inches from mine, gives me a slight nod, as if she understands, almost as if she has read my mind. We pull apart slowly, watching each other's eyes—hers dark, almost black; mine pale and blue. We stare without blinking, and I understand this meeting of our gazes to seal a pact between us. We are *the two*.

The contestant removed next-to-last will receive modest rewards—more than enough to compensate her time and effort, but little compared to what the producer has promised to the final contestant. For her, there will be immense satisfaction, wealth, notoriety. If I am the one, it would mean that museums begin to mount my pieces. I know that my work is good. It has been praised privately; offers were made, which somehow came to nothing. But all this and more would be remedied if I were to be the last one.

We never know when a period will end. The producer has arranged it this way to heighten the interest of the audience. His assistant may arrive at any time with a notice of removal for one of the contestants. These removals have occurred at moments both intimate and mundane. Matteus was removed, literally, from my bed. There was a knock at the door, and I could hear the camera pointed there become suddenly alert. We both realized what was happening, but neither knew whom the summons would be for. There was a moment of fearful suspense, and then the door opened. Matteus covered himself, as if for protection. The assistant entered and nodded at him. A short time later he was gone.

But the current period seems particularly long. There is no doubt in my own mind now that I am pregnant—I missed my last menstruation—though Eve tells me that when women live close together their menses can be synchronized. It could be that I am merely responding to the irregularity of her own cycle.

The largest, best-lit mirror in the house is in the exercise room. Lately, I have begun to go there every day to examine myself. I stare at my belly and breasts, searching minutely for any sign of my pregnancy. Though I know it is too early for me to show, I am desperate to confirm outwardly what I feel inwardly to be true. The camera watches silently as I pose and stretch, focused on the imaginary rectangle of space that contains me in front of the mirror. I have lost interest in speculating about any of my audience, except for one: the producer himself. It is impossible to know if he is watching, but a further question has begun to germinate in my mind. Could it be that he is the *only* viewer, that he has brought us here exclusively for his own amusement?

Eve tells me that, following her training in engineering, she completed three years of medical school before deciding that medicine did not suit her. I let her examine me, but she remains cautious about declaring my pregnancy. Meanwhile, she and I pair off in an alliance against John, who takes it badly. Up to this point he has survived on his insouciant attitude and intriguing smile. But now this poise begins to disintegrate. His drinking increases and he fails to complete a number of the small tasks he was assigned. One night he takes Eve aside; they go to her room and close the door. My heart beats hard, but I continue about my business. After perhaps an hour, John comes out. I recognize his footsteps down the hallway and the squeak of his door as it closes. Eve stays in her room, and I don't dare to look for her there.

The next morning, John's time comes. His room is empty, his presence obliterated. The producer's assistant must have removed him while we slept. Eve and I ought to feel elation, but instead we are subdued. The period's ending came so suddenly, so shockingly. Eve takes my hand, squeezes it hard, and we go about our small tasks. Finally, in the late afternoon, we drink a toast that needs no words. For this solemn occasion, I break my abstinence with a small sip of vodka.

More and more, I find myself staring into the camera. I move one way and then the other, making its roving eye follow. I imagine the producer at the other end, watching. He and he alone. Perhaps he is old or crippled and can't do what we do, can only experience these things through us. But could he really be the sole audience? Surely, the contestants who have been removed would learn this quickly and complain. But no sooner have I thought this than I visualize the imposing skyscraper of glass and steel rising above the Avenue of the Americas. The producer is a powerful man. What could a band of disgruntled contestants do against him?

The next time the assistant comes to give us our assignments, I ask if John's room can remain open, explaining that I would like to put up an installation. He remains quiet for a moment before turning toward Eve. What do you think? he asks. I have not discussed this with her—I hold my breath. But beautiful Eve smiles. Of course, she says. The assistant is noncommittal, but two days later a small truck arrives, loaded with the materials I requested.

I leave John's sparse furniture in place, along with certain personal items that he must have forgotten in his haste to pack: a bathroom scale, a hairbrush, a pair of balled-up briefs, a half-empty cigarette pack, a book. Around the furniture, Eve and I begin to construct a replica of the skyscraper from which the producer exerts his power. The tower is severed at odd angles and split into sections: three in the bedroom, one in the bathroom, one in the doorway between them—with John's items placed inside the sections, one in each. The constructions are heavy with glass, which mirrors the light oddly, producing multiple reflections.

Eve and I begin to plan even grander installations for the other rooms. My pregnancy is still uncertain—there are signs and countersigns. I realize that I should have made more use of John while he was here. After a week or two, Eve moves into my room. It seems impossible that one of us will be removed. Perhaps the contest will end with *two* of us remaining—why not?

But one morning, the producer's assistant arrives with a stern rebuke for Eve. She has failed in one of her small tasks, the planting of certain flowers out on the patio. Despite her diligent efforts most of the flowers died. The assistant says nothing about removal, only warning her to do better. Still, Eve and I are terrified. That night, we stand before one of the cameras, hand in hand, pleading to be allowed to win together. Our tears are real. Will the producer be moved by our pleas? Is he listening at all?

The final period continues. At night we hold each other, by day go on with our small tasks and with the installations. What else can we do? We remain hopeful. If I am truly going to give birth, even the producer would hesitate to break us up. Indeed, the next time his assistant arrives it is with a promising signal. He tells us that our ratings are higher than they have ever been. We are elated, and that night we leave the light on in our bedroom as the cameras record us.

But at the same time that I hope, I rehearse in my mind Eve's removal—just in case. Perhaps she is doing the same. Though it now seems like a consolation prize, I imagine the wealth I would have, imagine traveling around the country and the world to museums that will host my installations. Already, a vast audience is viewing my work—mine and Eve's, though I am the creative force. She would never claim otherwise.

The producer's assistant opens up further space for us, rooms that have long been locked away. In many, we find remnants of the person who was removed: a decaying banana skin in a drawer; a torn t-shirt; a tampon; a lock of hair; a baseball cap, rimmed with sweat. These are like the bones of a departed civilization. There are no photographs of the former contestants. It was forbidden to take them, under penalty of immediate removal. But, hidden beneath the mattress of one of the beds, there is a drawing, a self-portrait of a woman, Maxine, who was among the last five of us. Her hair shimmers in streams, as if scattered by the wind, and she wears eyeglasses, though she never did in real life. Eve and I upend the mattress and lean it on its edge, exposing the drawing as we found it. These will comprise the central motif of the next installation we are planning.

In our own bed, Eve whispers into my ear, too softly for the audience to hear. To them, it must seem like an endearment, and in a way it is. If I win, she tells me, I'll share. Everything. Her breath gathers in my ear like a cloud that has released its rain. Gently, I turn her head and reciprocate: For me, the same, I say. The same. Could the producer ever have imagined that his last two competitors would conspire against him?

The final period has already lasted more than four weeks, the longest ever. Eve and I are out sunning ourselves on the patio. The weather is cool, the summer ending. Eve says she has still not been able to determine whether or not I am pregnant. This seems unlikely. I think that perhaps she knows, but can't bring herself to disappoint me. We are both dozing in the weak sunshine, when I feel an odd sensation. Opening my eyes, I look up to see the producer's assistant. An unscheduled visit—he is carrying a briefcase. I feel intense anticipation and a pang of fear. Eve … I say.

But the end has come for her—brutally, and without warning. The assistant looks at her. Pack your things, he says. Tears fill her eyes, and then mine. I come into her arms and we embrace for a long moment. To our left and right, I hear the soft buzz of the cameras as they move to record everything in intimate detail. As we part, they shift again. I'll see you soon, I say. But Eve smiles and shakes her head. You'll be famous. No, I tell her. I take her hand. I remember what I promised you—half of everything. Thank you, she answers, almost formally. Then she turns and walks away.

There is nothing holding me here any longer. I have been told that the producer will meet me sometime after I leave the house. Though I am free to go, collect my rewards, I have asked to stay a bit longer. The producer's assistant tells me it will be all right, provided the ratings hold up. The audience—or is it the producer himself?—seems to be interested in me still. I have the feeling that the cameras are closer than ever now, following my every breath. They have made me conscious of all my actions—each intake and exhalation of air, my tiny movements as I eat, or sit on the toilet, or build up my installations, bit by bit.

One night, my period comes, neither heavier nor lighter than normal. Now, it is clear that I am not pregnant and never have been. But, if this was not the Main Task—then what? Somehow I must have completed it; otherwise, why would I have been chosen over all the others? With this on my mind, I wander the rooms. My installations are everywhere now, growing organically from the walls, the floors, the furniture. The cameras watch inertly when I am not present; but, when I enter a room, they follow me, the installations seeming to come alive under their robotic gaze. I feel the producer watching with his many eyes. I stand still and take a breath, which the cameras record from above and below, left and right; from this angle and that; from all angles. Could it be that Main Task is *me*?

The Headache

A woman approaches me in the street. She is not very tall, her hair pale yellow and stiff as straw, her face empty. At her neck she wears a green scarf. Her left hand presses the side of her head near the temple.

I turn and follow her—she doesn't look back. The streets are crowded. The people are short here—I can see the tops of their heads, rows and rows of them, as if I were looking down from the roof of a building. I keep ten paces behind. She is easy to track: her hand keeps going to her head.

The street branches into three and the rows of heads break up. The rightmost fork leads to a museum housing the works of a famous painter. Most go there. The middle branch is the narrowest; an alley, really. I follow the woman down it. After fifty meters she begins to slow her pace and I get closer. She still doesn't turn. I have soft shoes, but I think she hears me. She stops, takes a key out, opens a low wooden door. The medieval houses in this sector have doors in unexpected places, like the orifices of the women in some of the famous artist's paintings. The woman enters easily, but I must make a deep bow. We climb a helical staircase and, at the top, she turns to look down at me, watching as I approach with my head still ducked. On the landing, when I straighten up, I see that I know her. We attended the same secondary school, long ago. I have always been intensely curious about the lives of my former classmates; perhaps this interest is a kind of radar that leads me to them in the streets.

141

She was pretty as a schoolgirl, but now her mouth is a red lipstick streak, not completely horizontal. There are lines on her forehead, and her cheeks need powdering. *Do you want a girl*, she asks. *You're early.* Her left hand goes to her temple and the lipstick slash contorts and compresses.

No, I don't need a girl. I tell her my name. *You*, she acknowledges. She opens a door. When I follow her through I see that we are indeed in a brothel. There is a red rug and shabby divans where the girls will sit. The light, which comes from shaded lamps, is dim; perhaps the girls do not merit close inspection.

We mount a short flight of carpeted stairs and enter the first door to the left. I must again duck my head. The woman sits on a banquette, her head thrown forward, arms dangling limply between her spread knees. Her stiff hair seems pasted to her head; it hardly moves. I sit on her wide ornate bed, across from her. When she finally lifts her face, I examine it. Her eyes are black points, dabbed below plucked brows. Her nose is fleshy, its lines indistinct. Her hand holds her temple.

Years ago, she was the youngest in our class, and looked even younger, a naïf. Her hair was darker, then; she had long legs and a thin neck. The skirts she wore were short and showed her legs, a bit of a scandal. She tempted us, but as if from a distance. There was a younger brother who sometimes came to meet her after school. When they stood together, she looked like an innocent child.

While I've been ruminating, she has left the room. Next door there is water running. I am curious to see her nude, but by the time I reach the bathroom she is already in the tub covered by bubbles with only one of her legs sticking out, dangling over the side. *My head is splitting apart*, she says.

I have a vision: A man cleaves a coconut with his axe. The two halves leap into the air, fall and roll, finally stopping far apart.

Water hisses in the pipes, voices float up to us. There must be another bath in the room below. Some of the girls are bathing. How did you get into this trade? I ask. I remember your family was well-to-do. She tosses her head angrily, though her hair remains still. *What does that have to do with it? I was always attracted to the* trade, *as you call it. My father used to attend on Wednesday nights. My mother knew, but pretended he went to political meetings. One night I followed him. I knocked on the door, and the proprietor recognized me and took me to the kitchen. She gave me a Coca Cola to drink, then told me to go home and not come back. I didn't know what kind of establishment it was until a boy at school told me.*

Which boy? She slides her leg further out of the bath and raises it, examining her toes. *Pablo.* Yes, I say, I remember. He was short, but self-contained; he laughed a lot. *I was drawn to the trade,* she tells me. *I would walk by at night, using any excuse. The shades were usually down, but I could sometimes see a woman's face in one of the windows.* The fascists were in power, I remind her. *My father was among them,* she says, *don't you remember?*

I want her to wet her head. Her plastered-down hair looks abnormal, as if someone had ripped patches from her scalp and spread the remaining hairs over the bare places. In fact her whole head seems distorted; the lipstick slash, which ought to have been vertically below the center of her forehead, is instead a few degrees to the side. No doubt, it's her headache that has disrupted her.

Pablo was in love with you, I say. I watched him watching you. She rubs the left side of her head up and down with her fingertips, seeming not to hear. She turns toward me, but her eyes are closed.

The priests condemned the trade from their pulpits, she tells me, *but their superiors knew it was indispensable for public order.* What did your father think when he found out about you? *What did you think?* she counters. I was not completely surprised, I say. *Pablo was. I was spread out on the bed when he saw me; my breasts were exposed, but I had my legs crossed, hiding my sex.* What did he do? *He gave me this.* She rubs the lipstick slash and red comes off on her fingers. *Let me have a cigarette.*

I put it into her lipstick mouth. It gets wet, but not so much that I can't light it. After she inhales, I remove it so she can blow the smoke back out. When I put the cigarette in again, she lets it hang from her lower lip, trailing smoke. You could have married at the time, I tell her. I would have married you. *You?* she says. *You were always so far away.*

She takes a last puff, then lets the cigarette fall from her lips to the soapy water. *My head hurts terribly, thank God it's only on one side.* Perhaps the offending side could be chopped out, I think. I ask where the boundary is and she uses her finger to draw a meridian, beginning at her neck, up over her scalp, down her forehead and across the middle of her left eye. I could cleave it with an axe, but then her brain-matter would slide loose. What would that look like?

You must wash your hair now, I tell her. She watches me with her pinpoint eyes, shrugs, picks up the shower spray and turns it on her head. The water splashes up from her scalp, the mist of particles filling the air around her like a halo of light. *Pull the plug,* she orders. The stopper is suspended by a brass chain, now pulled taut. I lift it and, after a moment, the soapy water shudders. Kneeling, I look from the far end of the tub. The surface of the water seems to slope upward, a trick of perspective. I watch her body as the tub slowly drains. Bubbles of soap adhere to her: they are not white, no, rather gray, with bluish interiors; they cover her body like drab blue flowers.

I say: you have never allowed me to see you fully nude. She shrugs. *Others have seen me.* I take the spray and run it vigorously across her, back and forth, until the soap is gone. Her skin looks like polished wood, the pores large, her breasts stark and pointed, the left one slightly higher. Her cunt is a thick black line, moist as fresh ink. She stands and I wrap her in a towel, except for her left arm, which is free to hold her head. Rubbing through the abrasive flesh of the towel, I dry her body. But when I try to remove her hand so as to dry her hair, she resists.

A door leads out from the bath into her dressing room. Shedding the towel, she sits at a dressing table in front of a mirror that stretches the entire length of the wall. I position myself on a stool behind her, watching her reflection. The mirror alters her face. Left and right are interchanged, reversing the asymmetry of the lipstick slash. The black dots of her eyes widen in the glass and there are slight smudges, perhaps in the mirror itself, suggesting eyebrows.

Pablo became a police officer, you know. It made him quite self-assured. He used to come around to my place. It was near the zoo—do you remember? It was before you became a whore, I say. She smiles, the red slash parting. *The apartment was just one large room, but it had a high ceiling and a skylight. The bed was in a corner, under a painting which portrayed a magician and his female assistant. The woman was dark haired, nude to the waist. My bed was hardly large enough for one—I never let Pablo sleep with me.*

Liar!

She turns, holding her head, her face contorted. She is suffering. Her pain is inflicted by God—I am nothing more than a witness. Pablo and I were rivals, I remind her. You gave him one hand and me the other. We went to a cafe together once, the one near the port. You reached across the table to lay your fingers over his, while underneath I felt your leg on mine.

Rub me, she says. Her head feels malleable, as if I could push down to her brain and pull it to the surface in places, forming little convoluted hills which would rise from her scalp. *No, not there.* She takes my hand and moves it to the place where the pain is greatest. My finger touches a little bony knob. *Yes*, she murmurs.

Her head slumps on my chest and I rub for a time, attaining a sensual rhythm. When I raise my eyes to the mirror our images bring to mind the magician and his assistant. Noises come from the floor below, muted laughter. The other whores must be getting ready. After a few minutes, she lifts her head and removes my hand. *Thank you.* I return to my chair behind her, watching in the glass. She unstoppers a bottle, wetting a handkerchief with clear liquid and dabbing at her lipstick. I am afraid that her mouth will vanish altogether, but a thin, horizontal line persists.

Her face looks abnormally pale. She has repainted her lips, getting the lines straight this time, but the color is even redder than before. She powders her cheeks, making them white; she looks like a kabuki performer or a clown. Her wardrobe is open; a clown's costume hangs where I can see it. Put it on, I say. She steps into the leggings, pulling the top up to insert her arms, flinching a bit as the material touches her naked skin. I zip her up in back and close her clown's collar. She stands with her back to the mirror. The broad clown's cuffs extend almost to the floor, her feet bare below them. The costume is checked with large squares of red and white; its baggy contours hide her figure. Above the collar: her white face and red mouth; her hair hanging down, still wet from the bath; her left hand on her temple, fingers spread wide, pressing so hard that her veins stand out in long, ropey lines. THE HEADACHE.

When she removes the costume, her body is flushed; it must have been hot underneath. Her breasts have softened, lost their wooden starkness. Why did you choose Pablo? I ask her. She comes over to me, presses against me. *It was touch and go then, don't you remember? The fascists still might have hung on. Pablo was a churchgoer, a rising star in the police force. My father pressured me.*

More lies. You have always done exactly as you wanted. You joined the trade because it tickled you. Your father must have been wounded terribly. He'd have had you thrown in prison to teach you a lesson, but by then it was too late—the fascists had become impotent. And Pablo? He was a minor official, nothing more. The new government allowed him to stay in office; he might have advanced from there, but he wasn't up to it.

While you became famous, she adds. She is combing her hair now, pulling out the difficult tangles, doubly in pain. We watch each other via the mirror. *You had too much imagination. No woman can survive with that sort of man. Your bizarre visions overwhelmed me. I began to see myself with your eyes.*

You are not suggesting …?

That I finally entered the trade because of you? Admit it, it was your vision of me—a whore.

Only because you behaved like one. It was not only Pablo and I—there were certainly others. When you became pregnant, we might have held a lottery to determine the father.

Her back straightens. In the mirror, the reflection begins to work on its eyes. The brows become darker, the lashes stretch. Mascara is applied. Gradually, the eyes widen, taking over the face. These eyes have seen everything, yet remain solemn and innocent.

Only Pablo loved me, though I didn't love him. He took his place beside me in the church, before God. My father was in his uniform. He stood at attention as I walked down the aisle. You were also there. I saw you in one of the rear pews, sitting alone. You were so tall and thin.

As tall, I say, as Pablo was short. Even you towered over him. Your hair was too long that day, snaking about in all directions. Your fingers stuck out greedily to receive the ring. You made quite a picture, the two of you, standing before the priest—a dwarf and a woman who resembled nothing so much as a tree.

Yes, she replies. *You made it quite clear how you saw us. How cruel you were!* I watch closely as she rouges her cheeks, applies the blush lightly on her forehead, even a touch to her nose. The white, clownlike pallor slowly disappears. Now the finishing touches—she sweeps her hair up, pins it; long earrings pulling at her earlobes; a green necklace. She stands, faces me, posing in front of the mirror. There is a long scar on her abdomen, above the spreading bush of pubic hair. *The fetus went bad in the seventh month,* she explains. *They had to remove it surgically. I was relieved, actually.* She seems to rise from her own hairy bush, a pink stalk, her breasts like fruit, hair a crown of vines. I feel my head begin to throb, the left side. I think I am getting your headache, I tell her. *Poor man!* She touches me briefly, then goes to her wardrobe to dress. A green skirt, tight blouse; nothing under, as befits a whore; finally, soft boots and a hat with a green feather.

I follow her down the red staircase. My footfalls resound through my body, the vibrations in my temple growing stronger. Sounds fly up to us; a bluish tinkle of giggles and chatter. In the sitting room, the whores are lounging on one of the divans. They are in various stages of undress, toilettes incomplete; some sit on the cushion, some on the floor, some lean in from behind. Their limbs intertwine, bodies mingling, a head on a breast, a pair of knees that don't match, red lips blowing kisses. They are like a dense bower of wild flowers, different species, come upon suddenly in the woods. *Half an hour,* she tells them, *then you must get ready.*

I realize I am holding my head, on the left side. The pain is suddenly intense. Surely, she cannot have suffered as much as this. How do you treat your headaches? I ask. She turns to face me, her feather and necklace glowing green. *Nothing does any good. You have to wait—didn't you know that? This can't be your first time?* No, I say, I had them when I was young, but it was years ago. *Won't you choose one of the girls? It might help—at least take your mind off it.*

Where is Pablo? I ask. I should find him, apologize; I had no right to subject him to ridicule. A tear forms in her left eye, dropping suddenly, heavily, like a pellet of translucent steel. *There were two bombs—hadn't you heard? He arrived just after the first; he was first on the scene. Then the second explosion came. It was in every newspaper—how could you not know?* A red blast, brilliant, with fiery edges, body parts scattered on the ground, an arm with a wristwatch, the sky white. I hardly ever looked at the papers, I tell her. I used them to line my floor, to wipe spatters up.

I sit on the bottom step to wait, holding my head with both hands, though only the left side hurts. The pain is terrible—I don't know how long I can stand it. After a time, two of the whores come over. She must have sent them. I can see her at the far end of the room, straightening a picture on the wall. Her green feather glows as if caught in a beam of sunlight. The whores have green eyes, lipstick mouths; they look at me with pity. I know how I must seem to them—my unshaven face black with shadows, my forehead tiny, eyes narrow with suffering; perhaps there is blood dripping from one ear. SELF PORTRAIT WITH HEADACHE. The two whores are rather old, their bodies slack, breasts hanging. Their faces seem familiar; perhaps they are also former classmates of ours, whom she has taken in. Yes, I tell them, I know you. I kiss one and then the other. Why not—while I'm waiting, until the pain goes away?

The
Ballad of
St. Katherine

The short, dramatic life of Katherine Turley contained the stuff of Hollywood movies and country songs. *The Ballad of St. Katherine*— would that have suited her?

Jody Hopson, in
Religion in America
"Katherine Turley: Healing Without Creed"

Part I

She was Katie, then.

She grew up in the Bronx along a winding street that followed the Harlem River: Proud Hill Road. The building stood high on an embankment protected by a stone wall. From the windows facing the street, there was a view over the river into Manhattan. On clear evenings the sun setting into the Hudson filled the rooms with burning light.

Katie was a child with funny ideas. She thought that birds might carry messages from the dead; that there was a roof beyond the sky; that September ought to come after October, instead of before. Thin-lipped, with a tentative smile, she wore her hair braided or in a ponytail, once in a while pinned up. Her face was freckled and angular, Irish looking.

In seventh grade, she shot up—a thin stalk with freckled cheeks and translucent eyebrows. On Proud Hill Road she jumped rope with two other girls; towered over them—dark, squat Iris and petite Joan. Her eyes were closed as she jumped, her expression beatific. One afternoon, Iris and Joan argued. "Drop dead," Iris said. Katie put her hand on the girl's shoulder. "Don't talk like that." She believed that words might have magical power.

Katie's father slept late on Sundays and didn't shave. He worked nights printing the Daily News, coming home to eat breakfast before hitting the sack. Waking him prematurely was the worst sin. In the lobby of the building, he scowled when he passed people, his head down. He didn't talk to Katie in the street. When they met he'd summon her with a motion of his head, then whisper a few words, sometimes matter-of-factly, sometimes with vehemence. He seldom hit her, hardly touched her at all. But one time, on a Saturday morning, he taught her to cook corned beef and cabbage.

Under her bed, she kept a box of holy relics—a broken-off piece of cross, a statuette of Jesus with blue skin, a vial of Holy Water. These had been sent out from Ireland by her aunt, who'd married a Catholic and converted. Each of these pieces exuded heat, as if charged by a secret power.

The building had a laundry room in the basement. The super, a German immigrant who lived in a subterranean apartment with his wife and two sons, kept it well heated. Katie's mother, Ginger, did the wash frequently. She was a strawberry blonde who stared at you with crossed eyes. Women in the building swore that whenever they entered the washroom she was there. She told one of the women that the sound of the machines soothed her.

Ginger brought her knitting to the laundry room. She had a favorite chair, two down from the washing machine. If another woman got it first, she would remove the chair closest to the washer, then sit beside the woman—in the formerly third chair, which she had made into the second, restoring the favorable geometry.

Katie had her first date. She and the boy hit it off and they went to the movies a few times. Her father was at the Daily News, so the coast was clear. Ginger told him nothing about these dates. The boy brought Katie home at eleven, kissing her goodnight, progressive kissing. But he made the mistake of calling one afternoon, and her father answered. Afterward, he removed his thick belt and laid Katie across the bed and strapped her, while her mother was made to watch. When it was over, Ginger grabbed whatever laundry she could find and fled to the basement.

Mr. Buschbaum, the super, found her in the steamy washroom. Clean shaven, his face and hair both cropped close with a razor, dressed in a white undershirt and drawstring pants, he took the sobbing Ginger in his arms. "Don't cry, missus."

Katie's friend Iris invited her for a weekend on an uncle's farm in Pennsylvania.

Her father allowed this—he was unpredictable, ran hot and cold. Away from the city lights, she saw the Pleiades for the first time. The stars shivered. She stared at them. Iris's uncle set up a small telescope and she looked. *The Seven Sisters.* The brightest of them glowed with bluish veils, surrounded by their subdued companions. The stars shouted at her, and her fingers on the cold skin of the telescope could feel them.

She got a Commercial Diploma and became a secretary in Manhattan, referring to herself as Katherine. Receiving her first paycheck, she announced to her parents that she would move out, taking a tiny apartment on 102nd Street, south of Columbia. Her father reacted angrily, while her mother was stunned and bewildered. In the laundry room, Ginger deposited her wash, opening and closing the machine, over and over. Finally, the super had to stop the repetitive clicking and slamming, gently shutting the door one last time.

The secretarial job was at the Joint University Space Institute (JUSI), nine blocks up from her apartment, along West End Avenue. Katherine was eighteen. A fast typist, and a fresh and shapely, though certainly not beautiful, girl, she had gotten in on the ground floor of the space research boom. She walked to work while everyone else was stuck in the subway. Her heels clicked on the sidewalk, while a voice in her head matched the rhythm: *uptown ... JUSI ... uptown ... one ... two ... three ... four ...* until she climbed the stairs of the remodeled brownstone and said good morning to the receptionist.

Her office was on the second floor, high-ceilinged but dark. The click of her typewriter filled the room and the sound glowed like light, canceling the dimness. She could type effortlessly for many minutes on end, until a page had to be turned or the phone rang or McReady called from his office. Baby-faced and heavy-set, McReady was a dour, graying Vermonter. He had three daughters all older than she and was a grandfather by two of them. His gray eyebrows rolled as he spoke, and his Adam's apple bobbed in a slow rhythm.

On Sunday mornings, Ginger came down on the subway and the two of them walked in Riverside Park or attended a church service. Afterward, they'd go back to the apartment and Ginger would prepare a meal. This was possible because of Sunday's role as a sleep day for Katherine's father, who would not require Ginger's presence until he awoke at four or five in the afternoon. Then, she'd cook a second dinner at home and sit with him, forcing herself to eat without appetite while he glanced resentfully across the table. If they spoke, their daughter's name was never mentioned.

One Sunday, Ginger became increasingly uneasy in Katherine's tiny kitchen. This was unusual—she had been doing well on these occasions despite the stress of having to cook twice. When Ginger's agitation wouldn't dissipate, Katherine filled a bag with her clothes, some of them clean, and walked her mother to Broadway where there was a laundromat. There in the hothouse atmosphere, Ginger selected a washer and found a seat suitably juxtaposed. The machines hummed and clicked, each seemingly with its own rhythm and individual language. Katherine listened. Perhaps everything in the world could talk to you, provided you knew how to listen.

A boy came over and started speaking to her. Brent. A Columbia boy—slim, with soft-looking sandy hair and large clear glasses through which you could see brown eyes. He came on to her the only way he knew—with talk about injustice, corrupt institutions, the war. She introduced him to Ginger, who smiled. She was calming down. The machine was working; her washing was far along.

Katherine went on a date with Brent. He talked about his parents in Connecticut, part of the cesspool of capitalism that would have to be destroyed. She told him how she had taken Ginger to the laundromat to calm her. "Weird," he said.

Katherine didn't think so, not particularly. She compared her with the mother of her friend Iris, a woman who smoked cigarettes ceaselessly, but only the outermost inch, lighting them up and stubbing them out. It seemed natural to her that Ginger liked the warmth and controlled hubbub of the washroom. This had been true from the earliest times she remembered.

But Brent didn't linger on Ginger's peculiarities—he was much more interested in Katherine's father. In Brent's eyes, his vocation—printer and late-shift worker—conferred on Katherine an immediate status. She was authentic, a daughter of the proletariat.

Brent was studying philosophy. He wanted to be an existentialist and communist, follow in the footsteps of Jean-Paul Sartre. He took her downtown to a tiny theater where *No Exit* was performed. Afterward, when they discussed it, he told her that the play was allegorical—it was actually about the "hell" of capitalist society. He asked if she understood.

"Yes," she told him. She did, but there was also another impression that overwhelmed her while she was watching the play: That hell was a basement. There, the three characters tortured one another; but, above, there were warm apartments where people lived happier lives, the higher the floor the greater the love, until, at the top, God ruled in heaven. She told Brent nothing of this.

JUSI's Director was Miles Tobin, a smart-dresser with a crew cut and brown-rimmed glasses. Barely forty now, he had gotten his PhD in three years, eventually going to Washington D.C. and rising fast. He was infamous for calling staff into his office and giving them tongue-lashings for the most trivial offenses, as if JUSI were filled with unruly children and he was the father. Katherine was afraid of him, though she had never experienced his anger. In fact, he hardly seemed to know who she was.

One of the prime recipients of Tobin's tirades was P. J. Marshall, the Public Affairs Officer, a thin elegant southerner who looked thirty-five but was probably ten years older—some even said twenty. Behind his back, he was called JUSI Fruit, though largely without malice. Tobin and he actually got on fairly well, despite the frequent rants.

Katherine was considerably younger than anyone else at the office and had been excluded from extramural socializing. But one night, JUSI Fruit invited her to a gathering at his place. She realized he was homosexual. At first it had shocked her—her father had always derided fags. But looking around P. J.'s apartment, she realized that the others didn't care about his queerness. Even Tobin was there. And, apparently, he knew who Katherine was after all. When they came across one another, he acknowledged her and they exchanged a few words.

Brent took her to a meeting at Columbia. They crowded into a small auditorium, all the seats full, some sitting on the floor, some standing. Katherine felt a vibration in the room, like wings beating. She wondered if the speakers were allowed to say what they were saying. That the police were pigs and deserved to be "offed." That all power came from the barrel of a gun. That Columbia should be burned to the ground. Weren't there laws against talking that way?

The crowd began to chant. Before each shout she could sense the inhalation, a giant vacuum that drew away the air so that she couldn't breathe. She tried to align herself with the collective respiration but quickly breathed in when it should have been out and found herself choking. Her panic increased and she remembered a time at Orchard Beach when she'd inhaled water and her father, who couldn't swim, had to wade in to get her.

"What's wrong?"

Brent grabbed her hand and led her up the aisle through the crowd, all standing now, the syncopated one-two-three of the chant repeating in her head, her breath suspended until finally they reached the hall and she inhaled in desperate gasps, Brent's arm around her, his eyes blinking.

After her failure at Orchard Beach, Katherine's father had never taken her swimming again; but Brent, she realized, was not like her father. Patiently, he brought her literature. At first, there were brief pamphlets that mentioned the injustices of U.S. society, their arguments so simple that they were often conveyed in cartoons. Then, as she progressed, the pamphlets gave way to essays and the slogans swelled into truths, universal and grand.

The Indochina war intensified. Brent imposed a duty on Katherine to watch the CBS Evening News every night. Villages burned and, in the hubbub of artillery and women's screams, Morley Safer could hardly keep the indignation out of his voice. For her, these were horrible ordeals. Pain rose from the screen in enveloping waves, and Katherine saw evil shapes roiling in gray smoke or outlined in the foliage.

"This war is no miscalculation," Brent said. "It's a conspiracy of the rich against the poor, and Columbia is right in the middle of it."

"I know."

He stared at her, focusing through his glasses. "JUSI, also," he told her. "Never forget it."

"JUSI?" Katherine had to laugh. She tried to imagine McReady as a cartoon Nazi in a stiff uniform, with fangs for teeth and a knife in his hand, dripping blood. It was too much.

But Brent told her that NASA's weather satellites actually gathered data on Soviet and Chinese military activities or peered down on the Earth to discover natural resources ripe for plunder by America's voracious corporations. The Space Program was a vital part of the military-industrial complex that Eisenhower had warned against.

Katherine wasn't sure. She typed McReady's research papers and sometimes those of others. They concerned the interiors of stars, nucleosysthesis, interstellar matter. Only one scientist that she knew of at JUSI actually studied the Earth—Weisser, who made climate models and tried to predict the weather. Could it be that Weisser, a bluff, red-nosed man with a wild crop of white hair, was in reality a kind of spy?

JUSI Fruit invited her again. His guests smoked pot, usually in the bedroom, and drank wine out in front. Katherine did neither.

Occasionally, she would have a few sips of beer. P. J. liked to play parlor games—charades, psychological quizzes, spontaneous limerick-writing. Katherine usually tried to stay out of these, and nobody forced her; but one time, when the game consisted of trying to predict coin tosses, she decided to participate. She got six of the first ten flips, then seven of the next ten, then six again. JUSI Fruit declared her the winner.

Katherine smiled, but she felt uneasy. Preceding most of the correct calls, there had been an unpleasant sensation and then a kind of voice in her head saying heads or tails. It had not happened before the wrong guesses.

"Very good."

She turned to see Tobin standing beside her. He seldom came to JUSI Fruit's parties, but he was here again tonight. He guided her to an opening on the sofa and they sat down together. He wasn't married, she knew; a magazine had written an article naming him one of New York's most eligible bachelors. He told her about his undergraduate college days at Duke, where he had actually worked with J. B. Rhine on ESP experiments before deciding to go on in physics rather than psychology. He sat close to her; she could feel the warmth of his leg against hers. In fact, there was an overall warmth coming from him and directed at her. She felt it on her skin, like sunshine. But she was afraid of him, too—not that he would harm her, but that she might disappoint him.

There was also a tension in his body. When P. J. came by, Tobin asked for some aspirin. "A headache," he apologized. He watched her. "Your hands look cool." She reached out and touched his forehead. There were taut vibrations. She stroked him with her fingers. Sometimes she had helped Ginger's headaches this way, but without really understanding what to do. Now, however, she found herself searching for a precise rhythm. She hadn't known to try this before, but just the other day McReady had explained to her how opposite trains of waves exactly juxtaposed in time and space would cancel, leaving the wave-medium calm. She had this calmness in her mind.

Tobin closed his eyes and leaned straight back on the cushion. She stroked faster and felt the vibration subside, then faster still and felt it rise again. She slowed down slightly, almost imperceptibly. "That's good," he told her.

She supposed that Brent was her boyfriend. One night when he was dropping her off she put her lips in his way and he kissed her. Obviously, he was inexperienced at it; even the boy in high school had kissed with greater ease. From then on, there had been a progression in their physical contact, but it proceeded at a crawl. Though she was comfortable with this slow pace, her new sophistication led her to suspect him. Perhaps Brent was not merely shy or extra considerate with her; perhaps he didn't like women that way at all.

They went to another meeting. This one ended in a demonstration that spilled out onto Broadway, stopping traffic. That risked arrest, but they left before the cops came. The next day, there was an announcement that fifteen thousand more troops were being sent to Vietnam. The Pentagon claimed that these were not new forces, merely replacements, but no one believed it.

She had coffee with Brent at a Greek luncheonette a few blocks from JUSI. He told her that an "action" was coming. In the lexicon of The Movement, that meant an outburst, some planned violence. She could imagine the mob of people filling the street, the suffocating closeness of all their bodies, the nauseating smells.

"I don't want to," she said. She felt better immediately, but also guilty about her selfishness. She knew that Brent was right about the war—that it was evil and it had to be stopped. "I want to do something," she told him, "but not in the street."

To her surprise, Brent's face remained neutral, without accusation. "Maybe we can accomplish something by ourselves."

"What?"

He asked if she had access to JUSI's computer, if she could run an input deck through the card reader.

"Of course," she said. She did it for Dr. McReady all the time.

"What if we could sabotage the computer, put it down for weeks, maybe forever?"

"What good would that do? The programs they run have to do with stars and gasses in space."

"And spy satellites, and weapons development," Brent said. "They're in constant contact with Los Alamos and Livermore."

That was true, Katherine knew. McReady worked closely with colleagues at Livermore. They corresponded frequently; she had typed many letters.

"I've never seen anything about weapons," she told him

"Do you think they'd show you? There are secretaries at JUSI with high security clearance."

"Who?"

He shrugged. Katherine thought of whom it might be. No name came to her at first, but then, suddenly, a clear voice in her head said: Beth Forsberg. Tobin's executive secretary.

"Look," Brent said. "JUSI's got an IBM 7094. It's bigger and faster than anything else in the world, except for the weapons labs, which we can't touch. It would be a triumph for The Movement to take that computer out."

The Movement, Katherine thought. It was a body with many arms and legs, like the statues of Hindu gods she'd seen in the museum. The legs walked and the arms delivered blows, sometimes singly, sometimes jointly, but never in total coordination. Brent was a hand at the end of one of these limbs and she a finger on the hand, an appendage of an appendage. If The Movement had a brain, Brent was far removed from it and she farther still. Yet, at times, she heard a whispering noise, a rustling that came from everywhere, as if all the limbs were stirring at once, driven by an instinct that required no central intelligence.

The door to the luncheonette opened, letting cold air in. Katherine looked up to see Beth Forsberg. Speak of the Devil.

Beth acknowledged her with a slight extension of the close-lipped smile that was her perpetual expression. *I know something that you don't … something amusing.* She hung her coat up and sat at the counter. The door was closed now, but the cold stream spread through the room. Katherine could sense that it was coming from Beth—her behind, spread on the stool; her straight, rather thin, back; short hair. In the mirror behind the counter, her image flashed a moment then subsided. The cold was emanating precisely from there. Her gaze crossed Katherine's but in a different plane so that meeting was impossible. She realized that whole worlds could exist which interpenetrated but never touched. Beth said a few words to the counterman and her lipstick radiated from the mirror in red waves.

Katherine slid her hand across the table and burrowed under Brent's hand. "I don't know," she said.

McReady went skiing for two weeks, and Katherine was "borrowed" by Tobin. She moved temporarily to a desk in his office suite, outside the large, bright room where Tobin himself sat, but past the anteroom that was Beth Forsberg's realm. Brent said that if she got the chance she should look around for papers that might be interesting. She had access to the inner office; she would often leave the letters she had typed on Tobin's desk when he wasn't there. One morning she saw a report from the NASA Inspector-General's Office. She felt her heart beat; she could sense Beth's presence waxing and waning in the outer room. She read quickly. As far as she could understand, Tobin was in hot water for a number of purchases he had made—some trips to Hawaii, cases of expensive wines for parties he had thrown and two oriental carpets he'd put in his Westchester house. But there was nothing about links to the military-industrial complex. She decided not to tell Brent what she had found.

Tobin asked her to cure another of his headaches. He sat on the couch in his office, while she stood above him, touching his forehead. In the midst of this, Beth appeared in the doorway. "Come in," Tobin told her. "I want you to see this." Beth wore her usual smile and her lipstick; she was narrow above, bigger below but still shapely, a soft skirt swelling over her belly and round behind. Her powerful vibrations interfered with Tobin's rhythm; Katherine couldn't get it right. After a few minutes, she stopped. Though she felt she had done nothing, he said it was better. Beth looked at her, the little smile on her face.

When McReady returned she moved back to her old desk. She hardly saw Tobin now. When they passed in the hallway, he acknowledged her but didn't stop to speak. She followed up on an offhand comment he had once made about her hair and had it cut in a short, gently-layered style. The first time he saw it, he complimented her. But Brent was upset—the new hairdo struck him as effete and bourgeois. They had a fight about it, their first. The next day, Brent apologized. A liberated woman of the revolution ought to be able to wear her hair as she pleased.

The Movement continued its program. There were two successful actions—a sit-in at the Columbia physics building, Pupin Hall, and a raid on a Draft Board in Washington Heights. The masked students filmed themselves pouring ink on the draft records, and sent a print to CBS, which ran part of it on the Evening News.

Brent came over to Katherine's apartment to watch. In the gray, unsteady light of the TV, he kissed her in celebration and they lay together on the couch, performing their limited repertoire. Red blotches burst out on Katherine's cheeks, and her lips became sore from kissing. She spread her arms, one stretching up along the upholstery, the other trailing to the floor. Her legs remained crossed, knotted at the ankles; she lacked the will to open them, he the courage to push them apart. The picture came to her of her body on the cross, but she fought it off and it disappeared.

McReady's usual computer programs required a box and a half of cards, about four times the size of the deck that Brent had given her. She had decided to do it after a week of heart-wrenching horrors on her television set—a fishing boat hit from the air, killing everyone aboard; a burning village; a mother and her baby, dead in a rice paddy. As they had planned, she inserted the poison deck behind McReady's cards, fronted by an ID card that she had copied from one of the graduate students. She had worried that the student would get in trouble, but Brent had argued that an investigation would surely clear him.

McReady's program took ninety minutes to complete. Afterward, the poison deck ran immediately, but seemingly without effect. It had been designed to work only after the subsequent job began execution. In practice this took sixty minutes more, so that the cause of the sabotage and its effect, the taking down of the 7094, were separated by nearly two hours.

Katherine called Brent from JUSI to tell him the good news, communicating via their pre-arranged code.

"I'm afraid I have to call off our date tonight."

"That's too bad," Brent said.

They met in her apartment. Brent let himself in with the key she had given him. He hung it on the leftmost of the three hooks, but she transferred it to the right; her key in the middle, his at the right, the left hook empty. She was wearing body lotion; it was a brand she had seen advertised, horribly expensive though she'd bought the smallest jar.

Brent expected to make out on the couch the way they always did, but Katherine led him to the bedroom. She pulled back the bed covering and sat down to begin removing her clothes—shoes, stockings, rolling them down (her legs felt cold); opening her blouse. She took off her bra and let her breasts fall out. No man had ever seen her naked before, not even the doctor, Dr. Robinet, a staunch Catholic, almost a priest, who examined her gingerly when necessary, through her clothing.

Brent stood watching her. He was hard; it was obvious to see. She stood and opened the buttons of her skirt, letting it trail to her ankles. Her only training for this had been a foreign film he'd taken her to see months before, shortly after they had met. The film made a political point, but the only scene she remembered was the woman taking off her clothes, slowly, while a man watched, smoking a cigarette, his face serious. Shocked, she had wanted Brent to say something to her, take her hand; but he had remained sitting tensely in his seat, staring straight ahead.

"Katherine ..."

He reached a hand out and felt her breast, touching only with his fingertips. His eyes looked gigantic behind his glasses, swollen up by some trick of magnification. His face was serious, even reverential, she thought, like the man's face in the movie.

He still had his scarf on; she unwound it and pulled it loose, then opened his shirt. Underneath, his body felt warm. The light touch of his fingers was making her breasts rise. Her nipples hardened. She wondered what would happen if they stayed that way and never went down. That was frightening, but the thought comforted her that she could ask the JUSI receptionist, Helen, with whom she was becoming friendly. She would know what to do.

She leaned forward and raised her face, inviting Brent to kiss her. "Let's get in bed," she told him. Before they did, she went to the kitchen one more time to check that the keys were on the proper hooks.

Tobin's office was on the top floor, reached by climbing a narrow, creaking staircase. Katherine had been up there many times—during McReady's two-week absence and, also, routinely, carrying papers for Tobin's signature or to bring him a copy of McReady's latest article. But this time the summons had come out of the blue.

"Dr. Tobin wants to see you."

Beth Forsberg had called her in the morning, ordering her to appear for a two o'clock audience. Beth, with her cold voice and superior smile—if Miles Tobin was God, she was his merciless angel. What was going to happen?

The only thing Katherine could think of was the computer, but she tried to force the idea from her mind. Brent had reassured her that it would be impossible to prove her responsibility, even if it were realized that the 7094 had been sabotaged and even if someone suspected that she had been involved. Besides, she already knew about Tobin's outbursts. Why should she have escaped what virtually everyone else had experienced? It was probably something trivial.

There were twenty-one steps going up to the top floor, twelve until the landing, then nine more. She counted them in her head. Three times seven. When she reached the top, Beth was waiting. She'd put on a new coat of lipstick and her lips glowed cherry red. JUSI Fruit said that Tobin had been sleeping with her, but Katherine didn't believe it, though she did believe that Beth might be in love with him.

"Come in, Katherine."

Tobin waved her forward with a little motion of his fingers. He was young and he looked it; he liked to appear in shirtsleeves, his collar open, tie loose, hair combed casually down onto his forehead. Recently, she had heard P. J. call him "The Boy Who Would Be King."

He made way for Katherine, then followed her into his office, with Beth behind him. Beth closed the door.

He sat down at his desk. At his back, sunlight entered through a floor-to-ceiling window. "Katherine, do you know why you're here?"

Beth was sitting next to her, taking notes on a pad. She jotted the stenographic symbols like an artist making brush strokes, the little smile always on her face. Her perfume had a nauseating smell that forced Katherine to choke back an urge to vomit.

"I don't know," she said. Brent had admonished her never to admit anything. The Movement did not want credit for this action; on the contrary, it wished to leave the impression of a secret force which could strike suddenly and not be traced. They were counting on Katherine.

Beth, ramrod straight in her chair, seemed to grin at Katherine's denial. Tobin scratched his head. "The 7094 is up again, you know."

How could that be? Brent had said it would be down a long time, maybe forever, but only a week had passed. She knew she should say she was glad, something that an innocent person would say, but the words didn't come out.

"We had to call IBM in," Tobin said. "They couldn't restart the machine—at first."

She had seen the IBM troubleshooters, of course; two men in jackets and ties, their hair cut short, like soldiers. They huddled with the Computing Group, then came in to have a long talk with McReady. They had young-old faces, serious expressions. Katherine had typed conspicuously as they passed her desk.

Tobin said: "Beth, would you leave us for a few minutes?"

She closed the steno book, stood up, smoothed down her sweater. Katherine's heart was beating fast. *Poom poom poom … poom poom poom poom.*

The door closed. Though they seemed to be alone, Katherine knew there was an intercom that led into Beth's office. She strained to see if the light was on, but it was hard to tell.

Tobin looked at her sternly. "Why did you do it, Katherine? Didn't we treat you well? Didn't I? What do you have against us?"

A cloud came across the sun, and the room grew suddenly dim. She could barely see him across the desk. What if she had truly done wrong and God was striking her blind as punishment? She could sense Beth listening in her office, her back stiff, lipstick flashing, her perfume rising like a poisoned cloud. Had she made Katherine her victim, enchanting Tobin and turning him against her?

"Was it a political act, Katherine? I know you've attended some of the demonstrations at Columbia. What did you think could be gained by interfering with JUSI's computer?"

Don't say anything, Brent had told her. Don't say don't say don't say don't say …

Tobin sighed. Perhaps it was meant for Beth, a secret code like the one Katherine and Brent had shared. She felt Beth's presence in the outer office, pouring out her spell over the intercom, filling the room with poison.

"I've been advised to call in the FBI for a formal investigation. You could go to jail, Katherine."

"Jail?" Her voice was so weak she could hardly hear it. She could feel the spell closing in, choking off all communication.

"I'd rather that didn't happen," Tobin said. "I'm giving you the opportunity to resign. If you do, I won't pursue the matter any further." He paused a moment, watching her. "Well, Katherine, what do you say?"

She said nothing.

Medicine is barbaric. Surgery brutally wounds the body and drugs produce side effects rivaling the symptoms of the illness they are meant to ameliorate. Diagnostic and therapeutic devices are pushed into every orifice, often causing profound discomfort. Patients are usually helpless. The first injunction of medicine has always been to do no harm; but this standard was and is impossible. Diagnosis and healing inevitably involve harm. The only question is: Does the benefit of the cure outweigh the brutality of the method? Only the result can justify the means.

Jody Hopson, in
Religion in America
"Katherine Turley: Healing Without Creed"

Part II

Katie is thirsty—she's had nothing to eat or drink since nine o'clock the night before. Ginger dampens a washcloth and holds it to her lips. This is the limit of what she is allowed, lest she choke on vomit while anesthetized. A nurse comes in and carefully removes the pins from her hair, brushing it out in long strokes to make sure nothing has been missed.

"Jewelry?" she asks.

Katie removes bracelets from her wrist and ankle, a ring she's had since high school. Last comes the piece she bought in a shop on Broadway—a necklace with seven stars. "I'm afraid," she says.

Ginger trails her fingers through Katie's hair, now grown long. "I'm here." She has been a rock through all of this, finding the strength from somewhere, perhaps God.

The gurney feels cold when Katie gets on. Ginger holds her hand until the entrance to the Acute Care Unit; she must remain behind in a waiting room. The nurse summarizes the procedure one last time. She has a soft musical voice and looks very pretty, like an actress playing a nurse. Finally, she asks: "Are you ready?"

Katie nods and closes her eyes.

The nurse keeps talking, describing things, as she attaches monitors for ECG and blood oxygen. She cuts hair away with a razor and bathes Katie's scalp with astringent liquid. Katie closes her eyes tighter but can't keep the sharp smell from entering through her nostrils.

Now, a sticky gel and the cold of the electrodes. She flinches. The nurse whispers to her. "Katherine, these are just to monitor your brainwaves, nothing more."

But the next pair of electrodes is not so innocuous. The psychiatrist steps forward. He wears a cropped beard and is old, perhaps sixty. The younger practitioners have rejected ECT categorically, sticking with drugs and talk, no matter how ineffective.

"Try to relax, Katherine."

He points at two spots toward the front of her scalp, paired left and right. After the nurse has prepared these sites, the doctor places the electrodes himself, moving each around slightly until he is satisfied.

Katie calls for Ginger.

The nurse squeezes her hand.

The IV is inserted and she is ordered to count backward from one hundred. She expects it to go slowly, like falling asleep, but the darkness is sudden and complete. At one tick she's there, the next gone.

The psychiatrist nods, bending to administer the stimulus. Suddenly, the EEG monitor goes crazy. Giant spikes appear, propagating across the screen until they fill it. The jagged lines grow, crossing in grotesque patterns, unintelligible until the nurse turns the gain down and the spikes reappear in steady rhythm. Katie is in seizure.

Her body twitches only slightly, restrained by straps and by the large dose of muscle relaxant she's received. Apart from the monitor, it is hardly obvious that anything is happening until, suddenly, a sharp, unmistakable odor rises from the table. The nurse wrinkles her nose and the doctor grimaces. Katie has voided her bowels.

The seizure lasts thirty seconds; a minute later, Katie's breathing regularizes and her oxygen mask is removed. They wait, alert for trouble, but the patient's condition remains stable. A new nurse arrives, who'll clean her and monitor her vitals until she awakes. As soon as the first nurse is outside the door, the psychiatrist confronts her.

"Why the hell didn't you fix her properly?"

"She had an enema," the nurse explains.

"You do it twice, goddamit, to make sure. Do we understand each other?"

Nodding, she backs away, as if from the presence of a king. The doctor, looking on, says nothing more.

Katie awakes with a headache. She grabs her forehead with both hands and moans; her eyes roll. The new nurse makes a cold compress and lays it on. Katie thanks her, but when the psychiatrist asks if she can say where she is, she shakes her head. After an hour, they wheel her back to her room. She can multiply three times four, but not nine times seven. She either doesn't know or won't answer to her name.

"Who is the President of the United States?"

"Kennedy," Katie replies.

The doctor shrugs. "It's normal at this stage," he tells the nurse. "Nothing to worry about." Kennedy has not been President for six years.

The hours pass and she begins to recover. She remembers who she is and her relationship to Ginger. When they tell her what has transpired, she acknowledges it, but has no memory of the time surrounding the treatment, except for counting backward. After a night's sleep, her memory has improved further, but her daze has given way to renewed depression. Today is a rest day; the ECT regime will resume tomorrow.

Following the second and third sessions, Katie's amnesia worsens, while her emotional state barely shows improvement. Perhaps her compulsive counting and morning gloom have diminished a little— it's hard to tell. Ginger wants to stop the therapy, but the psychiatrist prevails on her to allow one more treatment.

This time, when the anesthesia wears off, she definitely seems more tranquil, although her daze lasts well into the evening. The next morning she is still confused, but gives her mother a kiss and a smile. She is able to take a little walk around the corridors and to watch television. Ginger agrees to treatments five and six.

Now, the change in Katie is dramatic. The spring that has wound tighter and tighter begins to relax. A soft fog seems to envelop her, blunting every sharp edge. Even her face looks softer and rounder, her nose and cheekbones less prominent, all the angles wider.

After three days of rest, she is moved to a clinic near Fishkill, New York, seventy miles up the Hudson. This place houses a small experimental program, affiliated with Columbia-Presbyterian. Currently, they are studying the aftermath of ECT, using sophisticated new EEG devices connected to computers. This is a good program to be in—the care is comprehensive and the regimen far from onerous. Ginger wonders how her daughter was chosen out of all the people who have had the shock treatments. Though she hates to leave Katie so far away, she knows it's the best thing for her.

She wakes in the night—wide awake so suddenly it is as if the instant blackness of anesthesia were reversing itself. There is no sound. A thought she had in her sleep has now escaped—her head is empty. She doesn't have many clothes, only the contents of an old valise that Ginger hastily packed. She finds her jeans and pulls them on over her pajamas; a heavy sweater. Her boots elude her. She puts on socks, and then her furry, childish bed slippers. She tiptoes down the hall. At the desk by the door, Stan Womack is sitting his all-night vigil.

"Hello, Katherine. Up again?"

She smiles at him. "Can I go out for a while?"

This is not a closed institution—the participants in the study are free to leave any time. But neither are the doors open at night. The key is in the lock; Stan turns it. "The stars again?" he asks. "Don't go further than the front lawn, okay?"

As soon as she gets outside, he switches off the big front light. Katie stands on the porch for a minute, getting her eyes used to the dark. It's winter. Though the last few days have been unseasonably warm, the air tonight is cold and sharp. Her sweater has a collar, which she pulls up.

She walks out on the lawn seven steps, then another seven, trying not to count them. She knows she shouldn't. In the west near the horizon, she sees Rigel, then Orion's belt. She follows it up, quickly passing Aldebaran, twisting her head to see the Pleiades shining like blue jewels. The stars bathe her with benevolent rays, sing in her ears a song without words. If God lives anywhere, it must be there.

At first, she tries not to look to the east, but then she purposely does. Arcturus is still beneath the trees. She is not as afraid of it as she once was but she knows that, as the Pleiades disappear, the Red Star will rise high into the eastern sky. So far, she has not been brave enough to wait for this, but tonight she feels she will.

She closes her eyes, waits. The stars move slowly. Her new psychiatrist, Dr. Richter, a neuroscientist as well as a shrink, told her that the sight of the stars has made a profound impression on many. Belief in astrology is common. There is nothing wrong with it, provided she doesn't become fixated and lose her judgment. Whatever happens tonight, she can tell him tomorrow. But what if Dr. Richter is powerless against the stars?

She opens her eyes. The Pleiades are gone. She forces herself to look at Arcturus, which beams red arrows over her head and screams like a deranged mob.

Katie has visitors. JUSI Fruit and Helen have driven up from the city to see her. She is not really surprised—she knows that these two have kept track of her during her troubles. What does surprise her is who has come along: Miles Tobin. And he seems to have brought a date, a young Indian woman who came to do thesis research at JUSI about the time that Katie left. She remembers her as a small, exotic girl in a sari; today, she has traded that costume for a skirt and sweater, but still looks striking and unusual. She's called Indira, after Gandhi's daughter.

JUSI Fruit kisses her and then they all do. She takes them into the sitting room, where all the chairs are free; Katie's fellow clients, or patients, have fled before them, disappearing like pale ghosts. She sits on a loveseat, P. J. beside her. Helen and Tobin and his friend are on the adjacent couch. They could be back on the West Side in P. J.'s apartment.

If Katie is ashamed of her current residence or of the shock treatments, she doesn't show it. Her smile, however, is foggy—she's a little off. The conversation lags—even P. J. can't keep it going. After a while, he excuses himself; he wants a little air, out on the porch. Tobin follows.

"We can go for a walk in a little while," Katie says.

Indira takes P. J.'s vacated spot on the loveseat, while Helen sits on the floor at Katie's feet.

"How are you feeling?" Indira's voice rises and dips like a bird flying.

"All right," Katie says. Helen takes her hand.

Indira leans closer. "I have a twin," she begins. "A sister ... Parnathi ..."

Katie smiles, perhaps in encouragement.

"My sister is ill, is miserable."

Helen squeezes Katie's fingers. She gets to her feet. "I'll see you in a few minutes."

Indira folds her hands on her lap. "Parnathi has tried to take her life. In Britain. Our father is highly conservative—do you know? He refuses her all strong treatment. I wonder ..."

"I'm sorry about her," Katie says.

"Yes. But, I wonder ... do you feel well now?"

"Yes."

"Truly?"

"Yes, much better."

"Thank you," Indira tells her.

Katie reaches out with both hands and touches Indira's cheekbones. She can feel her heartbeat, she finds, and her mind's rhythm. She has not been able to do this since she became ill, but now the sensations are very strong. After a minute, she removes her hands, and Indira stares at her. "I think your sister is all right," Katie says. "Don't worry."

Out on the path that leads through sloping fields in back of the house, Tobin and Katie walk a little ahead. Behind them are P. J. and Helen, and then Indira, trailing further.

Tobin is solicitous; he takes her arm, apologizes. "I feel sorry about what happened, Katherine. I hope you understand—I had no choice."

She doesn't respond to this, but instead, unexpectedly, asks about Beth. Tobin seems startled for a moment, as if he doesn't know whom she means. He rubs his chin.

"She left three or four months ago. Actually, Katherine, I had to let her go. There were some irregularities ..."

"Where is she?"

"I'm afraid I couldn't tell you. I did write her a recommendation, but after that …" He shrugs, looking at Katherine directly, gazing in her eyes.

Katie understands. Beth has sunk beneath the horizon into a dark place, which no vision can penetrate.

"Katherine," Miles says, "after you've finished your rehabilitation, perhaps …"

She asks: "Do you know what happened to Brent?"

"Your boyfriend? I've been told that he's in Canada. Things have quieted down a lot. I think that if you wanted to come back to us …"

Katie is silent, as if she hasn't heard. She's looking at the little bang of hair, hanging down on Miles' forehead; concentrating, as if there's a puzzle to solve. Finally, she gives him her foggy smile. "I don't know," she says.

Behind her, where he's been listening in, JUSI Fruit raises an eyebrow.

When Ginger doesn't visit for two weeks, Dr. Richter urges Katie to call. She waits for the evening, when she knows her father will be at work. The phone rings four … six … eight times before her mother finally picks it up.

"I was doing the wash," she explains.

Katie opens her nostrils. The smell of the laundry seems to come over the wires. Ginger's voice sounds small and vague. When Katie was sickest, her mother was strong. Her father had carped about everything: that the hospital was a dump; that the drug companies would sell you anything, so long as they could make a buck; that the psychiatrist, with his little beard, looked like a smug, self-satisfied jerk. "Who says that she's sick at all?" he argued. "She was always strange." Ginger had stood up to him, then, as she'd never done before. But now that Katie is getting better, her mother seems to be going backward.

"How is daddy?"

"Oh, you know him." Katie can see her seated by the telephone table, in the small, uncomfortable chair, pulling at the collar of her green robe. Ginger likes green—the color of the ocean when the weather is rough. She saw the ocean for the first time when she was sixteen, and since then she's been partial to green sweaters and dresses, scarves, a little pillbox hat.

"When are you coming up?"

There are excuses—the weather is bad, the apartment needs cleaning. Katie knows the truth is that Ginger's anxious about leaving the city, hates even to leave the neighborhood. She overcame this fear when her daughter needed her most, but now seems to be sinking back into it.

"Maybe, if I can get your father to come with me," Ginger says.

Katie feels as if she's the mother and Ginger the little girl. She explores this feeling for a moment. It has a cold, crisp crust, like snow underfoot.

But later in the night, when she comes out of her room, things change. Stan is not at his desk; probably, he's in the kitchen getting a snack. The key is in the front door—there's no stringent security in this place; nobody is going to run away. Outside, the front light is still on. Shielding her eyes she looks up at the sky. The brightest stars blot out their neighbors. She can feel their arrogance across the distance. Backing up to the edge of the lawn, she looks for the Seven Sisters, but still can't see them in the brightness. She faces away from the light and lets her eyes rest.

"What is that red one?"

She's startled. Stan has come outdoors to stand beside her. She looks where he's pointing. "Arcturus," she says.

Suddenly, in the sky's tableau, she sees Ginger's death, so clear and compelling that it cannot be mistaken. Her shoulders slump and she collapses to her knees and a howl escapes her … and then again … and again …

She doesn't feel Stan Womack's arm around her, or hear the words he speaks, uselessly, to comfort her.

Part III

Each morning an invisible force woke her around six; sometimes it hurled her suddenly into awareness, sometimes she rose so slowly into morning that the upward pull seemed barely sufficient.

Her room was cold. Something was wrong with the radiator, but the landlord always shrugged off her complaints. Mr. Buschbaum had died three years ago and the service had never been good since then. One night, shivering in bed, she had prayed for heat, but God had not answered. Perhaps it was good for her to experience discomfort; or perhaps she should tip the latest super, whom she'd not yet met, with a bottle of whiskey at Christmas as her father had done with Mr. Buschbaum.

She pulled the quilt tighter around her and tried to shrink her body into the silhouette she'd already heated. When the weather became a little warmer, Amigo would sleep with her again; right now, he was stretched out beside the living room radiator, which still worked.

In a minute she would get up. At first, she thought it was Tuesday—the day for the foyer. There were six rooms—kitchen, bathroom, living room, foyer, two bedrooms—and she cleaned each once a week. Her heart sank a little. Sometimes, Tuesday was a difficult morning because the foyer wasn't much to look forward to. But no, she realized that it was the seventh day, Sunday, when she did no cleaning.

Sunday was the day for church. She had chosen the Catholic Church, St. Cecilia's, which was only a few blocks away. She liked its cold, stone interior, heavy with shadows. Looking upward from the right spot, you were caught by a trick of light: in the high, central, Italianate dome the air seemed of a different density, as if a buoyant presence hovered there, whose outline could be dimly sensed.

The priest was Irish, red faced, a priest of the old school. His thick hands were quick to tousle a child's hair, or cuff the side of his head; or, Katherine had heard, to fill a shot glass with Four Roses. Half of the congregants were also Irish, despite the fact that they were now a minority in the neighborhood, even among the Catholics. Perhaps most of the Irish families that hadn't yet moved out were represented here. They were now an anachronism in this particular church, they and the priest both. It was rumored that the Cardinal would soon send a new shepherd, a Mexican or Puerto Rican, who could recite the mass in Spanish.

Meanwhile, it was still Father Walker who was waiting to greet the congregants as they left the Sanctuary. "Hello, Katherine."

He held out his hand and she touched his fingers, which were rough and hot. She was amazed at the smoothness of his face, baby skin, as if he had never shaved. He held her hand for an extra second, then let go to beckon over her shoulder. A young woman came up, perhaps a bit older than Katherine, but with a little twin girl on each side of her.

"This is Rosie Mallory," the priest said. "Cary is on the right, I think, Carly on the left."

The woman nodded at her. "Rosemary," she corrected. She had sandy blonde hair, pinned up on her head, showing her ears. The girls pulled at her, and she let them drag her away. She gave Katherine a little wave. "See you again."

"I have to go, too," Katherine told Father Walker.

Some Sundays, when her legs wouldn't carry her, she sat at home and looked out the window with Amigo on her lap. The last leaves fell and their stiff remains blew in the street. Birds squawked in the diminished trees, getting ready to fly.

When it finally got dark, she forced herself to move. She couldn't remember having eaten during the day, perhaps in the morning. The refrigerator and the pantry were nearly empty now. At one time, she'd had jars of spaghetti sauce, frozen vegetables, tuna fish. Her father had gone shopping with her, picking this and that, filling the cart. But that seemed like months ago and now the food was gone.

On Sunday night, this late, the A & P would be dark, but perhaps the bodega would still be open. It was hard to think at the moment. Sometimes, thoughts would assemble themselves for her effortlessly from out of the air, while other times her mind went round and round like a merry-go-round, stopping nowhere.

She took the elevator to the lobby. When the doors slid open, there was an unmistakable mewling sound. In front of one of the big radiators a cat lay, with a kitten nuzzling her underside. The tiny being sucked without effect, then fidgeted away, only to return to the nipple again and get nothing.

The poor animals! They had been made without souls. Though God noted the fall of every sparrow, He had created the Earth for man and given him dominion over all its creatures. The suffering of animals was as nothing when balanced against man's suffering, which was itself as nothing when weighed against the fate of his immortal soul. But, in that case, why had the sight of this kitten so saddened Katherine's heart, and why had a plan so suddenly crystallized in her thoughts?

"Wait," she whispered.

She tried to visualize the location of the incinerator room. On her own floor the incinerator was three doors down from her apartment, around a little corner. Couldn't she project the chute downward to the lobby and find its location there? Confused, she stood a moment before she realized that she could smell the incinerator. There was a ribbon of invisible smoke in the air, a sharp, acidic smell which grew stronger as she followed it. Opening the door, she held her breath.

The current of smoke, still invisible, stung her eyes. She reached out blindly for the light switch and found it to the right of the door, just as it was on her own floor.

Good. There was a pile of newspapers that people had left for disposal, along with a couple of cartons stacked one inside the other. She took the larger and flatter of the two cartons and lined it with newspaper. Returning to the radiator, she reached down gently for the cat, whose body immediately stiffened. The animal raised its head and looked at her intelligently, but its body still resisted. What could it want? Perhaps …

Stretching out on the floor, she felt in under the radiator. Dust rose, filling her nostrils. She swept the hidden area with her hand, encountering something which made her jump. She fished it out—another kitten, small and furry, tinier than the first, its body cold.

"What are you doing, missy?"

She sat up and looked: a tall man in overalls and a denim cap. "I found these kittens. They're starving."

"You bring them in from the street? It's against building rules."

How could that be? People had dogs that they walked in the park, taking the animals up and down in the elevator. "No," she said. "They were here already."

The man squatted down next to her. "This here one's dead."

"No."

"His eyes are closed, missy, and he ain't moving."

"No," Katherine insisted. Carefully, she lifted the kittens and put them in the carton. The cat, docile now, allowed herself to be placed beside them."

"Do you have any milk?"

The man nodded. "I'll bring some. Which apartment?"

Katherine hesitated.

"It's all right," he said. "I'm the super."

He rang the bell fifteen minutes later, a quart of milk held in front of him. His hair was combed now, slicked down. "I'm Johnny."

He held out his free hand and she shook it. "Katherine."

"Where's your father?"

She didn't answer, didn't know for a moment, the question not making sense.

"I'll tell you," Johnny said. "I saw him moving out with his girlfriend. He's gone."

"Can I have the milk please?"

He smiled. "Can I have a kiss please?" He handed her the carton. "Just one, then we're even."

She closed her eyes, felt his mouth on hers, his lips pushing against her. She pulled away.

"Okay," the super said. "Deal is a deal." He backed up toward the door. "Look, Katherine. You need anything fixed in the apartment, just knock on my door. I'll come up right away."

She put the cats in the bathtub. There was a medicine dropper, she remembered, in an old blue bottle filled with fluid that her father used to melt the wax in his ears. She poured it out, then washed the bottle carefully and refilled it with milk.

Amigo came into the bathroom, mewing loudly. God had made him inferior to man, but among the animals he had his place and prerogatives.

"All right." She interrupted what she was doing and went to get his food, drowning it in milk this one time so he wouldn't become jealous.

She filled another bowl with milk and brought it back to the bathroom. The cat considered it, but wouldn't drink. The kittens had to be first. The smaller, colder one still had its eyes closed. The super thought it was dead, but Katherine could hear its heart beating weakly, fading in and out. She drew milk into the dropper and forced it between the kitten's lips. The liquid dribbled down its tiny chin; but, surely, some of it had gotten inside. Surely, the slight movement she had seen at the kitten's throat was real.

The other one spat up the first dropper of milk, but tolerated the second. Its miniature pink tongue crept out like a sign sent by

God. Though the tiny beast lacked a soul, there was still something of God in it, the same essence that birds and trees had, even stones.

The cat took her share of milk now, drinking decorously. When she had finished, she used her tongue to groom the larger kitten, ignoring the other.

The next morning Johnny brought her a bag of groceries, asking for a kiss and a touch in return. He put his hand on her bare arm, his face opening in a smile. She moved away, taking a deep breath and letting it out. Johnny looked at her chest. "I guess you must be one of them hippie chicks that don't wear no bra."

The air was heavy with his need. She could feel it in her own shoulders and neck, like a weight pushing down from above. God had made men this way, she thought.

"You have a wife. I've seen her." A tall, graying woman, who wore dresses that buttoned down the front, their belts tied loosely over her belly.

"I have two children," Johnny said, "a boy and a girl."

She pushed him away. "You'd better go."

"First I need my kiss."

He had hard lips, cracked in several places. She wondered when she had last brushed her teeth. She knew that she'd been doing it, but the last few days, with the kittens and all, she might have forgotten.

If so, Johnny didn't seem to mind.

Once he was gone, she dead-bolted the door and went to check on the kittens again. The small one was lying comfortably, while his brother sucked at the cat's teat. It seemed that the milk Johnny had brought the night before might have restored her. She looked in the grocery bag. He'd brought milk again this time, along with Wonder Bread, tuna, Kix, a package of cold cuts and a coffee cake.

She put two pieces of bread in Ginger's old toaster, which hummed as it warmed, louder and louder. There was nothing to spread on the toast (Johnny hadn't thought of that), but she made a dry sandwich with a slice of baloney. With it, she poured half a glass of milk. To be able to take care of the cats she, also, would need nourishment.

She washed in the tub, carefully scrubbing the place where Johnny had touched her arm. She brushed her teeth. There was no underwear left in the dresser, so she used the panties she'd just removed. Over them, a skirt and turtleneck. Then, her winter coat and Ginger's green scarf; long wool stockings on her legs; finally, her soft boots. She was running out of clean clothes, but there never seemed enough time to do the laundry. Every day, there was a room to clean, and, later, she would come home from the park and want nothing more than to sit and think about the wonders she'd seen.

Today was Monday—the kitchen; but she'd decided to reverse the order this morning, go out to the park first and then spend the afternoon doing her cleaning and tending to the kittens. The park was beautiful late in the morning, with the sun coming from above the buildings in the Bronx, lighting the river and the Manhattan shore.

The day was very warm for November; the grass presented its fragrance and even the leafless trees seemed to waft a smell into the still air. She sat on the rise overlooking the river, letting the sun warm her back. Everything had paused, waiting for winter. The grass and the trees would soon die, only to return in spring: the same, yet different—on the branches, new leaves; new blades of grass in the bare spots; in the old river, new water would flow.

She found herself sweating in the unseasonable sunshine. Removing her coat, she spread it on the ground, laying Ginger's bright scarf alongside. She opened her boots and took them off, and her high stockings, baring her feet and legs to the sun. She felt the grass with her toes. Brown and inert to the eye, it signaled the skin with electric insistence. There was life in the dormant grass, in the sky, in the sparkling flow of the river. One day, while she sat watching here, God would talk to her. God would tell her what to do.

But perhaps not today.

There was a vibration in the ground, a drumbeat; then, voices, rupturing the tranquility. "*Hola loquita.*"

They gathered around her, making kissing noises. "Hey, how 'bout I lay down nex' to djou?"

She ignored them, looking straight ahead, watching the flash of sun on the river. One of the boys sat down on the sleeve of her stretched-out coat, inching closer. A short boy with half-closed eyes; she'd seen him before. She turned her head. There were five of them, one bigger and more imposing than the others. He looked like one of the boxers that her father used to watch on the TV.

"*No la toques.*"

She understood. *Don't touch her.* The short one withdrew.

The other stood over her. "*Cómo te llamas?* You unnerstan'?"

"My name is Katherine," she said.

He watched her with his heavy eyes. "*Me llamo* Che."

She nodded. The Spanish she'd learned long ago in junior high, studied for hours at Iris's kitchen table, had now come back to her. The electricity they'd put through her head had taken so much away—things she couldn't quite remember—but her Spanish had been restored. God wanted that.

"I watch you call squirrels. How d'you do this?"

Sometimes when she sat here, two or three squirrels would gather near her, squatting on their haunches. They had seemed to come on their own—she'd never called them. "I don't know," she told Che. She felt them all watching.

Che put his hands in the pockets of his silky windbreaker. He rocked slowly, rising on the balls of his feet, then back down onto his heels. The jacket, which they all wore, had a totemic name written in black script at the level of the heart. *Brujos.* The Sorcerers.

"Why those guys don' come lookin' for you no more?"

"What do you mean?"

"One little *maricón*, faggot," one of them said.

Now, she understood. It must have been P.J. and Miles. They still checked up on her once in a while. It was usually by telephone, but now her phone was off. They must have come looking for her in the park.

Che laughed. His face was Indian—thick lips and high cheekbones; a wide forehead under blackest hair, oily and thick. He seemed very old, as if he had lived for ages. "Call the squirrels," he commanded her.

"They won't come if you are here."

The short boy said: "Hey, baby, wan' to do some fuckie fuckie with me?"

God was in the sky and grass, even the buildings behind her and the cars on the Expressway. He was in herself and in the boy, too. Nothing bad would happen.

"You wan' to?" Che asked her.

"No."

"*Bueno.*" He gave a sharp whistle to the others, delivered with a slight movement of his head. "*Hasta luego,*" he said to her. "Be seein' you."

As soon as she got back upstairs, she checked the kittens. The healthier one was standing up by his mother, trying his legs out. He made a soft mew as Katherine came close. But where was the other? She looked in the box and on the floor, then through the apartment. In the bedroom where her parents used to sleep, the window was open a few inches from the bottom. Outside, the burnt orange fire escape stretched down one story to the first floor. Below that was the ladder, pulled up now, six or seven feet above the raised garden.

This was the way the kitten must have escaped. He was so small to have climbed down all the steps and especially to make the last leap to the ground. But she'd seen Amigo jump from the table many times and once even from the top of the tall bookcase, up near the ceiling. He'd landed light as a feather and strutted away.

She opened the window wider and leaned out over the fire escape. She called quietly: "Kitty … kitty," but there was no sign of him, either on the metal steps or in the garden below. Should she go out to look? She hesitated. There was the kitchen to clean and if she entered the park those boys might still be around. She didn't want to see their faces again today. Besides, wasn't God there to protect the kitten? What could she do that He couldn't?

Each time she went to the Catholic Church, Rosemary Mallory was there. She sat in a back pew with a twin on either side. They made faces at each other across their mother's lap and kicked at the bench in front of them, while Rosemary tried to pull them apart.

Katherine wasn't a Catholic, had never taken communion or confessed. Each Sunday, she expected Father Walker to bring it up, but so far he hadn't. Perhaps he didn't want to scare her away, a young lady who looked Irish, a commodity growing scarcer among his new flock of murmuring Spanish women with their black kerchiefs and dark eyes, and their husbands who never came to church at all.

Rosemary's husband had never shown up either. He had a night job and slept on Sunday mornings, the way Katherine's father had. Rosemary didn't talk much about him. She looked fatigued. The twins kept pulling at her, one on either side. Little blonde girls, neatly dressed, each with a ribbon in her hair. But Rosemary's hair was falling down on her forehead, and she kept brushing it back.

"This is hell," she said.

They stood on the sidewalk in front of the church—a cold, clear Sunday morning. They had talked practically every week, beginning with one time when the twins were at Rosemary's cousin's house and she'd come without them. She was a neighborhood girl, but from up the hill near the elevated. She had gone to Catholic schools, so they didn't know each other growing up, but she looked so familiar. Perhaps Katherine had seen her on the IRT, or it could have been at the Cascades Pool on Jerome Avenue when they were teenagers—could she have been the reddish blonde girl posing on the diving board while the boys gathered around? Memory was so strange. Why should she remember that girl now, of all things, when she had forgotten so much else?

Rosemary yawned and leaned back to stretch her shoulders and neck. Katherine saw the swell of her belly—she hadn't noticed it before. "Are you …?"

"Five months gone, almost."

"Oh, my God!" Katherine said.

Rosemary made a face. "'Oh, my God!' is about right," she said.

When Katherine got home, Amigo was making a racket, prowling back and forth in front of the bathroom door. Inside, she found, as expected, the mother, Belle, and Hombre, her kitten, by now half grown; but, crouching behind Belle, there was another, gray and white, with a patch on his flank, shaped like a star. The marking was very much like the one the other kitten had had, the little runt who had run away. In fact, before his disappearance Katherine had actually been planning to name him "Star" by reason of the mark.

Could it be that Star had returned?

She held her breath and ran into her parents' room. The window was open. Of course! She had opened it the night before, when she was looking through Ginger's things and had spilled some perfume. Perhaps Star had smelled it and been drawn back to the apartment. Leaning out over the fire escape, she looked for the ladder. It was where she hadn't expected—slotted up, far above the ground. How could the cat have climbed to her window, then? It was much too far to jump, and the building's stone facade was smooth and hard to grip. What could have propelled him?

She put cat food in a bowl, soaked with milk, and offered it to Star, who seemed uninterested. He must have drunk something already out of Belle's dish. You could see how solicitous Belle was toward the new cat. Didn't that prove it was Star?

She took him in her arms and stroked his neck. The cat settled against her, but then jerked upright as the bell rang. Katherine opened the peephole and at the end of its dim tunnel saw Johnny grinning at her.

"I saw you come home."

"I didn't see you."

"I was up by the mailboxes, sweeping."

"Oh," she said.

He followed her back through the foyer into the living room. She had on her nice dress that she wore to church; her winter boots, recently soled. She'd taken them to the old Jewish shoemaker who was still hanging on in the neighborhood. His hands, covered with gray hair, had shaken as he marked the boots with chalk. His face was bloodless, without expression.

She said to Johnny: "I have a new cat."

"Yeah. Does he have a name?"

"Star." She went to the bathroom and brought him back.

Johnny grinned. "You like him?" He sounded as if they were looking at the cat in a store, and he would buy it for her if she said yes.

"He's the one who ran away when he was small."

"Sure enough," Johnny said. "You need anything?"

She shook her head. Now that he was helping her out she had plenty of everything. She got two government checks, cashing them each month at a place that had opened on Jerome Avenue. She'd used some of the money to pay for fixing the boots, and the shoemaker had returned them in mint condition.

Johnny noticed. "You got them shined."

"Fixed up with new soles," she told him.

"Let's see."

She knew where this was going to lead. All of his overtures led in the same direction.

Sitting her on the sofa, he pulled the boots off. They still smelled of polish on the outside, and on the inside the smell of her feet.

"Can I take your stockings down?"

"Oh, Johnny," she said, "was it you who brought Star back?"

He grinned again, looking older, his cheekbones shiny with stretched skin, ears pulled back, a circle of hairless scalp above his forehead.

"Where did you find him?"

"In the park."

"You thought he had died, didn't you?"

"Yeah."

"Then you saw him."

He nodded. "What about the stockings, Katherine?"

She said nothing for a moment, just looked at him as he rolled the stockings down and pulled them off.

"You think I'm simple, don't you?"

"No."

"What, then?"

"I think you need someone to take care of you," he told her.

The twins were with Rosemary's cousin again, and would remain there until the new baby was born. Rosemary's belly was huge. She walked flatfooted, with her narrow shoulders thrown back and knees spread to counteract the weight that was dragging her forward. In church, Father Walker had given her a long look—perhaps it would have been better if she'd stayed at home.

When the mass was over and they had their coats on, Rosemary said that she didn't want to go home yet. The apartment would be dark, her husband still asleep or waking up cranky. "How about your place?" she asked.

Katherine blushed. Suppose Johnny came upstairs while Rosemary was there? How could she explain it? But when she hesitated, Rosemary pulled at her sleeve. "Come on."

They walked slowly up Proud Hill Road, arm in arm. The weather was the kind that made your ears hurt. The sun, low in the sky, left long shadows. Crossing to the river side, they followed the sidewalk along the edge of the park, where the sun seemed stronger. Up ahead, on one of the benches, Katherine could see a couple of the Brujos, dressed in their thin jackets despite the cold. They lounged against the bench backs, smoking, legs stretched out on the sidewalk.

"*Mira, la loquita!*"

"Just ignore them," Katherine said. "They won't harm us."

"Hey, who's you' frien'?"

Katherine walked straight ahead, looking right through them, but Rosemary stopped and turned their way, her belly out in front of her. One of the boys flipped his cigarette in a high arc toward the gutter. "*Mira, soy el padre.*" I'm the father.

The other one laughed. "*No—yo soy.*"

Rosemary glared at them. "Fuck you, you creeps."

The boys laughed and whistled, but Katherine could hardly believe what had come out of Rosemary's mouth. Away from the church, without the twins, she had changed abruptly. Deep inside all of us, it seemed, there was another self, or a number of selves, just waiting for the right circumstances to emerge into the world. She thought of Johnny—the coarse, lazy Johnny who neglected his job and cheated on his wife, and the tender Johnny who rolled her stockings down and licked her thighs, the Johnny who had seen her kitten in the park and brought him back.

People were a mystery, though God had made them all.

Up in the apartment, Katherine sat Rosemary in a straight chair and went to make tea. The cats came slowly into the living room, Amigo and Star first; Belle and Hombre were shyer and preferred to keep their distance.

"Your place is bright," Rosemary said.

Though there would be no direct sun until late in the afternoon, light seemed to ricochet into the room from the fire escapes and sidewalks, even from the bright winter air itself. The radiator clanged and hissed; all the rooms were warm now—Johnny had made sure of that.

Star jumped up into Rosemary's lap, purring as she stroked him. "He's nice," she said.

"He almost died when he was small. I had to feed him milk out of a dropper. Someone said he was already dead, but then he came back."

"Did you ask God to save him?"

She tried to remember. Yes, she thought she had asked God—not out loud or even in unspoken words, but in her heart.

"I ask God things," Rosemary said, "late at night sometimes, when the girls are asleep and I'm alone."

"What do you ask?"

"Why my life is already over? What the twins would do without me?"

Again, the other Rosemary, the one she didn't know. She looked down at Amigo, and when he came up into her arms, she hugged him for comfort.

"I'm sorry," Rosemary told her. "I shouldn't talk that way to you."

"No," Katherine said. "It's all right. I never realized you had a hard life."

Rosemary shrugged. "I got myself knocked up at seventeen and I've had hardly a minute of freedom since."

"You're so brave, to have another. You have faith."

"Sure." Splayed out in Katherine's armchair, she rubbed her belly, round and round, her head thrown back, watching the ceiling. "Ritchie doesn't believe in rubbers. I was on the pill for a few years—he didn't know. My cousin was helping me out. Then she couldn't anymore—no money to pay for it. One morning, Ritchie comes home from work, three or four in the morning after a few beers, and jumps me."

"You let him?" Katherine saw Brent's face, his swollen penis, the need she had aroused in him. Should she have refused him?

"What else do I have to look forward to?" Rosemary said.

And Johnny, Katie thought, and Miles Tobin—all those men with their one need.

"Do you have a boyfriend?"

Katherine blushed. "Not exactly."

"I don't know much about you," Rosemary told her.

It was true. They had talked mostly about the neighborhood, high school, growing up. About her time in Manhattan, she hadn't said much. Only that she had a job, then she'd gotten sick, and now she was on welfare and disability until she recovered.

Star had jumped down from Rosemary's lap; now, he came back, stretching up from her belly onto her chest, staring at her. "Maybe I ought to get a cat. It's nice." She rubbed Star's head and he purred. "Look, Katherine, forget what I said. You don't have to tell me anything."

"No, it's all right. I don't have a boyfriend, but there's someone who comes around a lot—the super."

Rosemary laughed. "The super?"

"Yes."

"A single guy?"

"No."

"Jesus," Rosemary said.

"He's nice to me."

"I'll bet."

Katherine smoothed her hair back—one, two, three times. "I'm simple, aren't I?"

"You have to watch out with men."

"I know," Katherine told her. "They have this terrible need to get close to you, get inside you, lose themselves. I thought I could be alone here and listen to God, and learn His purpose for me. Then Johnny came to me …"

"The super?"

"Yes. He was kind to me. He brought my cat back, the one who almost died, and I thought that maybe he's a part of it …"

"Part of God's plan for you."

"How can a person know?" she said. "What if God sent him to me to relieve his terrible need? I know I can do that."

"That's what men always want," Rosemary told her. "Even this one." She flipped Star over and rubbed his underside, pulling him onto her chest. The cat purred furiously.

"Star was close to death," Katherine said. "You couldn't tell he was breathing, but I knew that the spark hadn't left him. The next

The Ballad of St. Katherine

day I went to the park, and when I got back he was gone. He went down the fire escape. Then, much later, Johnny found him in the park. He was grown already."

"The same cat?"

Katherine showed her the mark. "Star. That's how he got his name."

"Maybe that's your vocation," Rosemary told her. "Maybe it's animals."

She smiled at Katherine, eyes bright, her face animated; as if, this time, she had really come up with something.

Johnny told her about his wife. Emily. He met her in Missouri on a Greyhound bus. She already had the two children. Katherine could imagine how he'd been driven by his need.

He'd traveled all over, he told her—in beat-up cars, in buses, even as a bum, riding on freight trains. His first time in New York was in the fifties, when he worked at the Brooklyn Navy Yard. Since then, he had gone away and come back twice.

Emily was a white trash woman, but nicer and smarter than you'd expect. The thing was, she'd gotten cancer and had to have a breast removed. Johnny could deal with that, but Emily took it worse. She cooked and cleaned and ironed for him, but could no longer tolerate his touch. Eventually, she ejected him from her bedroom. He had another room where he kept his phonograph records and some of his tools. That was where he slept. The two children shared the other bedroom, even though one was a girl and one a boy, thirteen and nine, getting too old for that.

Katherine took a deep breath. "Is all of it true?"

"On my mother's life, I swear."

Rosemary had told her—you have to be careful about men. Katherine didn't want to be a simpleton.

Johnny never asked more than to touch her with his fingers or lips; briefly, tenderly. She confessed all this to Rosemary, who said that he was a pervert. But Katherine saw a kind of devotion in it, like a devout Catholic kissing a statue of the Virgin Mary. There was a look of devotion she could read in Johnny's eyes.

Dark, cloudy days came, with flurries and a sharp smell in the air. Katherine cleaned in the morning, finishing always before noon. Each room had a different surface, a skin. The kitchen with its porcelain, linoleum, formica—cool and reflecting, but bearing the imperfections of age; strangely enough, the marks that had been left were not her mother's, but her father's—the sink chipped where once he had hammered it in frustration, the black scuff of his heel on the floor.

In the living room, she vacuumed with her shoes and socks off, her bare toes curling into the rug. The old upright Electrolux had whined and puffed out dust, barely picking up more than it expelled. Johnny had worked on it twice, but without effect; it was too old to be repaired. The second time he'd brought up a new vacuum for her to borrow; stretching out on the rug, he'd fondled and kissed her feet, claiming his reward.

Johnny gave her a clock, a cheap, funky plastic oval shaped to look like a crescent moon in a black sky. When it registered noon, she pulled on her warmest clothes—tights with long stockings over them, a long, heavy woolen skirt, two sweaters, her winter coat, boots, mittens, a wool scarf (another present from Johnny) and stocking cap. Johnny had also given her a sleeping bag and a small thermos, which she had filled with sweet tea. In the park, there was a single structure, a locked utility hut made of stone. She seated herself on the sheltered side, out of the wind, alone with the dull skies and the snowflakes. The cars on the Expressway went by without noise, gliding mysteriously, as if through smoke. Behind the gray screen of air, Manhattan looked colorless and drained of perspective. Only the remaining wind, propelling flurries against her cheek, seemed real.

What was this world of wind and snow?—only a facsimile, a painting, one of many, hanging on the walls of a house of light. Split in two, as in a dream, she could see her flat presence on the canvas, while at the same time, brilliant light poured down around her and sweet voices called. She was certain that death would release her into this Luminous World.

She pulled Johnny's sleeping bag tighter around her. Johnny was in the basement now with his wife and her terrible wound. She could feel his need welling up from underground, a rising shadow that climbed the stone wall of Proud Hill Road, looming up above her. Silently, she asked God that Emily be made whole, not in her body (which would be a miracle), but in her mind, so that Johnny's need might be satisfied.

A squirrel came to her, hunched just at the edge of the sleeping bag, holding a morsel of food. Rosemary had said that *animals* might be her vocation. Could it be as simple as that? She held out her hand and the squirrel shuffled forward, the food dropping from its jaws. It stared at her, watching with its bright eye. Picking up the piece of food, she offered it on her gloved palm and the squirrel consumed it. This poor being, who could never enter the Luminous World, suffered hunger and thirst nonetheless, and one day would die.

She wondered how many days and weeks Star had risked being run down in the streets, or faced starvation? She could imagine children (boys) hunting him with rocks; the boys, who had souls, pursuing the hapless animal, who was lacking. Though God must be perfect, it seemed an error that He had failed to give souls to cats and birds and even to the smallest creatures. God was in everything, but not equally. The rocks and clouds were dead parts of Him, like fingernails; the grasses and trees were alive but immobile; the insects hopped and flew, and the animals had thoughts and dreams—but only people had been given souls. Why was that?

Upstairs in the apartment, the cats were waiting. She tried to imagine Hombre and Star chasing one another, Amigo tempting Belle into a skirmish. Had she fed them this morning? She remembered peering into the bag of cat food, which was nearly empty (Johnny had promised to bring more), but couldn't recall pouring it into the bowls. Perhaps the cats were hungry.

Amigo was at the door when she came in; immediately he began to scold her, his mewl loud and complaining. The depleted bag of cat food was gone, a new bag in its place, but still she couldn't remember if the cats had eaten. Belle came out and walked around her nervously, and she could just see Hombre, crouched at the end of the foyer.

Star, she thought.

She found him in the living room, stretched out alongside the radiator. There was nothing amiss in that—it was a favorite spot—but something seemed wrong with the way he was laying. She knelt down beside him and touched his fur, her fingers penetrating easily to the hot skin underneath.

"Star?"

He lifted his head and mewled feebly. She searched for the mark; it was there on his flank, but larger and more diffused. She smoothed his fur inward, trying to clarify the star, but her effort only seemed to make it more indistinct.

Johnny came upstairs to take a look. The cat was docile under his touch, his body hot. "Don't look good."

"Oh," she said.

"You prayed for him before, Katherine. You could do it again."

She took Johnny's hand, held it tight and tried to find God. They were both on their knees, the distressed cat just in front of them. She closed her eyes and let herself travel through the sky. She saw the stars, the Pleiades. As she watched, they combined, and the beacon of their merged luminosities shone out into space—God's light, shining everywhere.

That night she dreamed that she entered the Luminous World with the cat in her arms. In the morning, when she touched Star's fur, it was brittle and cold. She searched with her fingers for his spark, but it was gone. Star was no more.

Johnny said that the ground in the park was too hard for a deep-enough grave to be dug. Packs of dogs sometimes ran there, and if Star's remains were too shallow they'd tear him apart. The best solution, he thought, was the incinerator. Could Katherine live with that?

"What will happen to him?"

"He'll be ashes and smoke," Johnny said, "mixed in with the garbage—I can't burn him alone. They haul away the ashes in a truck and eventually they get buried somewhere out on Staten Island."

She saw Amigo looking up at her, all the cats, awaiting her decision. Star would become earth and air. "Yes," she said. "I give my permission."

They wrapped the cat in an old sheet and had a little ceremony in the basement in front of the furnace. Emily and her children came out, surprising Katherine, making her blush. Emily had on a gray dress, one that she had seen before. They had encountered each other a number of times by the mailboxes in the lobby. Emily had nodded at her, but said nothing.

Now, Johnny also surprised her, with a prayer. "Lord, take this animal into your infinite mercy. In the name of Jesus. Amen."

The furnace door was closed. Katherine could feel the heat from where she stood, the high flame visible through the iron grillwork. "Give him to me," Johnny said. "I'll drop him in from the lobby."

She pulled the towel tightly around Star and handed him over from her arms into Johnny's, the way you would hand a baby. Johnny looked at her for a minute, then he was gone. The children also vanished, running for the TV in the super's apartment. All of a sudden, she and Emily were alone.

"John told you about my trouble, did he?"

Katherine nodded.

"They gave me a choice—my breast or my life. I stayed up all night and prayed about it. I heard God's voice saying that my children needed me."

She moved closer to Katherine, slowly, almost imperceptibly.

"They said I'd be all right afterwards, but now I think it's coming back."

"No," Katherine said.

"I wake up every night with the sweats, and my body is so sour I can smell it myself. The cancer is growing in me again."

"No," Katherine repeated, but there *was* a smell coming from Emily, strong and sour like the sometime smell of alcohol on Johnny's breath.

"John told me that when the cat was a baby he was near death and you brought him back with prayer. I wanted to ask you ..."

"I can't," Katherine said.

"Please! I know you can. It's not for me, it's for the children."

Emily came forward into her arms. They were the same height, but Emily felt gaunt and hollow, pressing into Katherine with her sharp bones. Behind them, the furnace flared twice; once for smoke and once for ashes, Katherine thought, the barest elements of Star's being returning to the place they arose from.

Upstairs, the cats looked at her strangely, as if they knew; pacing, with their ears thrown back, tails in the air. She sat on the rug and waited until they came—Belle first, then Hombre, finally Amigo, who moved cautiously as a soldier on patrol.

She took them all in her arms, whispering to them until they settled in. Poor creatures—spark without soul—they could do little. But she, who had a soul—what could *she* do? What was the meaning of all she had suffered—those things sharp in her memory and those that only came back in dreams? Who would help her to decide this?—Father Walker with his failing church? Rosemary, in friendship? Johnny? Or, perhaps, more than any of these, it would be Emily, with her faith and her terrible disease.

She heard Rosemary's voice in her head. "Maybe your vocation is animals." The cats had grown quiet on her chest. It took no divine light to calm their fears, only the rhythm of her own heart transferred into theirs. The animals needed no light, but the thinnest ray from the Luminous World was enough to reform the human soul and repair the body.

"Oh God," she whispered. "Why did you choose me?"

Johnny came up later. She bared her breast for him and let him suck. Gradually, the need flowed out of him. When he had finished, he dried Katherine's breast carefully with his hand.

"You're a virgin, Katherine," he said. He stared at her for a moment. "Aren't you?"

She stroked his cheek, gently as she would the belly of her cat.

"Yes," she told him.

Part IV

The New York Daily News, May 11, 1972
"Bronx Gang War"
Sidebar: "Gang Chief: Local Saint Saved Us"

Armando "Che" Febres, jefe of the Brujos, and now self-proclaimed "King of the West Bronx," said in an interview yesterday that the victory of the predominantly Puerto Rican Brujos over their black rivals, the River Aces, was the result of intervention by a neighborhood "saint." Febres, who prefers the name "Che," said that the decisive three-day battle, fought with guns, baseball bats and two-by-fours, was won by the outnumbered Brujos after a young neighborhood woman invoked "the power of the stars."

"We were very preoccupied because the Aces had more soldiers. But we had La Santa on our side and we fought like God's angels."

According to Che, La Santa is a girl who lives near Harlem River Park. "She sits in the park and all the animals come over to her. Like they lose all their fear." When the battle with the Aces was going badly the Brujos asked for a blessing, and La Santa touched each of them on the forehead. She told Che to go to the roof of a nearby apartment building and look at the stars, especially "seven stars close together in a little triangle."

"I couldn't really see them very good, but I said a prayer like La Santa said. After that, we all felt strong."

Bronx Police Lieutenant Donald H. Costello verified that the Brujos were outnumbered. The Aces had allied gangs from across the river in Manhattan, he said, all together twice as many fighters as the Brujos. "We were prepared to deal with the Aces after the turf war. It was a real surprise that the other side won."

Asked about La Santa, Costello said that he had never heard of her.

Part V

Rosemary called from the hospital, ringing Johnny's number in the basement. The super came up to Katherine's apartment. "Your friend is on the phone."

She held the receiver to her ear and heard Rosemary panting. A contraction. When it was over, Rosemary told her that nothing much was happening. 'I have lots of these little contractions, but they haven't gotten me anywhere."

"Don't get discouraged."

Rosemary laughed. "Are you kidding? I'm on vacation here. I lift my pinky and the nurse comes running to see what she can get me."

"Is Ritchie with you?"

"Ritchie? What time is it?"

"Almost two." Katherine had been cleaning the bathroom.

"He's either still asleep or he's up on Jerome Avenue at the Blarney Stone."

"Oh, Rosemary. Should I come and stay with you?"

She realized that Johnny was watching her from the doorway. His hungry gaze was so familiar, comforting in its way.

"You want me to run you up there?" He had an old car that he and Emily had driven up from Missouri, that he'd kept running all this time.

But Rosemary said no; she was all right, she'd call again.

She saw Johnny looking past her, over her shoulder. Emily had come into the room. Her hair was gnarled, tangled, the twists of different color grown together, gray and brown. Her shoulders slumped forward. "I won't disturb you," she said.

Johnny touched Katherine on the arm. "I have work needs to get done."

"Don't," she tried to say, but in a moment he was gone.

Emily remained. Her gray sack of a dress had buttons down the front. "Please," she said.

Katherine hesitated. She looked at her hands. The fingertips were white and without sensation, as if she'd been out in the cold.

"Please," Emily repeated.

"I'll try."

She undid the buttons and pulled the wide bodice of the dress across Emily's shoulders and off her arms until it hung from her waist. She covered her chest with her arms, but Katherine gently pulled them away. The left breast was a horrible wound, overgrown with scarring. But the right breast was intact, the little apple that Johnny had picked.

"Lay your hands on me," Emily said.

She touched the destroyed side with her right hand and the intact side with her left. Her cold fingertips felt nothing; but then, suddenly, overwhelmingly, there was her mother's presence, as if Ginger had just walked into Emily's kitchen. "Turn the water on," Katherine said. "Hard."

Emily went to the faucet. The pipes hissed with the rising water, then quieted as it splashed down into the sink. The universal calm of water filled the room. Ginger's sound.

She put Emily in a chair and sat close to her, laying her hands on the dead side and the live side. When Emily's eyes closed, Katherine removed her hand from the destroyed breast and put it on Emily's forehead. Immediately, she felt the confusion of rhythms, the beating together of life and death. She had never done this before, never imagined it, the disentanglement of two beats. Was it even possible, since life and death were intertwined? She felt Ginger trying to help her. "It feels good," Emily said. But Katherine put her fingers on

Emily's lips and neither of them spoke again until the whole, long session was done.

Later, Johnny came up and asked if he could rub her with oil. He did it gently, his fingertips barely brushing her, her breasts first, nothing below, then up along her chest to her shoulders and under her chin. She raised her jaw, tilting her forehead toward him until his fingers found it, moving in small circles, branching out, slowly, slowly, her skin shimmering with the thin layer of oil.

"I could take care of you," Johnny said, his fingers still moving on her forehead. "Get you anything you need."

"You have your family."

"Emily says ..."

"Don't tell me!" Katherine ordered. "I felt the cancer in her breast, but it's still small, weak ..."

"She said to take her children to Missouri if she dies. To their grandmother."

She brushed his hand away and stood, pulling her robe closed and tying it tightly at her waist. "I won't let Emily die." she said.

A week passed, then two, and she didn't hear from Rosemary. She used Johnny's phone to call the hospital, and was told that the patient had been discharged. She tried her home number. It rang six times, then Ritchie answered, his voice a low growl. "She can't talk right now." The words were like blows.

On Sunday she went to St. Cecilia's, hoping to see Rosemary there. The heat wasn't working right; the Sanctuary was freezing. Father Walker performed the mass with a scarf wrapped around his neck. The crowd of congregants was sparse, Rosemary not among them.

When the service was over, she found Father Walker at his accustomed place by the door. "Have you seen Rosemary Mallory?"

The priest shook his head. "I was going to ask you the same." He took a handkerchief out and patted his nose. "Do you know if her child's been born?"

She had a sudden vision of all the new souls coming down like rain. Pale and transparent, they filled the sky, calling out in their tiny voices. She remembered someone telling her (could it have been Brent?) that tankers filled with oil sailed out vaguely to mid-ocean before finally receiving their destinations. Perhaps it was the same with souls, who floated gently on the winds, blown this way and that, alerting God with little whispers (Here I am; here *I* am) until He'd send an angel for each.

"Katherine?"

She recovered. "I'm sure the new soul is here."

"Well, then," Father Walker said. He turned to sneeze into his hanky, a series of exhalations that left him wheezing and coughing. "Ah … my, my …"

He was an old man, Katherine saw, with a moon face, its smooth surface marred by small pits and bruises. She realized that the traffic of souls went two ways, and the miracle was not so much in the rain of souls coming down, but rather in the rising to heaven of the old souls, like Father Walker's, weighted down with all their years in the world.

That night, Rosemary rang her doorbell. Katherine hadn't realized it was snowing out, until she saw Rosemary's hair covered with a white crust. The new baby was with her, its blanket also powdered with snow.

"Ritchie's drinking," Rosemary said.

Under her coat she wore a robe, her feet in bed slippers. The baby was silent, his skin icy cold.

Katherine ran water into the tub. The cats came into the bathroom, staring curiously. She was reminded of the night she found Belle, Star and Hombre, hiding under the big radiator in the lobby. "I'll call Johnny," she said.

Rosemary shook her head. "I don't want him."

Her belly looked like a deflated balloon, already scarred with stretch marks the twins had left. Katherine opened Rosemary's bra, letting her breasts out; they fell asymmetrically, one of the nipples discolored.

"The fucking bastard!" Rosemary said. "He pinched me as hard as he could."

Katherine helped her into the warm water, laying the little baby on her lap. "What's his name?"

"Robert," Rosemary told her. "After Bobby Kennedy." She said it listlessly, as if it didn't matter.

Lying back, she floated the baby on her belly. A steamy cloud rose in the room, fogging the mirrors. Amigo gave a sharp mewl and scratched at the door until Katherine let him out, the other cats following. The infant, little Robert, remained silent, though his skin puckered in the new warmth.

"Can you take him?" Rosemary said.

Katherine wrapped the baby in a towel and pressed him against her chest. She seemed to know instinctively how to hold him, and he to settle in against her. Had she done this before and forgotten it, as she had forgotten other things?

"He was drunk," Rosemary said, dreamily, her eyes shut. "He picked Robert up and the poor little baby started to scream. 'Fucking little brat,' Ritchie said. Fucking little brat. He gave him back to me and I put him on my breast but he couldn't get anything."

Rosemary's hair was limp with steam, her face flushed. "Katherine," she said. "I just want to rest."

"Can't I call Johnny?"

"I don't care," Rosemary said.

They put her down to sleep in the small bedroom, Katherine's childhood bed. Johnny took Robert, who immediately became restive and began to cry, a high-pitched shriek that seemed to penetrate the skin. They heard Rosemary call from her room: "Shut him up, please!"

The baby came back to Katherine, but she couldn't calm him. "He's hungry," Johnny said.

She searched Robert's face and found there (how strange!) the same look of male hunger that she'd seen in Brent and Johnny, her father, all the men she had known, as if this hunger were stamped in at birth; this need—for food, for a woman's touch, for ejaculation.

There was milk in the refrigerator, a carton of Meadow Gold. Johnny said that Robert couldn't digest whole milk; it would make him sick. He needed formula. Grand Union would certainly have it, but they were closed; all the groceries were closed at this hour on Sunday night.

The wind blew against the window, rattling the glass, while the cats strutted nervously, their fur electric. Katherine held Robert up and stared into his eyes, which seemed to change color as she watched, blue to brown to black, a trick of light, of the wavering light blinking in the storm.

"Arhhhhh," Robert howled.

Johnny said: "We have to take him in to your friend."

They eased open the bedroom door, tiptoeing ridiculously, as if Rosemary were not already disturbed by the infant's shrieks. She pulled the covers up over her head. "I can't stand it."

"You have to feed him," Katherine told her.

"I can't, I'm dry."

"Try it."

They propped her up with pillows and Katherine rolled up the sweater Rosemary had worn to bed. Johnny stood watching, leaning against the wall by the door. As soon as Katherine gave the baby to Rosemary, he stopped crying. Cocking his head, he went for her breast and began to suck. Katherine watched his tiny face, which got redder and redder, muscles tense with his masculine hunger. Finally, he broke contact with a violent twist and began to scream.

"For Christ's sake, get him away from me," Rosemary said. "I'll go crazy."

Katherine tucked her back in and took Robert to the kitchen. The baby kept howling. She moved him, gently, rhythmically, but it didn't help. His screams filled the room.

"We have to call the police," Katherine said.

Johnny was silent. Then he frowned. "We'd better not."

She looked at him.

"There's a reason," he said.

She continued to stare at him, while Robert continued to scream.

"We got into a little deal with the police in Missouri, Emily and I. Do you want to know what?"

She shook her head.

"Katherine," Johnny said. "You can give the baby suck yourself."

Her eyes widened. "How could I?"

"You brought Star back from death, didn't you?"

"He's just an animal."

"I know you can," Johnny told her.

Now, she remembered that her breasts *had* felt strange for a week or two, slightly swollen and aching, the veins standing out. She hadn't worried about it; her period was late, as frequently happened, reason enough for her body to feel unusual. But … could it be that God had prepared her in this way, with a purpose in mind?

Robert was silent for a moment. She felt him pushing at her, his lips seeking her breast through the thick sweater she wore. Her nipple rose toward him. Johnny held out his arms and she handed him the baby, who immediately began to shriek again.

Her sweater was green, a Christmas present from Ginger; she'd had it for many years. Her arms were cold now. There was a draft in the kitchen—Johnny had been unable to stop it. Reaching behind her, she unhooked her bra and let it fall to the floor.

"Your breasts are beautiful, Katherine, full of milk and honey."

She sat at the table and Johnny brought Robert close. The baby yearned toward her—body and soul, his entire being.

Part VI

One morning, when she came back from the park, Miles Tobin was sitting on the stoop in front of her building. He was hatless, in a thick-belted trench coat, his hair cut stylishly long. He was missing his glasses. His eyes were blue—had she never noticed that before?

"Hello, Katherine."

She didn't know what to say. She had never been alone with him, except in his office at JUSI, and then Beth had been nearby, just beyond the door.

"I was on the IRT, coming back from some business, and it occurred to me to just stay on and pay you a visit."

"Oh."

She had expected that if he came he'd be with P. J. or Helen, or one of his girlfriends—someone on his arm, or attending to everything he said His ears were red. The coat he was wearing couldn't be very warm. She had her winter coat on, and Ginger's scarf. But he didn't *look* cold. His shoulders were thrown back, thickening his chest against the pull of his clothing. His face also seemed thicker, heavier. For a moment he'd reminded her of Che.

"Did you have to wait long?"

"I don't know, Katherine, I was thinking."

"About what?"

He stood up. "Aren't you going to ask me in?"

She put him in her father's armchair. Under his trench coat he had been wearing a blue suit and a tie. As soon as he came in he removed the jacket, loosened the tie and rolled his sleeves up. Katherine supposed it was hot in the apartment; the radiators ran day and night.

It took only a few minutes for the cats to gather around, vying for attention. Eventually, Amigo retreated, while Tobin made friends with the other two. He stroked Belle under the chin, where she liked it, and let Hombre curl up on his lap. Miles was the only man, besides Johnny, who had been up here since her father left. The cats were neither warm nor cold toward Johnny; they treated him like part of the furniture. Miles, on the other hand, had made an impression.

She brought him a cup of coffee and sat opposite him on the heavy sofa. He drank a few sips, then bent his head back and watched the ceiling. A drop of blood appeared in one of his nostrils and fell onto his lip. "Christ," he said. He got a tissue from his pocket, pressing it against the offending nostril. "Nosebleed."

The tissue reddened. She didn't like to see his blood; she began to imagine it rushing out in quarts, his skin turning white, like the soft exterior of a bloodless insect that lives in the dark. "I used to have them when I was a child," he said. "They disappeared entirely; but, lately, in the cold weather ..."

She brought him a handkerchief, one of her father's. He had left them all, as if he wouldn't need them in Florida. In the same drawer he had left money, two hundred dollars in fifties. She hadn't had to spend any of it yet, with her government checks and Johnny taking care of her.

"You look good, Katherine," Miles said.

She wasn't sure how she looked. She seldom looked at herself; there was something a little frightening about a mirror, with its flat surface and uncanny depth. She had once seen a movie with Brent, in which a character lost himself in an endless regression of mirrors: an image, looking at an image, who looked at an image ... and so on, to infinity. Brent had had his arm around her—if not, she felt that she also might have been lost.

"Are you getting along?" Miles asked. "Are you working?"

She explained about the welfare and disability, but not about Johnny. Miles frowned. He was very clean shaven, but curls of thick hair sprouted from his forearms. He had rolled his sleeves up carefully, into nearly identical cuffs, just above the elbows. His chest was broad, his body strong looking, except for the blood running out of him, running and dripping.

"Even so, Katherine," he said. "It would be good for you to get out."

"I go to the park."

"Yes, I know," he told her. "The article in the Daily News—it was you, wasn't it?"

She had no idea what he meant, but he asked her to look in his suit jacket, the inside pocket. When she unfolded the sheet of newsprint, the photo of Che immediately caught her eye. He was staring into the camera *as if* into a mirror, seeing himself and infinity at the same time. The photograph had captured him, but the words that described her (it had to be her they were talking about) left her free: in the park, with the river behind it, and Manhattan further still, the sky above, the stars readying themselves, while the squirrels gathered around her. In the ambiguity of words lay their freedom.

"Can you really do magic, Katherine?"

"No," she said. "Not magic."

"I know you can cure headaches."

"Not always. Sometimes, I fail."

"Can you stop my nosebleed?"

The handkerchief was heavy with blood. She felt that he was testing her, the way her father sometimes had, to see if she would fail. But while her father expected little of her, expected failure, she saw in Miles' face that he was rooting for her. She felt his encouragement.

She touched the bridge of his nose and found his rhythm without trouble. It was singular and rose above the disharmonies. These disharmonies were errant channels that failed to turn back upon themselves; she could feel the blood flowing out along them.

Quickly, she closed them, one by one, and the blood flowed back through Miles' heart, the loop completing itself.

"Take the handkerchief away," she told him.

A drop of fresh blood fell onto his white shirt, soaking into the material, spreading, staining. For a moment, she saw Arcturus, low and swollen in the southeast. He must have noticed her face, because he asked: "What is it, Katherine? Don't worry about the shirt."

A second drop fell.

"Do you think about her?" she asked.

"Who?"

"Beth."

"No," he said.

She put a finger in his nostril. There were no more drops.

He went to the bathroom to wash. Katherine took his shirt and sprayed it with a cleaning solution Johnny had given her. The stains wavered, shimmering as if under water, the bottom of a pool, the pool's floor which fascinated and frightened her. At Cascades Pool on Jerome Avenue, she and Iris had spread out their towels on the long side of the deck, down toward the shallow end, where the littler kids stayed. The older children, sixteen, seventeen, eighteen, were encamped at the deep end, where Rosemary had stood provocatively on the diving board, her toes curling over its edge. Katherine stayed in the shallow water, looking down at her wavering feet, which seemed slightly unreal as if transformed permanently by the shimmer of light and water. Every moment, she was conscious of the deep end, where the floor suddenly fell away. She could feel the hole pull at her.

"Actually, I did see Beth."

Miles' face was clean, the nostril cleared. She had cured his nosebleed. He was in his undershirt, which he had tucked neatly in the waistband of his pants. The distance between them had been breached.

"There was a hearing," he said. "Beth testified. I saw her on the way out."

"What kind of hearing?"

"It was about money, Katherine. It's always about that. I bought some things, I entertained. It was a matter of hundreds, a few thousand at most. That was the focus—not the fact that I protected JUSI, kept it healthy, that it flourished under my stewardship. There were people who acted out of jealousy, Katherine, old men who had been around since the fifties, even the forties. I had plenty of enemies, and very few really grateful for what I did."

"What about her?" She could not bring herself to say the name.

"We were friends once. I don't blame her."

"No," Katherine said. "She's not your friend."

Miles laughed. His face looked boyish now, nothing like Che's Indian face. "Oh, Katherine, Katherine—you still have a lot to learn about the world." He took her hand in both of his. "Thank you for fixing my bloody nose. I'll visit again—is that all right? You should have a telephone, Katherine. Can I help with that?"

"No," she said. "I don't want one. I'm all right."

She got his shirt from the kitchen. The stains had faded, but could still be seen. He put the shirt on and knotted his tie in the foyer mirror. "Are you going back to JUSI now?" she asked him.

He moved a step closer to her. "I guess I didn't make myself clear. I'm not with JUSI any longer."

She looked into his eyes, which were steady. There was no reflection of herself there. "What are you doing, then?"

"Oh," he said, "I have a few things going on."

Part VII

Father Walker died, and the Archdiocese sent a young priest to replace him, a Jesuit, Spanish-speaking and severe. The masses alternated in English and Spanish, but the congregation still dwindled. The men of the neighborhood, who had seldom attended, found nothing now to change their minds. The women still came, but perhaps not so often as before, as if, despite the difficulties of life in the *barrio*, their need for God had lessened.

Rosemary's twins were now five, and Robert had his first birthday. Sunday morning, following church, they made a party for him at Katherine's. Ritchie was still working nights, still sleeping late on Sundays. Besides, he had no interest in birthday parties. Rosemary had the feeling he was going to leave her. She told Katherine that she hoped he did, but how could she make it with the three children on her own?

They had cake and balloons. Johnny had gotten her a used TV and connected it to the aerial on the roof. She hardly watched, but the twins turned it on when they came. Katherine also kept a jug of white wine in the refrigerator for Rosemary, who liked to have a glass or two.

She was on her second glass, Katherine drinking milk to keep her company. Katherine felt her best in the company of Rosemary and the children, better even than in the park. God had a softer presence here, and made no demands. Here, Katherine could be ordinary. Rosemary knew nothing about the miracle of the feeding, merely that they had found milk that night to satisfy Robert's hunger. Only she and Johnny knew the truth.

Rosemary put her glass down, and sat for a moment, very still. She raised a hand in caution. "Turn the TV down a minute," she told the twins.

There was noise from the hall, a man's voice. He was pounding on doors—an apartment down the hall, then next door, then Katherine's.

The neighborhood was so different from the way it had been when they were growing up. There was frequent noise, yelling. There were the Brujos and River Aces, condoms and beer cans thrown down against the fence that separated the park from the Expressway. "He'll go away," Katherine said.

Rosemary shook her head. "It's Ritchie."

Katherine went to the peephole and saw him. His ears looked red and mangled as if someone had rubbed them raw. He hit the door again. "Come out, Rose."

Rosemary came into the foyer. "Don't open up," she said

Katherine could feel the pounding of Rosemary's heart. "What will happen when you go home?"

"He'll be asleep by then."

The door shook, as Ritchie kicked it—one, two, three, four kicks. In the living room, Robert began to cry. "I'll go get him," Rosemary said. "Don't open the door."

But as soon as she was gone, Katherine told him through the peephole: "If you move back a few steps, I'll come out and talk to you."

She slipped out through the door, making sure it closed behind her. She could smell the sour liquor cloud, spilling out of Ritchie's skin to fill the hallway.

"Tell *her* to come out," he said. He held his hands up to show they were empty. "I won't do anything."

She could sense the animal in him, close to the surface—the quivering squirrel, ready to retreat, and the dog with his heavy jaws, his coat bristling with the forecast of attack. In the park, a new pack of dogs had started to run, often two or three, sometimes as many as a dozen. When they came close, Katherine found she could feel in her own skin the message of their intentions. So in tune did she become with these vibrations that she was able to cross their midst as a neutral presence, their thin snouts brushing her, sniffing without alarm.

"You can see her tomorrow, Ritchie, when you're better."

She put a hand gently on his shoulder, but he knocked it away. "Don't give me that shit."

Beyond his breathing, she listened for the building's murmurs—the fire like loud static in the incinerator, the rise of steam, the elevator starting in its shaft. She closed her eyes, feeling Ritchie's pull at her wrist, the pain in her arm as he twisted it up behind her.

"Open the goddamn door."

She tried to tune her breathing precisely to his, but he was beyond the limits of her gift. She willed her body to be limp, boneless.

"I'll break it fucking off," he threatened.

Behind the door, someone was listening—Rosemary, or one of the twins. "Don't come out," Katherine shouted.

Ritchie jerked her arm, and she could sense the bone about to break. The building grew hushed, as if waiting—except for the elevator's whine, which continued for seconds before ceasing abruptly. Katherine opened her eyes to see the doors open and Johnny step out. He had a long, thin knife, which he squeezed so tightly that his fingers were white.

"Let go of her, man."

Ritchie swung Katherine around, so that she was in between him and Johnny. "Who the fuck are you?"

"Let her loose before I come over there."

Ritchie dropped her arm, and she rubbed it where it hurt near the elbow. Johnny approached slowly, the knife in front of him. "I ever see you here again, I'll stick this between your ribs."

"Don't," Katherine said.

Johnny ignored her. "I'll gut you, I swear. She won't save you."

Ritchie retreated toward the elevator. He stared at Johnny, but didn't speak until the doors began to close between them. "You motherfucker!"

The elevator started to hum. Katherine massaged her arm, wincing as she rubbed. "You wouldn't have done it, Johnny?"

He retracted the knife's blade and put it in his pocket. "I would," he told her.

One morning, a knock at Katherine's door, not the bell.

"*Señora, por favor.*"

It was a woman whose face she knew vaguely, perhaps from St. Cecilia's. She had been cleaning the bathroom—the sink and toilet had needed it. In the past, each room had been done every week, but, lately, days passed without any cleaning, the thought of it slipping Katherine's mind as she read or walked in the park or Rosemary came over.

"*Señora ...*"

The woman showed her a medal of St. Christopher, which she said her husband would carry when he returned to El Salvador. It was becoming dangerous there. She entreated Katherine to bless the medal and increase her man's protection.

Katherine shook her head. "I can't."

"*Si, Señora, por favor.*"

She took the medallion. Its weight surprised her, along with a searing heat that seemed to burn her hand. She closed her eyes and the medal throbbed, the vibration rising to a peak, then gradually subsiding, until the surface was cool and still.

She handed it back.

"*Gracias, Señora.*" The woman curtsied slightly, then opened her purse and took out a couple of dollar bills, offering them.

Katherine stopped her hand. "I don't need anything," she told her.

But, then, when others came, every one a woman, they brought gifts other than money—a bag of cookies, a few bananas, a small article of clothing, knitted by hand—and these Katherine accepted. Some of the women had illness at home, a sick child; or perhaps sought luck in some endeavor; or believed that spells had been put on them, which had to be removed. Katherine would touch them—often on the forehead, sometimes the wrist or palm; then, she would feel something, immediate and strong; or else, nothing at all.

When something was there, it took the form of a disharmony—excessive heat or cold, for example, or a jarring arrhythmia, so powerful and discordant that it could stagger her. Spreading her fingers on the woman's flesh, she would feel the aberrant rhythm enter her own body at the Nine Portals; slowly, it would become harmonized in her blood, quieting, until the flow gently reversed and she could feel the woman's calmly beating heart in her fingertips.

But more often than not, she felt nothing, and could do nothing. These occasions frightened and dismayed her. What had gone wrong and why so often? She felt it must be some impurity in herself, or something she lacked, perhaps even her own sins, which had imprisoned her.

But Johnny told her she was the purest of women. He ran cool water into the tub and bathed her gently, anointing her breasts and forehead. Then, more roughly, he lathered her hair with shampoo and washed it out. She realized she had neglected her hair, letting it become coarse and filmy.

When he had finished drying her and rubbed her body with oil, they sat together on the bed, while the cats prowled around their legs, mewling plaintively.

She asked Johnny: "What should I say to them when I don't feel anything?"

He wrung his hands while he thought. "They need you. You oughtn't disappoint them."

"I can't make up things I don't feel."

"Something helpful, Katherine. Something without harm."

In the warm weather Father Rivera greeted his parishioners on the wide concrete porch of the church, just outside its massive metal doors. He was a short man, balding in front, his skin the color of weathered hemp. He had a high, squeaky voice, but otherwise gave the impression of maturity, his sunken cheeks and thin lips hinting that he had lived through difficult times.

These days Katherine seldom attended. When she did she'd sit in a back row and slip out as soon as the service ended. When Rosemary was also there, they would hook arms and walk in a convoy of Mallorys, the two women at the center with little Robert, the twins at their flanks.

One Sunday, waking early, she felt a strong need for the church. Foregoing breakfast, she fed the cats, who fidgeted around their bowls, mirroring her own restlessness. Rosemary and the children were away at the Jersey shore.

Alone in her pew, she felt the glance of others, heads turned quickly, discretely, to take note of her. Some she recognized—women who had come to her asking for blessings or protection; others were strangers who perhaps knew her only through rumors.

By the time the mass was over, her restless feeling had given way to a warmth in her chest, and she sat for a while gazing up at the high dome in front of her, lost for the moment in its illusion. Gradually her respiration adjusted to the expansion and contraction of the dome's light, so that finally it seemed that its pulses were driven by her own breathing, her inhalations sucking the rays from the dome, exhalations restoring them. Tears came down her cheeks and she wiped them with her fingers.

By the time she recovered, all the others had already left the Sanctuary. She got up and walked quickly out, only to be dazzled again, this time by the bright sunshine. She shielded her eyes with an arm, but colors still shimmered in front of her.

"Christ be with you, my child."

She turned toward the priest's voice, seeing him through sparkles of color, his forearms bare below the short sleeves of his black shirt, collar tight at the neck, his eyes hidden behind dark lenses.

"Hello Father."

"Lovely morning." He brought his fingertips together below his nose. "We haven't seen you so often of late—I suppose the beautiful days are tempting."

She didn't know what to answer. Father Walker had never confronted her in this way.

"Katherine," he said. "I've actually been looking for an opportunity to speak with you. Perhaps you have a few moments now?"

He led her down the narrow walk that bordered the church and through a side door topped with a sharp triangular arch. The sudden darkness blinded her. Inhaling briefly, she smelled dampness and the sweet fragrance of flowers.

Father Rivera's study was a mole's den, lit dimly with artificial light. He fiddled with the blinds, tilting them upward to let in weak shafts of reflected sunlight that rose through dust toward the ceiling. On one wall stood a small table filled with cut flowers and flowering plants, the source of the fragrance. Above the table hung three long fluorescent bulbs, which the priest turned on.

He smiled at Katherine with his thin lips. "My eyes are easily damaged by the ultraviolet. Eventually I'll go blind, but the more precautions I take the longer my sight will last. The plant light emits little beyond visible wavelengths."

"I'm sorry." She wondered what she would feel if she placed her fingertips on his forehead.

"Would you like some tea?"

She shook her head. She realized she hadn't eaten since five or six o'clock the previous evening. Johnny had made her a bowl of thick soup with bread and butter after the last of her supplicants had left. Since then she hadn't felt hungry.

"Please Father, make some for yourself."

"Never mind," he said. "I drink too much of it as it is."

He motioned her to a corner of the room where two armchairs stood close together, cater corner, their sides almost touching. Father Rivera took the more Spartan chair with its straight back and minimal padding. Her chair yielded slowly as she sat, the soft cushion smelling of dust.

The priest folded his hands on his lap. "Tell me, Katherine, how long have you been coming to our church?"

She shook her head. How long? Weeks seemed to her sometimes like days, minutes like hours. Johnny had often to remind her, orient her in time.

"A long time in any event," the priest said. "Two years since I arrived, and a number of years before that. And yet I have never seen you take confession or communion." His gaze seemed sharp, shooting into her. "Are you baptized, my child?"

She couldn't remember exactly, but surely Ginger must have had her baptized. Her mother would not have neglected *that*.

"I think so, Father."

"But not in the True Church?"

"No."

"Then why do you come, if I may ask?"

Why? Because of Rosemary? Because of the light breathing from the dome? Because God is here, however fleeting His presence?

"I don't know, Father."

He pursed his lips, gazing at her. "I could bar you, you know, forbid you the door. I've thought about it. You come here as an outsider, almost like a spy. What is your business here? Do you wish to be baptized into the Holy Roman Church?"

She closed her eyes and saw Johnny reaching out to her, his fingers moist from the bath, touching her forehead, her nipples.

"Do you believe, Katherine, that we have immortal souls?"

"Yes." She could sense Ginger's presence now, a calm sea, blue and gently rippled.

"You must know, then, that your own soul faces the gravest dangers."

Ginger's face was in the water, bathed in shimmering light.

The priest's hand shot out and slapped her cheek, the blow not very hard, but shocking in its intent. "I have heard stories, Katherine. I have heard that some in my flock come to you, that you have performed the Devil's rites, witchcraft ... unspeakable ..."

"No, Father."

"What, then?"

Suddenly she remembered the psychiatrist, his black sweater devouring the light, bearded face watching her, her wrists and ankles bound with straps that cut her flesh ...

"Well?"

What had they done to her? Some terrible thing that she would never do to any other! "I don't mean any harm," she said.

Father Rivera's voice softened. "No," he said. "Perhaps not. Perhaps you have done evil without intent, and have come here to be relieved of it." He stared into her eyes. "Go home now and think it over. If ever you return it must be to fully confess your sins, to see them as sins; only then can baptism in the Holy Church wash you clean."

"Yes," she said.

But walking home in the sun's brilliance, she saw Ritchie retreating before the thrust of Johnny's knife. She realized that Johnny and the priest could be brothers, their bodies were different, yet their faces strangely alike; something alike about their faces, only that Johnny's eyes were sunk a bit deeper into his head, and, on his upper lip, a moustache was always threatening to take hold. She needed to see him now. She would ask Johnny if *he* thought she had done the Devil's work, and whether she should throw herself on Father Rivera's mercy.

She entered the elevator and, as if the machine could read her mind, the inner door slid shut and the car descended. She rang the super's bell listening for Johnny's step, but it was Emily's daughter, Summer, who came to the door. Her long reddish hair was brushed out, her eyes green-flecked like her mother's.

"He's not here," she said.

"What about Emily?"

"Her neither."

"Is she all right?"

The girl shrugged. "Sure. You fixed her, didn't you?"

"No," Katherine told her. "Not me."

"She thinks so."

"Only God can heal." She turned to go. "Tell your father and mother I was here."

"Wait," the girl said. "Can I ask you something?"

They sat together in the kitchen. The formica tabletop had a worn patch where its inlaid pattern had been interrupted. Light spread across it, seeming to drift down from the overhead fixture, falling as slowly as snowflakes. The ancient refrigerator with its coil top kicked on in a series of ascending groans like a plane gathering speed on the runway. The room was full of the past. Ginger had sat here across from Mr. Buschbaum, who talked softly to her in his comforting voice, lapsing occasionally into German. Before him there had been another super, also German. The table and the refrigerator were first his, along with the light fixture and the cracked linoleum. Johnny had nailed patches over the worst places near the sink and door.

"My mother thinks you're a saint," Summer told her.

"I'm not."

The girl smiled. "*I* know, but *she* would do whatever you said."

"What do you want me to say?"

Suddenly the girl stood up. "I forgot. Can I get you a drink, a coke or something?"

"No, thank you." She wasn't thirsty, but felt hunger all of a sudden, an emptiness that spread through her.

Summer took a strand of hair between her fingers and twisted it. "Do you have a boyfriend?"

Katherine shook her head.

"But you have had."

"Yes." She'd had Brent. A long time ago, a thousand years.

"I have one," Summer said. "My mother hates him."

"What is his name?"

"They call him 'Juro.'"

"One of the Brujos?"

The girl's face lit up, green eyes sparkling. "You know him!"

"I know who he is." She had seen him in the park, a boy who stared coldly. "Why doesn't Emily like him?"

"Because he's a PR. She hates all of them. If she finds out I'm still seeing him she'll tell my daddy, and I'll get beat up."

"Johnny wouldn't hit you."

"No?"

The girl began to roll up her sleeve, but quit suddenly, pulling it down again and backing her chair away from the table. A moment later, Katherine heard Johnny's step. He stopped short in the doorway, staring at them.

"You shouldn't come down to the basement, Katherine. It's no place for a person like you."

"I need to talk to you."

"The washroom wants cleaning," Johnny said to Summer.

"All right." The girl rose slowly, lazily, and walked out of the kitchen.

Johnny had faith in Katherine. Lately, she realized, he had begun to look at her a different way, not the old male hunger, not exactly, but a more distant focus, as if he were in a dream. Apart from the anointing ceremonies, he scarcely touched her anymore, only stared hard with his rapt, distant expression. She was the most special of women, he told her. One day, people would come from everywhere to admire and adore her. Father Rivera, also. One day he would kneel to kiss the hem of her dress.

She rode upstairs in the elevator, which hummed and crawled. Johnny said that the landlord had missed two inspections, afraid of expensive repairs. Among other things, the walls needed attention; some of the boys in the building had scratched initials and slogans into the paint. Inside her apartment the air was heavy and still. The cats slept in the filtered sunlight; only Amigo seemed able to summon up enough energy for a tepid greeting. She ran water from the tap until most of the heat was out of it, then drank a large glass. It drifted slowly through her throat into her empty stomach, like moisture dripping from the ceiling of a cave.

In the bedroom she took off her dress and hung it carefully in the closet. Underneath, her slip was damp where it touched bare skin. It was too warm, really, for a slip, but she'd learned from Ginger to put one on with a dress, especially when worn to church. She opened the window from the bottom and was rewarded with a persistent breeze. Lying down on top of the bedspread she closed her eyes. She slept, then woke with no idea of how much time had passed. The room was still light. She felt hungry again now, but lacked the will to lift herself from the bed.

She shut her eyes again and now she dreamed—chaotic scenes that came and fled. This time when she woke, it was dark. Her bedroom seemed a strange place; nothing was familiar. The breeze had turned cold. Sitting up, she stretched her arms—toward the ceiling, the foot of the bed, out to the sides. She let her feet slip to the floor. The closet that had been Ginger's was straight ahead, about four steps. The old floorboards, loosened by time, creaked beneath her. But when she reached the proper place the closet wasn't there. Keeping one hand on the wall she inched along until finally the door appeared. Behind it, on a hook, she found Ginger's old robe, the green one. It was in the right place, exactly where she had expected, but the closet was wrong!

She put the robe on, pulling the belt tight around her empty insides. Now she felt hot again instead of cold. Feverish. Outside in the living room, the darkness was profound. Her mother's drapes were drawn, keeping out all light. But hadn't she left the drapes open when she went to bed? In fact, hadn't Johnny taken the drapes down for her altogether when the summer started?

She lowered herself to the rug and sat in front of the window, cross-legged. She waited. Behind the drapes, she knew, there was something terrible. "No, God," she said—but the drapes opened anyway. As she had feared, no familiar city was outside—rather a view she had never seen. A house—large, gabled, with three stories, its shape perfectly symmetric, rising above a foreground of yellow woods. Through these woods a path twisted, leading eventually upward ... a picture that frightened her more than she had ever been frightened ...

A house on a hill.

Religion and sexual feeling are very close. They spring from the same well of emotion deep in the soul, and share brain circuits.

Jody Hopson, in
Religion in America
"Katherine Turley: Healing Without Creed"

Part VIII

She hardly cleaned anymore. The place defied cleaning. Dust blew in on every breeze, penetrating the house's porous skin, collecting on the mantles, the counters, the intricate molding; mildew in the basement and bathrooms, the smell of damp; soot from the two fireplaces, stinging the eyes in winter. Besides, Katherine had no time to clean. It had become Emily's job and Summer's; and, sometimes, Summer's brother pitched in.

Upstairs, they lived with the dust; the central heating, inadequately installed and inefficient, ferried it up from the basement; the old windows admitted it. But downstairs—where the offices had been constructed, where Katherine's Sanctum had been placed at the geometrical center of the floor, where people entered with ills and woes and exited better, where reporters came for interviews and graduate students for thesis research—no effort was spared on the continual job of keeping the area clean.

She remembered the days when she had cleaned the apartment on Proud Hill Road, one room a day, regular as the stars—such a comforting rhythm. She remembered back further to her father, now dead in Florida, his last wife calling with the news. "He never wanted to talk about you," she said, "but he kept a kind of scrapbook—I know he was proud of you," and "if I came up north sometime, I mean, if I gave you notice before, I have an arthritic condition, I have pain all the time, do you think you could help me?"

She had told Candice, her secretary, to make room for the woman if she called, Candice grumbling how tight the schedule was, how she always had to juggle things, nothing in proper order. Johnny had said more than once they ought to get rid of her; she tore down the sanctity of the house, the aura of Katherine's presence. But Candice was good with the poor suffering souls who came for solace. Katherine saw how they grew calmer in her presence, more hopeful—a part of her own work already done. And, despite her complaints, Candice was actually adept in doing the schedule.

The trouble with the schedule lay in the stars—especially in the late winter and through the spring, when the Seven were weakened and Katherine became fitful. One didn't know day by day which appointments Johnny could get her to keep and which would have to be broken. A nervous gloom descended over the household; even the cats felt it—the aging Amigo who walked around out of sorts, his whiskers twitching; and strutting Hombre, in his prime, irritably mauling the new kitten. Katherine still missed Belle, who had died years ago, and she would have had more cats, except that Miles had objected. The animals wandered around downstairs, getting underfoot, interfering with the visitors, projecting chaos into the pristine environment of Katherine's ministry. It was Miles who had supervised all the construction on the ground floor, who had not spared their meager capital, creating—with Katherine's permission, always with her permission—the atmosphere in which her spirituality could blossom and their enterprise prosper.

And there were the glorious days in late summer and in the fall, when the Pleiades were ascendant and Arcturus had sunk into darkness. Katherine would be up at night, sometimes all night, sitting on the hill that looked east and south across the Hudson—the location that she had seen in her vision and Miles had found for her—praying for the sickest of the supplicants, the most unwhole in body or soul, with the Seven resplendent in the sky, and her powers, whatever they were, at their zenith. Afterward, she might be exhausted and sleep late into the day, and Candice would have to juggle the schedule accordingly.

Johnny was the one to wake her, his hand on her hunched shoulder. He opened the curtains first, letting in the breeze that was blowing off the river. The day was cloudy; there had been storms in the morning and more were forecast. It was barely past noon. He hated to wake her so early, but if the overcast remained into the night she would be able to get some sleep later. She responded sluggishly to his touch, her body warm and a bit clammy. He rubbed her shoulder more insistently. "Katherine, get yourself up."

Sometimes she was so deep in sleep that he was afraid she had parted her body. One day, he knew, her soul *would* fly away, leaving him behind. He thought about it at night, staring at the wall that separated their bedrooms, a wall so thick that nothing could be heard across its boundary—not the moans that she made in the night, her heavy breathing, not even Amigo's loud mewls as he prowled the ledge outside Katherine's window.

"Please, Katherine."

She was worse than a child to wake, worse than Summer had been as a child when he'd ripped the covers off her, leaving her with hands raised across her chest for protection. At least, the baby had been quiet this morning. Johnny had heard Summer changing him in the bathroom, sound traveling easily through the halls in this house and up and down the stairs, despite the nearly impervious walls. Afterward, she must have fed him and put him back down to sleep.

231

"Johnny, what time is it?"

When he told her, she groaned and tried to turn back over, but he managed to get a hand behind her and sit her up. She bathed in the sumptuous tub, in the bathroom that Miles had allowed to be built into Katherine's bedroom, the only construction of any consequence above the ground floor. When she was through, he brought a towel. Katherine's skin was smooth and rosy, but she was too thin, her bones sharp and ribs showing when she lifted her arms. There were lines on her forehead and down under her eyes. She took the towel from Johnny and dried herself carefully. He no longer was allowed to touch her body; it was hard to remember that he ever had been. After she was dry, she anointed herself at the Nine Portals—eyelids, earlobes, nostrils, mouth, anus, vagina—a tiny drop of oil at each, so that angels could enter her and disharmony escape.

She was awake. "Get me a cup of coffee," she told Johnny.

Her appointment was at two, with a graduate student from the Psychology Department at Duke, who wanted to study faith healing. He had proposed an intensive period of six months, during which he would spend hours and days around Katherine; not staying at the house, of course, not venturing above the ground floor, but living nearby and coming over frequently. Johnny was dead against it, but it wasn't his department; his job was security, grounds keeping, house repairs, and, of course, catering to Katherine's needs. Miles had arranged the interview. They all knew what Katherine could do—why not show it to the world? Miles was a risk taker; he had plans for another building on their land—a residential "faith hospital," where people could stay, close to Katherine, while she tried to fix them.

The student's name was Jody Hopson. Need radiated from him like the light of a tiny, powerful lamp lit suddenly in a dark room. Katherine was overwhelmed by it; it was hard to believe that Miles couldn't feel it also, though she had ceased to be amazed by this. Miles had brought Jody into the office, where Katherine sat behind her plain desk. At her back, a large window looked south over the Hudson. Miles had added this window in the renovation, and the first time Katherine saw it, the resemblance to Miles Tobin's window in his long-ago office at JUSI was not lost on her. The view had its effect on Jody, taking the focus off Katherine and allowing her to watch him for a moment. He was thin, slight, intense; he wore a small beard. The waves of desire filled the air around him.

Katherine came out from behind the desk and took his hand. Johnny had combed out her hair today and let it hang loose beneath a white ribbon. She was wearing a long casual colorful dress—one of Ginger's, the last remaining. It was still Johnny's favorite. Miles had hinted that the colors were fading, but wouldn't suggest outright that a dress of Ginger's be tossed out. Jody looked obliquely at the dress, his eyes on Katherine's eyes.

Miles excused himself. He had some traveling to do—first, down to the city; then south on a three-state tour to get Katherine's word out. He had just completed two consecutive weeks of sleeping in the house. This was a rarity for Miles, who often was absent for days, or even weeks, on end. When he returned, his room, on the third floor, smelled of dust and disuse; Emily, in her plodding routine, in her days of bed rest and malaise, had chosen his room to neglect.

"Do you mind if I touch you?" Katherine asked. She and Jody sat on the curving divan, coffee in front of them that Candice had brought. She felt him flinch slightly from her before he gave permission.

She put her hand on his forehead and felt terrible confusion there, a clashing of waves. He shut his eyes, perhaps expecting her to do something; the waves roiled and beat at the Nine Portals, but she closed herself off; enough, today, just to touch him. She was almost sure she would give her assent to his project.

She asked him: "Where will you stay?"

"I can rent a room in town. I've looked at a few. It's only a few miles—I have a bike. A motorcycle, that is." He spoke quickly; he was breathless

"What will you do when you're not here with us? It seems lonely." She thought of the long nights on Proud Hill Road, before the cats were sent to keep her company, before she met Johnny.

"I can ride and hike around here," he said. "Maybe take the train down to New York sometimes, see some museums. I have a lot of reading I need to do."

She poured coffee, handed him a cup. He looked at her hands, then back into her eyes, keeping his eyes on hers. Miles had talked to Jody's thesis advisor, Hardy Brekstrup, a longtime pillar at Duke, famous for his studies of the Psychology of Religion. According to this Brekstrup, Jody had a brilliant mind and was destined for great things. Brekstrup himself was fair minded, Miles said, not hostile to revealed religion or even toward phenomena that bordered on the miraculous or supernatural.

They sipped their coffee as thunderclouds boiled up from the south and the room grew darker. Far down the river, lightning flickered without sound. The water turned muddy, then slate gray. Katherine usually stayed away from the river—the steep banks unnerved her. But the sound of the rushing water made her think of Ginger, and she would get as close as she dared. Johnny was usually with her; he held onto her and kept her safe. In a dream, she had seen Ginger drowning, although she had actually died choking on her own vomit, a kind of drowning, but on land, asleep on the couch in the living room on Proud Hill Road. The water beckoned to Katherine; she felt as if the dream might be a portent for her own future.

For a few minutes they watched the river silently—Jody seemed comfortable with that. Katherine tried to find the brilliance in him, something hard and bright as diamonds or steel. She could feel the rhythm of his breath. He sat up straight against the meandering lines of the divan, looking taller than he had while standing. Perhaps there was a bar of steel anchoring his ascetic frame.

Breaking the silence, she asked him: "What do you hope to find here?" They hadn't addressed each other by name. He had called her "ma'am" once or twice. How old could he be? Twenty-five or six? Not so far short of her own age, but of course she was older; older than Miles, than Johnny, older even than ageless Che—as old as the stars. "You can call me Katherine," she said, "or some call me 'Sister.'"

He still wouldn't use any name. "I want to learn your theology, observe your practices, the laying on of hands, how you speak to God. I want to observe the healing."

"And for yourself?" she asked. "You don't want anything for yourself?"

Even in the dim light, she could see him redden. "No," he told her. "Nothing for myself."

Summer had been seeing the boy called Juro on and off for more than a decade. Of course, he wasn't a boy anymore, nor Summer a girl; she was a woman who'd had his baby. She had gotten pregnant in the city, where she went periodically to meet Juro, sometimes to stay with him, when they weren't estranged. Even before the pregnancy, Johnny and Emily had wanted to kick her out. But Katherine had prayed with Johnny one night, a long time on their knees on the hill out under the stars, and Johnny heard God saying that Summer had a place in His plan.

And not only that. Now that she was going to stay put for a while with the baby, she could also be of direct use in Katherine's ministry. At the moment, they were near drowning in the flood of requests that came in, day after day, pleading for Katherine's intercession; in the past week alone there were more than six hundred letters, and in some weeks the traffic had been even greater. Someone had to read all these letters, remove whatever money might be enclosed (sometimes nothing; often, two or three singles or a five- or ten-dollar bill; sometimes, as much as a few twenties; rarely, a check for a much larger amount) and then write three relevant sentences on the postcards that Katherine sent in reply. First sentence—thanking the writer for putting her trust in Katherine, and for the contribution if there was one; second sentence—to the effect that Katherine was working on the problem; third sentence—please remember Katherine in your own prayers.

Of course, there was no question of Katherine reading all these letters; she was already at the limit of her strength. Instead, she chose a few—touching dozens of envelopes before her sensitive fingers would finally select one, taking the ones she had selected out with her under the stars or putting them beneath her pillow while she slept—representative tokens of all the misery in the world and of the small but steady light that she could bring against it. At first, Candice had written the replies; but when they began to take too much of her time, Miles had suggested that Summer help out. She had a nice handwriting and was certainly intelligent enough to compose the substantive middle sentence on the postcards. Miles, himself, would randomly monitor her work to make sure it was all right.

The new moon appeared in the western sky and began to wax, day by day. On the night it turned full, Katherine began to menstruate. She was shocked and told no one. Her periods had terminated abruptly, years ago, at about the time her "gift" had matured. Now, just as suddenly, they had returned. Bathed in moonlight, she asked God what was meant by this—but no answer came. She entered Summer's room when the girl was away, and took one of her pads. The next night the flow stopped. The moon was lumpen, misshapen, roiling in the hazy sky. Katherine breathed quietly.

But the next month, her period returned. After the first day, it didn't disappear as she expected, but instead grew stronger. This time, it was a little later; the moon was already waning. Outside, the air had grown cooler; fall was coming. Johnny was prowling the grounds, as he often did when she was out at night. The moonlight reflected from his cheekbones, highlighting them while the rest of his face sunk into the darkness. Suddenly, she saw him in a coffin, a collection of waxy bones.

"What's wrong, Katherine?"

She told him about her menstruation.

Johnny thought for a moment. "Maybe it's because of Summer," he said. "You should send her away—I told you."

"Where would she go?"

Johnny shrugged. "The baby has a father."

"No," she said. "I feel that God wants something of me."

"What could He want, more than you're already doing?"

When the answer came, it was so simple she was amazed she could have missed it. God had made her fertile again. He wanted her to have a child.

She didn't tell Johnny what she was thinking.

Jody rented a room in town, in the house of an older couple. Katherine sent Johnny down to the Greyhound station in Beacon to pick up his trunk and help him move in. Johnny was grudgingly reconciled to his presence. With Katherine's acquiescence, he read Jody a set of rules: Above the ground floor were private living quarters—stay out! Katherine's permission was necessary to enter her office. Permission from Katherine or Miles was also needed to look at any papers or files. If Katherine was tired, Johnny would tell him to leave her alone.

Apart from these rules, Jody was free to wander the house and grounds as he chose. He came around most days, usually arriving late in the morning and leaving before dinner. But sometimes he would remain through the meal and, then, late into the night. One morning, Johnny found him asleep on the floor of the living room; shaking him roughly, he got him to his feet and marched him to the door. After that, Jody never slept in the house or stayed beyond dawn. When the hour was very late, he would walk his motorcycle down the road a little before starting it; even so, you could hear the bark of the engine all through the house.

Johnny had emptied out a small room near Candice's office and put a desk and cabinet in for Jody to use. If Katherine slept into the afternoon, he would sit at the desk and transcribe his notes or look through the scrapbook that Miles had compiled of Katherine's history, or, sometimes, talk with one of the others—Candice, Emily, even Johnny. Otherwise, whenever Katherine was willing, he would simply follow her around.

Some days it seemed to him there was nothing extraordinary about her. He sat with her in the kitchen drinking coffee and she would seem like a housewife, like his own mother; she talked about a shopping list she was drawing up for Johnny, about Summer's baby, about the dripping faucet in the bathroom. She received a note from Rosemary Mallory, showing him the photographs that were enclosed. One of the twins was already married, the other an airline hostess; little Robert, the baby, was in high school.

But there were also times when he'd sit on the divan and watch her at her desk. She had grown used to him; his presence no longer disturbed her. Eyes closed, her fingers on one of the letters she had chosen—one of the people in terrible trouble (how terrible, he knew, since she shared the letters: the women with cancer, with mortally-ill children, the cripples, the fearful, the abandoned)—Katherine would sit straight-backed, motionless, barely breathing. He felt sure she was in a trance of some sort, a high state of meditation or prayer; he had seen such states before, interviewed practitioners, read much of the vast literature. It would be difficult, impossible really, to fake such a state time after time; and, after all, why would you?—how much easier to simply bar outsiders from your headquarters and do what you did in private?

And there were other letters Katherine showed him, testimonies for miraculous cures, medically impossible, people restored from the edge of death. And there was one case he had seen in person—a man who visited Katherine the first week Jody had been with her. He had arrived in a wheelchair, rolled out and lowered from the back of a van. There were tubes in his arm and side, a nurse with him. His complexion was sallow, and he spoke weakly, as if he had lost interest. That night, Katherine had taken him out under the stars. Jody had not been allowed to accompany them, but the next day, when he saw the man, something seemed to have changed. His appearance was the same, his voice barely audible, but Jody could no longer sense the same resignation in him. A month later, he returned in a chauffeured limousine, walking now with the aid of a cane, and, despite his frailty, speaking with an authority that seemed natural to him. He handed Katherine a check. What the amount was, she would not say—Miles Tobin had forbidden all talk of money.

Yes, there was Tobin. Katherine had been vague about him, but Jody had taken the information he had and gone to the library with it. He found newspaper articles chronicling Tobin's whirlwind academic career—his Doctorate at age twenty-five, after he had made up a full slate of undergraduate physics courses; his appointment at MIT; then, his jump to Washington and rise through the NASA bureaucracy. When JUSI was created, he was made Director, and there was speculation he was being groomed to ultimately take over as NASA Administrator. Then, the scandals broke—charges of misappropriation of funds; and further rumors, not quite charges, of kickbacks from NASA contractors. The Justice Department began to build a criminal case, but dropped it when Tobin resigned. After that, his name disappeared from the newspapers for a decade before emerging again, associated with Katherine. Jody supposed there was more information to be had, if he were willing to spend the effort. But this was about her, not him. And what would it matter if Tobin turned out to be even more unsavory than the written history indicated, provided that Katherine was real?

She was wearing a simple dress, white, high cut to cover her shoulders but expose her collarbones, emphasize her delicate neck, Adam's apple prominent, her chin a bit pointed, mouth larger than you'd expect, slender nose but the nostrils large, minutely fluttering with her breath. She opened her eyes, looked around; she picked Jody out, but stared at him as if she were seeing him for the first time, watching him with her cat's eyes that changed color, right now dark green, almost black; then, finally, as if she had at long last realized who he was, a smile.

"What are you thinking?" she asked him.

He shook his head.

"Let me touch you."

She stumbled a little getting up, and Jody went to her and steadied her. They sat together on the divan. In the altered light, her pupils looked larger and lighter in color. Her hair, pinned at her forehead, more reddish today, hung loosely down her back. She circled his wrist with her cool fingers, felt his blood respond to her. There was nothing malicious in him, only his need, neither evil nor good. Johnny had not stopped being suspicious of him. Johnny kept whispering in her ear to watch out. She felt that Johnny's nerves were frayed. The baby cried at night, and Summer walked him up and down the hallway. She was soft, blowsy, her milk-filled breasts rolling softly as she moved, as if caught in the swells of some mild sea. When she passed, Johnny would stare at her with a hard look, almost like hatred. He had been happier in the city, Katherine thought, in the hard stone of Proud Hill Road, the ants' nest of apartments, the stopped-up sinks, leaky toilets, radiators that never got hot; and the tenants who sought his services, women alone in the daytime, anonymous women, each behind an apartment door that looked like all the other doors.

"What will you do," she asked Jody, "when you finish here?"

"Write my dissertation," he said. "Maybe a book after that."

"About me?"

"I think you would have a prominent part in it," he told her.

She was still holding his wrist, circling it loosely. "What was it like in the seminary?" she asked.

"You know about that?"

Miles had told her. Brekstrup had showed him Jody's records; it was only fair, given that Jody had been asking to be admitted into their household.

He pulled his hand away. She could feel his vulnerability. She was his sister, she felt. She would pray for him to get what he wanted.

"I had no vocation," he said. "It took some time for me to realize it."

She told him about Father Rivera, how he had expelled her from St. Cecilia's; the hard face of religion, Father Rivera's face. The dome of St. Cecilia's exuded shimmering light, but the priest's face had been dark, as his robes were dark, and his living quarters underground where he was safe from sunlight.

"You never attend church anymore?" Jody asked. He had never seen Katherine anywhere but in the house or out on the grounds. He had come on weekdays and Sundays, daylight and dark, and Katherine had always been present.

"God is everywhere," she said. "God is here."

Since Miles had found the house and they'd moved from the city, she had never been away—not to any church, not to the IGA just two miles distant, certainly not back to the Bronx. Her strength was here, she told him; the stars were right, rising over the river. She had no need or desire to go elsewhere.

"Are you afraid?" As soon as it was out, he regretted it. He had no right to ask her that. It was too personal, cutting to the bone.

But Katherine only smiled. Amigo had come into the room, wandering through the open door, jumping into her lap. "I was very fearful once," she said, "but it was ages ago." She scratched the cat under his chin. "*He* was only a kitten."

Jody nodded, looking at her face, always her face. "Me too," he told her. He had also been afraid.

He interviewed Miles Tobin. It was a duel of minds. Though he was much younger and clearly less experienced in the world, he felt at no disadvantage. If he could hold his own with Hardy Brekstrup, Hardy treating him as an equal, then he could approach Tobin with confidence.

Miles was just back from one of his trips. His office was a mess, not a place meant for conversation, anyway. Jody suggested the coffee shop in the village. It was the place he went to sit and think, organize his notes; one of the three points of his existence, along with the room he lived in, a few blocks away, and, of course, the house.

Jody was formal at first, but Miles soon put him on a first name basis. In their other interview, at the beginning, when Tobin was asking the questions, they *had* been formal. But, given the hothouse atmosphere of Katherine's realm, with Summer feeding the baby, and the cats strutting around, and Johnny appearing suddenly where you didn't expect him, it seemed silly for them to maintain a formal distance.

Jody had made up his mind beforehand not to bring up Tobin's former problems; he was a scholar, not an investigative reporter, after all, and Tobin was really peripheral to his research. However, he did ask about Tobin's scientific career. He was a nuclear physicist and had published thirty papers before his involvement in Washington had curtailed his research. Jody asked how he, as a scientist, could believe in Katherine's miracle cures?

Miles was wearing jeans and a plaid shirt, looking rustic. His hands were on the table, one cradling his coffee cup, the other arched slightly, tapping with all five fingers. He had on two rings, both squarish and heavy; Jody looked, without thinking, for a wedding ring, but, of course, there was none—how could there be, considering the way Tobin lived his life, his unswerving devotion to Katherine?

"I don't believe in miracles," he said. "Nature is governed by laws amenable to scientific investigation. One day we'll understand how all this works."

"Then, you don't think God exists?"

Miles smiled. "I didn't say that. Wasn't it God who made the natural order? Isn't He present in it?"

"A good answer," Jody told him. He asked: "Is there a placebo effect in these cures?"

Miles raised his glasses, looked at Jody beneath them. "No doubt. Your Professor Brekstrup once proposed to me a double blind experiment, in which Katherine would pray for one group of ill people, but not for those in a control group, neither group knowing anything about her."

"You didn't agree to it?"

"Katherine has nothing to prove," Miles said. "She's not a magician or a carnival act. Sometimes she succeeds and sometimes fails. She has no rational understanding of what she does and neither do I. If someone were to suggest an experiment that could shed light on that question, I would be sympathetic to it. Though, of course, Katherine would have to agree."

Jody wrote on his yellow pad, head down, intent. He had already filled a whole page, not just with what Tobin told him, but also his own thoughts, ideas for further questions, links to the existing literature.

"Drink your coffee," Miles said. "It'll get cold."

He took a sip. It *was* cold. Around them rose a mild buzz of conversation, three or four tables occupied, all the customers women at this hour. He saw two of them looking over toward their booth, watching for a moment before turning away. They couldn't know who he was—it must be Tobin they had stared at. He was known in the village, of course; he handled any community relations problems that Katherine might have, gave money to local causes in her name, kept things smooth. Katherine, herself, never appeared; very few people in the village had ever seen her.

He asked Miles: "How would you compare her to other faith healers? Put her in context for me."

"I think Katherine is unique, comparable only, perhaps, to Jesus—I don't intend any irreverence or disrespect by that. What I mean is the following: all the others you can think of, the names that come to mind, were connected in some way with a religious creed, usually Christianity, either well established, Roman Catholicism, for example, or newer but still formalized, like Christian Science; or some creed that was individual and idiosyncratic, but also formalized in its way, a cult. Katherine never proselytizes, has no religion to promote, no advice to give; she prays for people—period. I suppose even the comparison to Jesus breaks down there. I meant it in the sense that he preceded Christianity and had no formal system to advocate—but, of course, he did preach and he willingly collected followers."

"Then," Jody said, "is Katherine's isolation integral to her mission. It's very striking to an outsider that she never leaves the grounds—almost as if she were in prison."

"Is that your metaphor for Katherine?" Miles said, contemptuously. "A prisoner?"

"All right, point taken. What would be a better way to put it?"

"I don't know," Miles said. "I suppose you might call the house and grounds a monastery of sorts."

They sat facing each other, both with hands under their chins, almost as if there were a chess board on the table between them. Jody broke away, leaned back, smoothed his hair back with his fingers. "But there are no other monks. Everyone else in the house is more or less part of the outside world. And Katherine, though her life is simple, certainly doesn't live in poverty. Nor in true isolation, either; there's a television set in one of the offices—does she ever watch it?"

"On occasion," Miles told him. "Have you talked to *her* about it?"

Jody hesitated, waited a beat. "I got the impression that she feels safe on the grounds, that, in a way, she's afraid to leave."

"You're mistaken. She's never afraid."

"I know," Jody said. "But in the past?"

Now Miles paused. "She said something to you about that?"

Jody felt he might have gone too far. "Not really."

"I've never known Katherine to be afraid," Miles told him, closing the subject.

November came. The Pleiades appeared at sunset in the eastern sky, crossing the meridian at midnight. Katherine menstruated again, the fourth month in a row. Johnny had brought her some boxes of pads from the village. She put them in the back of her closet and swore him to secrecy. The question of what God wanted for her stayed with her more and more. Her original idea, that He wished her to have a child, had struck with the force of revelation; but, as time passed, this force weakened and the thought crept in that she might have been mistaken. She took Summer's baby in her arms and he yearned toward her, as if she had given him birth. Summer was growing slim again. She fit into her tight jeans, and her breasts made modest bulges in her sweater. The baby had been put on formula and solid food.

Katherine dreamed that Belle gave birth. There were three in the litter—Hombre, Star, and a new kitten, a female, white as cotton. She came to Katherine, climbing up to her breast, mewling contentedly.

Still, she wasn't sure. One night, impulsively, she brought it to Johnny. "I'm coming to understand God's plan for me."

They were outdoors under the stars. Jody had just left, the sound of his cycle fading into the distance. The Sisters climbed over the river, shining like seven diamonds. Johnny had brought her out a sweater, thrown it over her shoulders. "What?" he asked.

"He wants me to have a child. Why else would He make me fertile?"

Johnny jammed his hands into the pockets of his overalls. He suddenly looked stooped to her, his shoulders bent. When he failed to shave for a day or two, his whiskers grew in gray. Hadn't she noticed before, that he was getting old?

He thought for a long time. "A virgin birth, like Jesus; or will there be a father?"

"I don't know." She had never considered this.

He nodded, reaching over to touch her forehead. For a moment, she thought it was the pattern of anointment—forehead, neck, breasts—that he hadn't performed for years, ever since Miles had brought them here. But his arm fell, listlessly. "You are a pure woman," he said. "Don't soil yourself."

A woman arrived for Katherine to pray over. She had first sent a letter; Jody had seen it, a plain envelope also containing a ten-dollar bill. Katherine had chosen her. When she came, she had documentation of her illness—an autoimmune disease, with terrible effects on the body. The doctor at a free clinic had treated her with steroids, which ameliorated her condition, but also had their side effects, swelling her face and limbs, attacking her kidneys. Katherine took her out under the Pleiades—early, as soon as it got dark.

This time, Jody was allowed to come with them. He had wanted to watch Katherine during one of these sessions; he had asked her a number of times, and she had always said talk to Miles. Invariably, he had found Miles reluctant about this, even dismissive. But now, he had agreed; subject to conditions, of course, as usual. Jody was to make himself so unobtrusive as to be all but invisible He was not to take notes or carry a recorder; he'd need to write everything up afterward, from memory. The woman, interviewed by Miles, was told that Jody was doing scholarly research on healing. She quickly gave permission for him to be present. Miles promised her anonymity, but she said it didn't matter to her; they could use her name if they wanted—all she cared about was Katherine's prayers.

The woman, called Elizabeth, was heavy set, with dark hair spread thinly across the top of her head. In the pale light of the stars and a sliver of moon, her face was puffed out, but not extravagantly so; she seemed almost rosy—illness and health not so easily distinguishable from the outside. She was bundled up in a coat and scarf, while Katherine wore one of her sleeveless dresses with a turtleneck underneath it. The two women kneeled on the grass, facing one another, with Katherine's hand on Elizabeth's forehead. A few feet away, Jody was also kneeling, aiming for invisibility. But Elizabeth's eyes were closed, and Katherine was gazing at the Seven Sisters with such rapt attention that he needn't have bothered at all to conceal himself.

He, also, looked at the sky. Above him the Great Square of Pegasus established itself. He got a glimpse of Orion, headless, on the eastern horizon; shifting his eyes, he found the Pleiades, which seemed to recede as he watched, into infinite black space—then, suddenly, a flash; he could swear the stars had flashed, some optical illusion, certainly, but he heard Katherine groan, then whisper under her breath, turning away to sit breathless in the grass, while Elizabeth opened her eyes and looked wildly around, as if she had just wakened in a strange room.

The next morning, Elizabeth left early, telling Miles she was anxious to get home; she had two children and a husband waiting for her. Jody was able to speak with her only briefly. He noticed no improvement in her appearance; perhaps she even looked a little worse in the daylight. But she told him that Katherine had cured her; her body felt only a little better than it had last night, but in her mind she knew that she was whole now, and that the healing of her body would follow.

Sure enough, not three weeks later, in the doldrums before Christmas, a time of sleet and gray clouds, another letter arrived. It was not one of those Katherine chose, but Miles had opened and read it; after he had shown it to her, she sat for a long time, transfixed, her head bowed, murmuring through slightly moving lips. Later, Jody saw the letter. Elizabeth had written that the pain in her joints was gone; she was sleeping full nights, six or seven hours, and waking refreshed. The doctor said that both her heart and kidney function had improved; indeed, she had enclosed a copy of the report her doctor had written—he had been skeptical before, but now he had added a couple of handwritten sentences: "There are many things we still do not understand. We can only be grateful."

There was a change in things. Emily noticed it—it had dawned on her slowly but surely over weeks of observation. It expressed itself in Katherine's face, which seemed softer and more pale; in her languid movements, as if the air in the house had grown heavy. She saw it in the men of the household—Johnny and Miles and that boy, Jody—the looks they gave Katherine, the way they had begun to position themselves close to her, sliding in toward her half a step, leaning inward, nothing obvious, a matter of inches; it could be they weren't even conscious of it.

It could be Summer's doing—Summer, with her blowsy good looks, her low necklines, feeding the baby haphazardly in front of any of them; her body soft and plump, then thinner and harder; she, flaunting it provocatively in skin-tight clothes. At times, Emily had wanted to slap the face of this daughter of hers, to beat her black and blue; but how could she allow herself to disturb the peace of Katherine's presence? And it was true that neither Miles nor Johnny seemed to give Summer a second look—at least, *that* sort of look. Only the boy had looked; Emily had seen him a few times, glancing over out of the corner of his eye when he thought no one was watching.

Something else was strange. Johnny had told Emily not to bother cleaning Katherine's room anymore—he was going to take over the job. Why? she asked. For her, the cleaning was a labor of love, one of the few things she could do to serve Katherine, to pay back the enormous debt she owned. Johnny had said merely that it was Katherine's wish. When she tried to question him further, he had turned his back and walked away.

She went to Katherine, one day when the house was empty for an hour, only she and the baby around. She had hoped to find her in her office, but instead Katherine had gone to the Sanctum, that tiny place that Miles had had constructed for her at the very center of the house, with its door on the east and its total darkness, broken only by the pale, indirect lighting that rimmed the room, just below the ceiling.

Katherine was not to be disturbed there, she knew that; but she felt that this was an emergency—she might not have the chance again. It was becoming more and more rare for Johnny to leave; he spent his time prowling around, coming up on you silently. He had always been secretive and silent, the inside of his head a mystery; but now there was a look about him, with his thin hair the color of moldy bread, cheeks parched, his shirtsleeves rolled up above the elbows, thin arms bulging with veins. If the Devil had an earthly appearance—Johnny looked like *him*.

She pushed open the Sanctum's door. She knew she ought to have knocked, but what if Katherine had told her to go away without even having looked at her? The room was dark; there was only the light she had let in, and the palest possible light from the ceiling. Katherine was kneeling before the thick drape that Miles Tobin had found and brought back from what used to be Persia, he said, darkest black like the night, embroidered with seven greater stars and multiple lesser stars, the greater ones fringed with soft blue nebulosities that identified them as the Sisters.

Emily said nothing, but got down on her knees next to Katherine, who seemed not to have noticed her. Her lips moved soundlessly with the Lord's Prayer. Katherine was the new Jesus; no, that was wrong—better to say that Jesus' hand had touched her. She had cured Emily's cancer, and Emily knew she was keeping her alive, even today. She felt a tear come from her eye, then another, a trickle of silent weeping running down her cheek.

Suddenly, Katherine started, looked around her.

"I'm afraid for you," Emily said.

Katherine took a breath, steadying herself. She reached out and touched Emily's neck with her fingertips. After a few seconds, Emily felt her own breathing calm.

"What is it?" Katherine asked.

"The way they look at you—it scares me. Like three hungry dogs."

Katherine was tranquil, not upset at all. Could she be smiling?

"It's because I've become fertile."

So that was it! Now, Emily understood everything. A woman become fertile sent off a message as unmistakable as any female animal in *her* time. You could see it in pubescent girls; not so much in the way they looked, but in the way men looked at *them* —a glance one day, passing without interest; then, the next day, that look of the animal, eyes narrowed, lips pressed together, as if they had discovered prey. It was just how God had made things, so that humans, too, could be fruitful and multiply, and spread over the Earth.

"It's God's will," Emily said.

Katherine took her hand, squeezed it hard. "Thank you."

They sat back against one of the Sanctum's walls, opposite the dark drape. Emily couldn't believe it—Katherine had leaned back against her, let herself be taken into Emily's arms.

"God wants me to have a child," Katherine said. "I wasn't sure— but last night my mother came in a dream and told me."

Emily understood. Of course, she did. "Who will the father be?" Her body stiffened. "Not Johnny."

It wasn't jealousy—she had no care for any man. It was just that Johnny would be wrong. Johnny would be a defilement.

"I don't know," Katherine told her. I've asked God, but He hasn't answered."

Emily hugged Katherine tightly, rocking her gently forward and back. "Not Johnny," she repeated. "Anyone but him."

In the little office they'd given him, Jody typed up his notes. Three months—more!—were already gone, less than half his tenure with Katherine remaining. He had asked Hardy for more time, but his advisor had flat out refused. "We don't want you becoming part of that operation," he'd said.

But Jody felt he needed more data, more evidence. Apart from Katherine herself, what had impressed him most were the living cases he had seen. Much more than the letters, which had no faces. He decided to try to follow these cases up. There had been fourteen all together—most impressive of them, the man in the wheelchair and, more recently, Elizabeth.

He put in a call to the Free Clinic in Youngstown, Ohio, where Elizabeth had been treated. Her doctor's name, the man whose report with its handwritten comment hinted at a cure bordering on the miraculous, was Weinberger; Jody was anxious to talk to him. But the receptionist at the Clinic insisted that they had no Dr. Weinberger. She was a woman with curt speech, flat and unenthusiastic. "No Dr. Weinberger," she repeated. "Not now, not six months ago, not a year ago." Her tone said that he was keeping her from something more important.

He rechecked the letterhead on the report Weinberger had written. The telephone number was the one he had called. Trying Information in Youngstown, he verified the number again; when he asked if there might be another clinic in town with a similar name, the operator could find none.

The Winter Solstice came. This was the day Katherine had chosen to celebrate instead of Christmas, which was four days later. There was no slight to Jesus in this, she told Jody. Years ago she had learned from Miles that the commemoration of Jesus' birth had been merged with the age-old Solstice holiday—the true date when Jesus had been born was lost in history.

As the sun crossed the southernmost point on the Ecliptic, Katherine prayed in the Sanctum, while the others waited. Among them, only Emily fell to her knees—near the big fireplace with its comforting blaze, imploring Jesus to keep Katherine well. Johnny had put up lights, inside and out—the atmosphere was festive. When Katherine came out, she was cheerful, even more so than in previous years. She was wearing a dress of star-blue; in her hair, a tiara, which also glistened like the stars, flashing and sparkling in the light from the fire.

Miles had just returned from the latest of his trips. He still had his suit on, his blue shirt with the collar undone, his loosened tie. He greeted Katherine, lightly kissed her cheek; he was the only one who seemed to have this privilege; he went further back with her than anyone, even Johnny. She said: "You look tired."

He took his glasses off, rubbed his eyes. Katherine looked up at him. She was barefoot. "Do you have a headache?"

He waved the idea off. "It isn't bad."

She took his elbow, guided him to the sofa. "Sit," she said—a mock order.

His eyes closed as she touched his forehead. They had done this so many times it had become as routine as popping a couple of aspirins; except that aspirins didn't give you the spectacular feel of Katherine's hands on you, and aspirins didn't work nearly as fast.

When Miles seemed better, Katherine went over to the playpen to sit with the baby. He made a noise in greeting, smiled at her, pushed himself up to his knees. When she picked him up, he reached for the tiara, twisting it on her head, until she laughed and pulled his hand away, crushing him against her chest. Suddenly, there came back to her the feel of little Robert sucking hungrily at her breast; little Robert who was six feet now, Rosemary said. So long ago. She had forgotten over the years; it had escaped her, but now returned; in its new fertility, her body had remembered.

Miles and Jody were sitting together on the sofa. Jody had taken Katherine's seat as soon as she got up; he was anxious to talk to Miles. He had not been able to locate Dr. Weinberger, and had no address for Elizabeth either. Also, he wanted to interview the doctor of the other man whose cure he had personally witnessed, the man who had returned in a limousine; he knew his name, Joseph Kitchel, but not the name of the doctor. He wanted to interview these doctors, perhaps others, to find out if the illnesses Katherine cured had something in common. Were they, for example, illnesses which might be thought to have a psychosomatic origin, as perhaps an autoimmune disease might be thought of, or were some of them more on the physical side? He hadn't wanted to bother Katherine with these questions—according to the ground rules, Miles controlled the access to all documents; he was the right one to ask.

Miles seemed astounded when Jody told him that Dr. Weinberger could not be found. He had taken his jacket off, rolled up his sleeves. He had a broad chest, muscular in the arms and shoulders; there was a set of weights in the basement that he used. He shook his head. "There must be a misunderstanding. What reason could Elizabeth possibly have to conceal the name of her doctor, or, even more, to go to the trouble of fabricating a report?"

Conceal? *Fabricate*? He had not been thinking in those terms—only that, perhaps, some error had been made, confusing Elizabeth's case with another's; or, at most, that this Dr. Weinberger might have some desire to stay out of the public eye. But could it be that the publicity surrounding Katherine had induced someone like Elizabeth to fake an illness and the subsequent cure in order to direct the spotlight toward herself? If so, that, in itself, would be an interesting aspect of the whole story, something worthy to follow up.

He realized that Miles was looking at him, regarding him quietly but at length—measuring him, perhaps. He had always wondered about Miles' role in Katherine's life: promoter, manager, detail-man, acolyte—perhaps all of these. It was another interesting aspect of the story—must every Katherine have her Miles?

But this particular Miles had a history—that rather shady past that Jody had decided not to go into with him. He was not one to think the worst of people, but there was, of course, another explanation for the insubstantiality of Dr. Weinberger—namely, that he was a fiction, an invention used to establish Elizabeth's illness and thus her subsequent "cure." Jody could not bring himself to believe that Katherine was a liar, but Miles was a different story. Could it be that he had manufactured the "cures" without Katherine's knowledge? Or, perhaps, that he had merely embellished the evidence of her powers to remove any doubts that Jody might have had? And, in that case, had he done the same with others?

Miles was still watching him, peering through his square glasses, intent, concentrated. For a moment, the strange idea occurred to Jody that Miles was reading his mind.

They had all gone to bed. Jody was the last, walking his cycle up the road, then blasting away, louder than usual, as if there were some urgency for him to leave. Katherine took Miles into her office, sat him on the divan, standing behind him, her fingers circling his forehead. She whispered in his ear. "Miles, I'm fertile. I've started to menstruate."

He leaned back, submitting to her hands, which moved across his forehead and into his scalp. "How long?"

"Four months now."

He took a slow breath, let it out. "Why didn't you tell me?"

"I don't know," she said. "It seemed much more momentous to tell *you*."

"Others know, then? Johnny?"

"And Emily."

"I see."

"Miles," she whispered. "Don't be angry."

He raised his arms to his head, covered her hands with his. "I've never been angry with you."

She asked him: "What should I do?"

She sat next to him, and he put his arm around her, as he had in the old days, when she had been frightened and tentative, before God's strength had filled her.

"You once told me your greatest sadness was that you had been made barren. But remember, Katherine, what a great gift you got in return."

She squeezed his hand. "Miles," she said. "I want to have a child now. God has given me the chance."

"You are a public person," he told her. "Your life is not your own. People will want to know who the father is."

"Maybe God will make me pregnant without a father—if it's His will. Johnny told me it could happen."

"Johnny!"

Miles said his name, vehemently, dismissively; as if Johnny were just the super, the handyman, and knew nothing beyond his realm of the furnace, the plumbing, the grounds. But hadn't he been Katherine's first spiritual advisor, hadn't he comforted and encouraged her; hadn't he anointed her body, and witnessed the miracles she'd performed?

"Katherine, what would you do with a child?"

"A little girl," she said. "I know. I'm sure that Ginger will be in her." She had a picture of the child in her mind—a girl with dusky blonde curls, thin and quiet, the way Ginger had been when she was small. There were photographs of her, but what had happened to them? Had they disappeared when Katherine's father went to Florida with his new woman? "I don't want Ginger to be gone from Earth when I die. I want there to be something left of her. And the powers God gave me?—*she* will have them."

She. The new baby, who would appear spontaneously in Katherine's womb, God's work; or, would be deposited inside her by a man, the chosen man.

Miles shifted position on the divan and took her hands in his, looking at her, his brown eyes large and steady behind his glasses while her eyes flashed and changed, green to black to gray, a trick of the room's light, perhaps, a flicker of electric power. Whatever it was, Miles never ceased to marvel at Katherine's eyes. She was waiting for his answer, staring back at him.

"All right," he finally said.

Who had put the idea in her head that it should be Jody? She wasn't sure how the thought had come. Could it have been Miles? She couldn't remember, but even if so, the true source had surely been God; speaking through Miles, using him for His purposes, as He had used Katherine and all of them.

Certainly it was Miles who had suggested that Jody be given a room to sleep in. The weather had turned beastly—rain, which froze as soon as it hit the ground, days and nights of it. The road was dangerous; Jody had skidded once, ending up in a field—no harm done, but the next time it could be much worse. Johnny had objected, of course; he thought that he and Miles had been in agreement that Jody should not stay the night. But Miles had been firm, hinting even at the possibility of lawsuits if Jody were injured. In the end it was up to Katherine; Miles and Johnny could advise, but the final decisions were hers. One night, Ginger came in a dream, weeping for Jody, tears of compassion. He got his room.

There was plenty of space. Apart from Miles' room, the third floor was used mainly for storage. There was a bathroom along the hall that Miles used and Jody could share. There was a bed among the stored furniture that Johnny carried into a room he had emptied next door to Miles. Jody's window looked out onto the gray Hudson. Above him, he could hear the freezing rain tinkling into the gutters. Below, sound traveled up the heat pipe from Katherine's room. At night he could hear her sneezing, four or five times in a row, an allergy that she seemed to develop late each winter, lasting into the spring.

Miles seemed ready to forget the disappearing Dr. Weinberger, but when Jody pressed him he was forced to admit that he'd had no luck in finding him. However, he did put Jody into contact with Elizabeth again. She sounded bright and chipper on the phone, a striking change from the phlegmatic woman that Katherine had prayed with under the stars. She told Jody that she was well, that she hardly even thought of her illness anymore. When he asked about Weinberger, she said that he had left Youngstown, for where she didn't know—he had always been a strange bird, this Weinberger.

Miles also gave him the number of the doctor of Joe Kitchel, the other major cure Jody had witnessed. This doctor was accessible—he called Jody back the same day. He had permission from Kitchel to discuss the case. His illness had been colon cancer.

"Are you sure?" Jody asked.

"There was a positive diagnosis, plus a reevaluation following a round of chemotherapy."

"Do you believe in miracles?"

"I believe in God," the doctor said.

Jody had a telephone conversation with Hardy Brekstrup, who thought that the amount of material on Katherine was sufficient to use her as the center of the dissertation. There were the two instances that Jody himself had witnessed, his conversations with the principals, including Elizabeth, Kitchel (who had agreed to an interview) and Kitchel's physician; there were the written testimonials, hundreds of them, that Katherine had received over the years; there were Jody's interviews with Katherine, Miles, Johnny and Emily, Candice—plenty of material.

But Jody wasn't sure. There were things that still bothered him: the case of Dr. Weinberger; the voice of Elizabeth on the telephone, sounding almost like another woman; Miles, everything about Miles.

"All right," Brekstrup said. "Let's start at the other end. Have you found any evidence of fraud?"

"No," Jody admitted. "Nothing tangible."

"Do you have any reason to believe that some of the letters have been faked?"

"No. I believe that Katherine is legitimate—let me make that clear."

"Well, then …"

"I know," Jody said. "I'm not making a lot of sense."

Brekstrup was silent for a moment. "What do you propose to do?"

"I'm not sure. Gather more information, keep my eyes open. If I could stay a few extra months …"

"I don't think that would be a good idea," Brekstrup interrupted. "We have already discussed it, I believe."

That was that. He had less than a month left.

February came. It was not the month Katherine would have chosen. Arcturus rose rapidly to dominate the sky, while the Sisters sank. But the birth would come in November when the Pleiades rode the sky throughout the night, while the Red Star would rise only near dawn, snuffed out by the sun. And, even in February, there were propitious hours, early in the evening, the Sisters in the west and the Red Star still below the trees. But there was something else. Katherine wanted her daughter conceived under Ginger's brilliant eye, a sharp, clear night when the stars glittered like jewels. Ordinarily, there were many February nights like this, but winter this year had been warm and rainy, the sky full of clouds. Also, there was Johnny, prowling around as if he suspected something. She never should have told him she was fertile; it was just that it had taken her so much by surprise, and there was a reflex in her to rely on Johnny, something from long ago.

The month waned. Letters poured in—there was so much woe in the world. Candice was overwhelmed, even with Summer's help; Miles had to cancel a trip, staying home to lend a hand. He told Katherine that they had to hire someone else, at least one more. The crazy idea came to her that the front door would swing open one day and Beth would walk through—Arcturus glowering in the sky, pouring down red rays. But Miles chose a woman in the village, who had suffered with sleep complaints, whom Katherine had helped. He impressed upon her that loyalty was primary, offered her high wages. She accepted.

Jody watched. The letters came in and the replies flowed out with equal frequency. At one time, Katherine had handwritten the replies; then Candice had taken over; then, Candice and Emily—the short notes still done by hand. But now, Miles had constructed form letters, three different ones; in each case, one would be chosen, signed with Katherine's signature stamp, and personalized by a line or two, handwritten by one of the women. The new letters were also remarkable in that they solicited further contributions, something that had never been done before.

When Jody asked Katherine about this, she was short with him. Her tone was thin, bordering on sarcasm. But, then, immediately, she apologized, moving closer to him, her hand on his arm. Later, he sat in his room, looking out at the river. Perhaps he had deserved Katherine's rebuke. Of course, there had to be money coming in—to pay the salaries, run the house, for fuel, postage, food. Even Buddhist monks, who begged with food bowls, built their monasteries with donations from the rich. Miles had told him that Katherine had received a number of bequests over the years; these had kept them going, but would not do so indefinitely, especially if Katherine's work were to be expanded. Again, Jody had no doubt that she was sincere, that her presence was calming, that a certain power flowed from her. But ... the cures? There was, of course, the placebo effect—people getting better because they believed in Katherine's intervention, or merely because they knew someone cared—and, there was Miles' promotion and, possibly, manipulation. What did it all add up to?

Certainly, he had enough to finish his dissertation now. Moreover, Brekstrup had told him that the material might further be reworked into a book. After that, an academic career was possible, even likely, if he wanted it. Brekstrup had accepted relatively few students over the years; there was no heir apparent, unless it was Jody. This had been his idea all along, hadn't it? Why did it now leave him cold, empty?

Below him, on the lawn, Johnny was skulking around, wearing a waterproofed windbreaker and a stocking cap against the cold, thin drizzle that had fallen endlessly this winter. He patrolled like a soldier on sentry, Katherine's bodyguard—protecting her against what? She had no enemies, so far as Jody could see. The locals did not dislike her; they spoke of her with a sort of bemused tolerance, despite the strangeness of her never leaving the grounds; she had even helped a few with minor ailments, building up a small reservoir of good will.

He supposed that Katherine was a woman who brought forth protective instincts. To him, she seemed a paradoxical mixture of strength and vulnerability. Her strength came from faith, she told him, her feeling of God's presence in the stars and in everyday things, the sense of her mother watching over her. The vulnerability was more subtle—something in the narrow structure of her bones, translucent eyebrows, her skin that sometimes seemed thin as paper. And, once in a while, he had seen a look on her face, fleeting, a flicker in her luminous eyes; something that, before it disappeared, seemed to him almost like fear.

Getting up, he stared at himself in the mirror above his dresser. He was in love with her, wasn't he?—a stupid sort of puppy love that he was too old for, almost thirty, he ought to know better. Some nights, he had lain in bed thinking of her, one part of his mind trying to create a sexual fantasy, while another part recoiled in humiliation and embarrassment. Miserable nights—sometimes ending in the fantasy's consummation, sometimes in the cold satisfaction of abstinence.

He envied Miles his ease with her, the way he could touch her casually, as if it were an act of no import—while Jody stared into her eyes, to avoid looking elsewhere: at her flowing dresses, her breasts, the fleeting outline of a hip, her toes with their short, blunt nails. Sometimes he imagined living in the house alone with her. In actuality, he *was* becoming more and more of a recluse since he had moved in, hardly going into the village; only twice, in fact—once for the call to Brekstrup, the other time to the coffee bar, to get away from Katherine's presence, actually, so he could think.

Perhaps Brekstrup's advice—his *command*—was best, after all: wind up, move out, write the dissertation, get on with his career and his life. Washing his face, he went downstairs to find Katherine in her office, Candice with her, going through the mail. The women looked up, Katherine smiling at him, Candice bending back immediately to her work.

"I wanted to let you know," he said. "I'll be leaving in a week or so."

The smile left Katherine's face. "So soon?"

"We've gotten used to him around here, haven't we?" Candice remarked. It was clear that she could just as easily accustom herself to his absence.

But not Katherine. "It isn't a good time," she told him. "The stars are wrong."

The stars? Should he tell her that he didn't believe in the stars—that whatever powers she had must lie in her own person, or in her relation with a mysterious God, nothing to do with the stars? "My advisor wants me back on campus. There's nothing more for me to do here."

Katherine stared at him for a moment, then closed her eyes, her lips moving silently. Candice rose. "I'm going outside for a cigarette." The door clicked shut.

"Promise me you won't leave until I tell you. I'll have Miles call your advisor. A few days or a week won't make a difference." She stood, motioned him toward her. "Let me touch you."

He knew he shouldn't, but he approached her anyway. She felt with her hand along his neck and chin, until she found the spot she wanted, just under the earlobe. He thought that if, years from now, he had forgotten what Katherine looked like, the feel of her fingers would still be with him.

The weather stayed cloudy, recalcitrant, unnatural. Miles talked to Brekstrup, who was unsympathetic. The spring semester was well on its way—he wanted Jody to take over one of his classes for a few weeks. Katherine felt the sky closing in on her.

Then, one night, a west wind came up suddenly; within half an hour the air had turned sharply colder and the stars emerged. This change had not been forecast; it was, in fact, contrary to the forecast. Waking in her bed, Katherine could feel the change in the air. She had been dreaming—not a pleasant dream, but she couldn't remember it. She had gone to bed early, shortly after dinner, feeling exhausted. What time was it?

She went to the window. The sky was washed clean, the stars brilliant; in the west, the Seven Sisters hung down like jeweled fruit. How long before they set? Two hours, she judged, perhaps three; she had never been good at such estimates. She removed her nightgown, which was stained from her body, and pulled on a simple, flowing white dress, like pulling on purity. Opening the door a crack she looked out into the hall. It was empty. She listened for the baby, but heard nothing; he was probably asleep, perhaps Summer, too, behind their closed door. Emily, she thought, must also be sleeping; she rose

261

early in the morning, and it was her habit to be in bed by nine. And Johnny—where was he? She didn't want to be seen by Johnny, he of all people. She shrank from his judgment, his condemnation, even from the narrowness and intensity of his devotion. Ever since she had revealed her fertility, something had become strange in him, foreign; touching his skin, she'd felt the blood sliding through his veins with a shifting, hesitant rhythm, as if, at any time, it might reverse itself and start flowing the wrong way through his heart.

She eased the door closed behind her and moved silently up the hall, feeling with her bare feet the worn-smooth boards of the house's wooden floor with its age of centuries. Willing herself invisible, she entered the stairwell and climbed to the third floor. There was a light under Miles' door; she heard his radio playing. She glided past, her feet quiet, though it was no matter if Miles happened to hear her. When she found Jody's room, she stopped a moment, waiting, before turning the doorknob.

The room was completely dark. She called his name, and, getting no answer, worked her way over to his bed, feeling in the darkness—blanket, turned-down sheet, his two pillows. The bed was still made—Jody wasn't there. She didn't dare turn on the light. Johnny was probably outside—what if he had just seen Jody, then the room lighting up? Lately, he was so unpredictable—would he come running?

She sat on the bed to wait. The taste of sleep was still in her mouth, her eyelids heavy; she felt the languor of her fertility, a soft, white flower, spreading gigantic petals. She lay back. The room was a world without light or sound—only the taste in her mouth and the light pressure of Jody's mattress on her back to bind her in space and time. Time passed, perhaps she slept. After a while, she got to her feet and felt for the window, pulling aside the shade to look out. Jody's view was to the south, but not far enough west to see the Pleiades. On her meridian, she spotted Regulus, and then Procyon, a little to the west of that. She moved to the window's edge and looked the opposite way, east, straining to make sure that

Arcturus was still not visible, bracing for its red, pulsating rays, but seeing nothing. But Arcturus would be there very soon, she knew, perhaps a half hour, perhaps only minutes. Jody had no clock in his room—what time was it?

She decided to go back to her own room, but when she eased open the door she heard traffic in the hall downstairs: Summer's voice—she had not been in bed after all; some soft moans from the baby; and Johnny, she was sure it was him—she recognized the tread of his heavy boots, the knock of his knuckles against the wall every few feet, dragging his hand along the wall and then rapping it, as if testing for hollow spots. She waited. She heard someone in the bathroom, water rising in the pipes; the baby's cries grew louder. Shutting Jody's door, she went back to the bed and lay down.

When she woke again, she saw him standing in the doorway, framed in the light that entered from the hall. He could also see her—he was staring. She whispered: "Come in," but he stood, frozen. "Close the door," she said.

He did. She felt him move toward her in the dark. It was late, she thought—how much time had passed? Could the stars still be right? Tomorrow night would be better—just to be safe. The cold weather would remain for a few days, the clear skies. They could set a time for her to come to him. But now she felt his body on hers. His need ballooned up to fill the room, to fill her up, entering through all her portals—her nostrils, the taste in her mouth, his lips on her eyes, her ears; his fingers finding her.

"No," she told him. "Not yet."

"Katherine," he said.

He kissed her, his tongue entering her mouth, filling her so she couldn't talk. She felt a sweetness in her veins, moving all through her. She thought about Brent—had it been this way, really like this?

He had no time to take her dress off. He lifted her, rolled it up, over her thighs, her hips. She looked above him at the window, the pale glow of starlight transfusing the shade. "Jody, no!" She squirmed under him, but he held her. The room swelled with his need. She had put on sheer panties that had once been Ginger's; perhaps her mother was looking down on them—from Regulus, from Procyon; or Rigel—was it still in the sky?

"Don't tear them," she told him. "Wait."

She raised her hips and helped him slide the pants down to her ankles. She kicked them off. His entrance was hard—she hadn't been ready for him, not really. As he moved inside her, harder and harder, grunting and crying, she prayed to Ginger, to Jesus, to the God who ruled the stars, that no evil befall the seed he was planting.

After it was done, she felt Jody's tears on her face. He wept like a small child, full of overflowing emotion, his cheek on hers, his weight, still pressing, pressing, pressing into her. He would have kept her forever, if he could, joined to him forever; but she moved, sliding under him, extricating herself. She kissed him quickly, feeling on his soft, fervent lips the well of emotion that bubbled inside him, and, again, the sweetness running through her own blood. It would all be all right—wouldn't it?

But when she returned to her room and raised her shade, Arcturus was at the center of her window, smiting her eyes with a pair of red rays that seemed to originate separately but come together as they struck: one for derision, one for death.

At the time, when Jody had been inside her, she had been sure she'd become pregnant; but the next morning it looked a little different. What if conception had not occurred? What if the red sky she had seen, the evil, shimmering eye high on the meridian, was thus irrelevant? What if there was another chance?

She went to him again, in the evening when the Pleiades were high, as early as she dared. It was reckless; she could easily have been caught—by Emily, by Summer, even by Johnny himself. One night, Miles came out of his room and saw her; they looked at each other, but didn't speak.

Each night had been clear, and she had raised the shade to let Ginger and the Seven Sisters bear witness. Swollen with hunger, Jody pierced her. She shoved her wrist in his open mouth so he couldn't cry out. Afterward, she lingered in bed with him, waiting for the coast to be clear before she returned to her room. She would never let him enter her a second time in any night—the later the time grew, the further the Sisters sunk in the west, while Arcturus waited on the eastern horizon just below the trees.

Jody began to talk of the future. Katherine had not bargained for that—no one had ever been in love with her before, she realized, not even Brent, not even Johnny, not like this. Jody said he could have his degree by June; August at the latest. There were many colleges in the area, where he could teach—there was Vassar, there was New Paltz, even the city wasn't so far; or, he could work on his book first—grants were available, Brekstrup would help him get one. Katherine kissed him, pulled him against her. Could it be true? Could it be possible?

All of Jody's doubts vanished. Miles located Dr. Weinberger. He was not in Youngstown, but in a nearby suburb—his "disappearance" had all been a mistake. A telephone interview was arranged. The voice on the phone verified that Elizabeth had been seriously ill, her life a misery of pain, sleepless nights, mental confusion, a rash that covered most of her body. The voice said that he had seen his patient recently, not two weeks ago, about six months after Katherine's intervention. The difference was astounding. Her mind and skin were clear; she was almost free of pain; she had returned to work after an absence of more than three years. Jody took detailed notes on his yellow pad, the thought never entering his mind that the voice on the telephone could have been anyone.

"He's done," Miles said. "He should leave."

She hadn't told Miles about the sweet syrup that dripped through her veins when Jody touched her, his tears on her face, his plans. How could she let him go now, when she hated to part with him for even the daytime hours, those hours that crept by as they avoided each other, never touching, hardly looking; until the night, when she could come to him, early or late, whenever it was safe, Katherine not worrying anymore how the stars were—she was sure she must have conceived by now.

And Jody wanted to marry her—she hadn't told Miles *that* either. It wasn't that she thought Miles would be angry. She could talk to him, make him see that Jody believed in her, heart and soul; he would never do anything to hinder her work—on the contrary, he was bright and capable, what a help he would be! But, so far she had held back, not with any doubts concerning Jody or Miles, or even Johnny, but because she wanted Ginger to approve her plans. She had expected her mother to come in a dream, the way she always had at times of difficulty or decision; but perhaps she was staying away now because Katherine didn't really need her, because Jody was the right person, because Ginger, looking down from heaven, was content.

But Jody *had* to leave. Hardy Brekstrup was to be away from his class for three weeks and needed him to take over. It was impossible to say no. Miles grumbled about Jody leaving his things in the house, but he wasn't too bothered; as far as he was concerned, Jody's return would be brief—he'd pick up his stuff and then be gone for good. Only Katherine knew differently. She had decided that, if Ginger hadn't made herself known by the time Jody came back, she would take her silence for approval.

The snows came, a series of March storms, covering everything in white, even the houses, obliterating distinctions—only the curve of river stood out, gunmetal gray against the snow; and the road to the village, restored, day after day, by the snowplow.

Johnny saw tracks behind the house—a deer, it looked like. They came down out of the woods, sometimes, when food was scarce. Though why it should be so this winter, with all the rain and warm weather, he didn't understand. He would never get used to this land, he knew—its hills and deep woods, its gray skies, and its changes that you couldn't see coming. He was a Missouri boy;

or more, he supposed, a New York City boy now—he'd come back there three times and would have been happy to stay, if *she* had stayed. He had liked it that the city never changed; rain, snow, heat, history—it shrugged all of them off, kept going. He had thought that he and Katherine would also keep on; but people always changed—he should have known. And he had been warned, hadn't he? After Miles Tobin had started coming around, Emily had told Johnny to watch out, that he wasn't the equal of Miles, that Miles would take her in the end. He could have taken care of Tobin with a knife between the ribs long ago, one of the nights when he was on his way back to Manhattan from Proud Hill Road, taken his wallet—in that neighborhood, who would have cared? But a violent death would have shocked Katherine; there never was a time when she seemed strong enough.

He should have done it.

Miles thought that he was stupid—a dumb hick from Missouri, the same as the New York City boys in the Navy had thought of him years before. But he'd been a super for ten years, first for the Jews and Irish, then the Puerto Ricans. The landlords were in Florida, far away; when people had needs, they had to ask Johnny. They all tipped Johnny, and some of the women answered the door barely dressed. He knew enough about those women to last a lifetime.

Katherine wasn't like them. She was thin, like a flower, her skin pale, blue-veined; he couldn't look at her without wanting to touch her. Remembering, he moved silently through the fresh snow. There was a statue he saw in the museum in Kansas City, when he was ten or eleven, a school outing, the year he and his parents had lived there. It was a Greek woman, a goddess or maybe a nymph, sculpted out of light-colored marble with pale veins running through it. The teacher had warned them, especially him, especially Johnny, not to touch anything; but suddenly he was beside her, as if by magic, running his hand up her leg, over her hip, her smooth belly. The teacher had pulled him away roughly, and that night his daddy had strapped

him, but the woman had always stayed in his memory. How long
ago that must have been, more than forty years!

He should have used his knife on Miles, and then taken her
away with him, back to Missouri, or to another city like New York,
where there were jobs for supers and he could have set Katherine
up in another apartment. She was his true daughter, Johnny knew,
his pure, spiritual daughter—not like slutty Summer, who had put
out since she was fourteen, who walked around Katherine's house
with her tits hanging out, nursing the brat she had made with some
Puerto Rican trash whose home was the streets. And Katherine was,
at the same time, his spiritual mother, as God was his Father; he had
never been brought close to God by Jesus, but only through her, by
her touch and by her miracles.

He wasn't a dumb hick, the way Miles believed. He understood
that there had to be money for Katherine's ministry. She had never
asked anyone for a penny; it was Johnny who had told her visitors
that they ought to give something; it was Johnny who had suggested
that their sisters, mothers, cousins, in Philadelphia or Baltimore, or
back in Puerto Rico, might write to her, putting something in the
envelope. And, in those days, Katherine had touched every letter,
handled it, the ones in Spanish translated for her by someone Johnny
had found. Was her work more perfect now, that letters flowed in
from all over the world, thousands of dollars with them, or even
millions; and the letters answered by Candice, or, so much worse,
Summer, who flaunted her state of sin?

And, the years had passed this way. Johnny had felt himself
growing thin and brittle, death in his bones. He had tried to speak
to Katherine about Miles, but she had been bewitched by him,
or maybe just fooled. He knew things about her that Johnny had
never known, that Katherine wouldn't talk about. He had taken
advantage of Katherine's goodness, enticing her with his weakness:
his headaches, weak eyes, failures. Slowly but surely, Johnny had seen
her turn away from him. He became the yardman, the janitor; he
didn't mind, he was a super by trade—but he couldn't stand it that

Katherine passed him by sometimes as if she didn't see him, that she hardly talked to him, except to say that the toilet was clogged, or that someone needed a ride into the village, or that Miles had remarked that the grass wanted cutting.

Though, Johnny also knew things. All along, he had known that Katherine never had monthlies. He had emptied her garbage in the Bronx and for a long time at the house; even after Emily took over the cleaning of Katherine's room, Johnny had continued to examine her leavings. He was not surprised that she was clean; he thought her an angel, one foot already in heaven—why should she be like other women?

But when, suddenly, she had become fertile, it was Johnny she had come to, confiding in him and none besides. She understood that Johnny was loyal, that she was everything to him—Johnny would keep her secret. And when she had spoken to him further about it, he had the thought for a moment that the old days had returned; his hand went out to touch her, but stopped when he saw her face, the face of a pure, unsullied angel, shining in the starlight.

Miles thought him naive, stupid, like a child you can do anything in front of because he won't understand. As if Johnny had not seen Miles touch her; off-handedly, the way you might drag your fingers across a wall or a piece of furniture as you passed, as if Katherine was just another woman, like Summer or Emily. And did Miles think that Johnny slept all night, hearing nothing, seeing nothing, like a sleeping baby? Not hearing Katherine on the stairs, not seeing the light on in Miles' room, not waiting until she returned to her own room late in the night?

But, still, he had not been sure until the day came when she should have started again; and not even then, because she might just be late. He waited a week, two weeks, carefully searching her room; he had counted the number of pads left in the open box, and none had been used. There was no sign of her monthly; and, at the same time, her visits to the third floor had abruptly stopped. Did they think he was stupid! But still ...

And then, one morning, suddenly, he knew. He could see it in her belly, a slight rounding; a small, extra heaviness in her breasts that no stranger would notice; and in her eyes a look he had never seen there before, the same as the look in Summer's eyes—the look of a whore.

He filled up the pickup and the Town Car, bringing extra gas home for the riding mower, the trimmer, the hedge cutters. It was one of his jobs—he was the driver, the handyman. The baby became cranky, howled at night, his ear flaming red. Katherine took him in her arms, squeezed him against her; the crying subsided for a minute, before continuing full force. Miles came up beside her, put his arm around her shoulder; as if she was his, as if he owned her.

The next morning, Johnny took Summer and the baby to a doctor in the village. When they passed the service station, a boy who was pumping gas waved at her. Summer waved back, held the baby up by the window so he could see; another man's bastard. Johnny looked straight ahead. While Summer and the baby were with the doctor, he drove back to the station and had the boy fill up an extra five-gallon can.

Night came, and he found Katherine out under the stars. Wispy clouds, blown by the wind, parted to show Sirius, the Pleiades, Orion. Katherine was standing with her hands in her pockets, looking up at the sky. She was wearing the leather coat that Miles had brought back on his last trip; high leather boots that shown dully in the ambient light. She looked more like a whore than a saint. "You have a child inside you," he said. "Don't you?"

She touched him. "Oh, Johnny. Aren't you happy for me?" Her fingers burned through his coat like hellfire."

"The father—who is he?"

She watched him, studying his face. Her eyes lied. "I know it's a girl," she said. "God made me fertile, then He put her there."

She kept looking at him. He knew what she saw—a broken-down man, shoulders rounded, chest caving in, a cough that came night and morning. He could read her mocking eyes: Go back to Emily—she's all you're good for.

"I gave my life to you, Katherine."

She touched him again, this time on his cheek. "It's God's baby," she told him. "There is no human father."

He took hold of her hand and removed it. "It's him," he said to her. "It was always him."

She wakes in the night, listening. Emily's baby is quiet. She listens for the wind, but there is none; except for the heaving and creaking of the floors and beams, water rising in the pipes, the house is silent, folded up into itself. Jody has been due to come home tonight, but he hasn't come. She imagines going to his bed, lying in his arms—safe from the Red Star that rules the late hours.

But no man is more powerful than the stars. She sees him in her mind—his carroty hair flares up suddenly flaming red, hips widened, chest bulging. Her lips move: Oh God. Jody is Beth. At her window, the red rays knock, tapping silently, almost politely. She has been wrong all the time. The baby was conceived the first night, under Arcturus—the Devil's child. She feels a great fear, her body hot, heart booming as if it would break. But then, strangely, a calm approaches. She goes to the window and lifts the shade. The red beams flood in, filling the room with brilliant ruby light. She hears Ginger's voice.

Jody made the short ride on his bike. The road was clear, easy, glowing in the light of the sky. He wondered how late it was—he hadn't looked at his watch in a while. There had been bad weather in the South, delaying his plane. In the airport, he had sat for hours, thinking of Katherine on and off, mooning over her, he knew, like a lovesick puppy; he'd turn the thoughts off, but they would quickly return—he couldn't help it.

By the time they landed in White Plains it was after midnight. It took nearly another hour before he finally found a taxi that would take him to the village. The driver had a bald pate and hollow, bluish cheeks, his look reminiscent of an actor made up for a horror movie. He bargained as if inevitability were on his side. The tab was outrageous, but Jody couldn't stand the thought of spending the rest of the night in an airport motel. Besides, he had had good news: a grant was available, and Hardy Brekstrup would shepherd his application. Not that Hardy approved his course of action. He had suggested two job possibilities, both at universities in the South. But if Jody had compelling reasons for doing otherwise—fine. Hardy was not one to interfere in the personal lives of his students. He wondered if Brekstrup suspected that he was in love with Katherine. Did it actually show on his face?

He was dropped off by the taxi behind the train station, where he had parked his bike. The driver took off immediately, leaving Jody alone under the stars. He was afraid the bike might not start, but after a few tries it did, despite the cold. A quarter mile out from the house, he stopped on the upward slope of a shallow hill. Though he was tired he wanted to walk the bike in. Katherine would probably be asleep, not expecting him anymore tonight. He planned to surprise her, to wake her with a kiss, to slide into her bed where he'd never been, to start making up for the three long weeks he had been away.

The night was spectacular—above the hill, a beautiful reddish glow, gorgeous as a sunset, some unusual atmospheric effect, caused, he suspected, by the intensely cold weather having capped off their long winter of rain. Reaching the crest, he could finally see the house. It was suffused in an aura of orange and red, a ball of flame that billowed out and up. There was no smoke. His first thought was that it must be an illusion of the moonlight, but, of course, there was no moon. He kicked his cycle on and rode in fast. As he got nearer he began to shout Katherine's name.